THE WISH

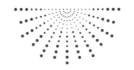

EDEN WINTERS

ROCKY RIDGE BOOKS

COPYRIGHT

The Wish © 2020 by Eden Winters

Cover by Perie Wolford

All rights reserved.

ISBN: 978-1-62622-099-7

First edition Torquere Press 2010

Second Edition Dreamspinner Press 2012

Third Edition 2020

Rocky Ridge Books
PO Box 6922
Broomfield, CO 80021 USA
http://RockyRidgeBooks.com

Many thanks and hugs to my support group: Pam, Meg, Mara, Lynda, Feliz, Jared, John A., John R., Doug, and Chris.

CHAPTER ONE

"I CAN'T believe he's gone. Even though I knew how sick he was, a part of me thought he'd get better."

A warm hand on Alfred Anderson's shoulder accompanied his friend's words, and he leaned into the gesture in subconscious desperation for the touch of another, now that his lover was gone.

"I thought so too, Douglas. Right up to the end, I never gave up hope." He still didn't believe the empty shell lying before them was the one who'd shared his life. He kept expecting to turn and find his partner, healthy and whole again, standing at his side.

The expected sympathy came as if by rote. "Well, if there's anything I can do...." Anticipated under the circumstances, the words were all the more welcome because of their sincerity. Douglas Sinclair would do anything in his power to make the burden lighter, and Alfred knew it.

The two gentlemen, one elderly, the other not so much so, stood together, dressed in plain black suits befitting the solemn occasion. The weak light of a midwinter's afternoon bathed them in its soft glow during their brief respite from the arduous tasks ahead. Neither spoke for several moments, as they stood vigil for someone incredibly dear to them both, and who they'd greatly miss.

In a shining mahogany casket before them lay the remains of a man, still handsome despite the ravages of time and cancer. Douglas reached out to stroke a shrunken cheek. "I can't believe this is actually my baby brother. Half brother. No, brother. How...?" He stopped and swallowed hard. "Who am I going to fight with now?" he cried in despair, sparing an apologetic glance toward Alfred, as if Alfred ever considered the constant scrapping between the two to be real.

"I know, Douglas, I know," Alfred said, reaching up and giving his friend's hand an understanding squeeze, knowing full well what Douglas meant. "I'll certainly miss the show." Though Alfred's own way of saying "I love you" was more conventional, the undertones of affection in the good-natured bickering had never eluded him.

After a few moments, Alfred asked, "Would you mind giving us some time alone, please?"

The hand withdrew, and a softly murmured "Of course" preceded Douglas's departure through the heavy wooden doors separating the secluded parlor from the world outside. Alfred glanced over his shoulder and offered a weary smile, one his friend and de facto brother-in-law returned as he secured the doors behind himself, warning others of the desire for privacy.

Heavy footsteps retreated down the hallway, growing ever fainter. When they faded into nonexistence, Alfred exhaled heavily, running his fingers through his full head of silvery hair, something his lover had enjoyed doing, particularly after Byron's own once-flame-red locks had thinned and fallen out.

How Byron had mourned the loss of his hair—a casualty of

the chemotherapy that failed to save his life. Then his body had begun to wither, and despite Alfred's best efforts to remain positive, Byron's inevitable death could no longer be denied.

"I know you wouldn't agree with me, but I think bald is a good look for you—very macho and sexy," Alfred whispered, fingers lovingly caressing the smooth pate of the man who'd shared his life for nearly thirty years.

"I didn't mind the weight loss, either, even if I did miss our afternoons spent by the pool." Self-conscious about his appearance, toward the end Byron only allowed Alfred and his doctor to see him undressed. And side effects of the unsuccessful chemotherapy had kept him out of the sun, something he'd once loved—slathered with sunscreen, of course, due to milk-white skin that never tanned, only burned.

"You're still as handsome as you ever were. But as attractive as you were on the outside, your outer beauty paled in comparison to how you were inside. You had the biggest heart of anyone I've ever known, and I'm deeply honored you gave it to me.

"It should have been me, you know," Alfred continued, his fingers now lightly brushing his lover's pale and cold brow. "I'm twenty-two years older than you. By all rights, you should have been around long after my time. It isn't fair." With those words, the tears he'd held back began to fall. Alone with Byron for perhaps the first time in days, Alfred mourned a life cut short by a foe that all the money in the world couldn't defeat. "I'm sorry, love: I couldn't let go, so you wouldn't let go. I'm terribly, terribly sorry." The last few months had been a kind of hell he'd never imagined. Through the entire ordeal, Byron hung on, readily agreeing to anything the doctor recommended, solely because Alfred wasn't ready to live without him. "I should have wished you Godspeed and saved you the pain," Alfred whispered.

Moving a chair to the edge of the casket and snagging several tissues from a conveniently provided box, Alfred felt very much a lonely old man as he wearily dropped onto the padded seat. "I'll always love you, you know." He folded his arms against the edge of the polished wood, resting his head on them while gazing down at the person he considered the best thing to ever happen to him. Fifty-four was far too young to die. Fortunately, they'd shared a great life, and while he'd be lonely and miss his lover terribly, the memories they'd made together brought some measure of comfort.

"I've given the matter some thought, baby, and I'm going to try to give you what you asked for. I still don't totally agree with the plan, although I know, as always, that you have every-one's best interests at heart." He stood once more, bending from the waist to kiss his lover softly on the cold, painted lips. "I hope you were right when you said they'd be perfect together if only they'd give each other a chance. I know I should have done this when you first asked, but you know how stubborn I can be." His lips quirked up into a ghost of a smile as he recalled the many times he'd been compared to a four-legged, braying mammal by this same man now lying still and quiet before him. How he'd love to hear the teasing again, just once more.

"They're both coming here. I'll make the introductions. The rest will be up to them, and you, if you're still around." It warmed his heart to imagine Byron still with him, maybe standing beside him, free from pain and worry, happy and at peace once more.

Despair suddenly crept into his heart, reality sinking in, truly sinking in, that his lover wasn't there anymore. No, Byron was well and truly gone, leaving Alfred alone probably for the rest of his life, short as that time might be. "Goodbye, my friend, my lover, my life," he whispered through trembling lips, knuckles whitening from the force with which he clutched the coffin. "You asked something of me, and I'll do my best to give it to you. However, I want something too. I don't believe I'll be long. Would you wait for me?"

Sorrowfully, he recalled the misery the poor man had bravely faced in the name of a few more months, days, and hours. "I'm sorry I wanted you to stay here when you were ready to go; all the pain you endured. But facing life without you...." Words trailing off in a sob, he finally did what he'd needed to do since his partner slipped away: breaking down completely and grieving, for himself, for his lost love, for the memories they'd no longer make.

In his sorrow, he didn't notice the shadowy figure emerging from behind him—a shadow that shouldn't exist in the sunlight washing over the room. Sinking back down in his chair, Alfred gripped the casket, oblivious to the shapeless mass taking form behind him, wrapping what appeared to be human arms around his trembling body. Although he took no notice of these things, deep within his heart familiarity blossomed, and he no longer felt so alone.

AFTER the rush of friends, family, and the merely curious passed, Douglas escorted him home, where Alfred sat alone in his office, the odd sense of peace settling over him again. The day took a toll on already frayed nerves, to the point where Alfred had been sorely tempted to cast decorum aside and verbally upbraid a thoughtless "mourner" who'd dared suggest he replace his dead lover immediately, and with the man's own widowed daughter, no less. Apparently the ill-mannered social climber hadn't noticed Alfred's recently deceased partner was a man, choosing instead to recall that he'd once been married to a woman, albeit disastrously.

Only the intervention of his dear friend and butler, Bernard, kept Alfred's name out of tomorrow's headlines. That is, if he wasn't already destined for front-page notoriety for the passing of his "long-time companion," as polite company deemed his relationship. In total defiance of his privileged upbringing, he snorted at the notion of Byron being anything other than what he was—Alfred's husband—in the eyes of anyone who mattered.

Oh, he'd tried to please his elitist parents, marrying a rich, shallow heiress with even less desire for him than he'd had for her. Theirs was a delicately balanced arrangement, one suitable to them both. While they remained childless, as a couple who refused to touch each other would be, they made their families happy, or as happy as upper-crust sensibilities allowed. Their agreement kept his and Susan's sizeable trust funds intact while providing them each with a built-in escort for social functions.

Susan grew careless, and when the scandal broke, she bore the brunt of public scorn and he received pitying gazes from some and knowing smirks from others. Throughout the accusations and innuendo, he'd done his best to stand by and support the woman who shared his name and little else. In the end she'd quietly filed for divorce before retiring from public life, taking her now notorious inamorata with her—a club singer of dubious background. Now, decades later, Alfred finally realized something genuine must have existed in Susan's relationship with the entertainer, for the two women had remained together until Susan's death three years earlier.

The post-scandal clamor died down after a while, only to resurface when Alfred himself slipped up, trusting someone who sold him out to a sleazy tabloid for less money than he'd have paid to keep the man silent. One horrible experience taught him to carefully guard his affections... until he met his lovely redhead, the one who'd captured his heart the moment they met. Suddenly the scandals, the reporters, and even his parents' threats no longer mattered. With Byron, Alfred found the courage to live life on his own terms, and damned the consequences.

He sighed and raised his glass of brandy—the one vice he refused to give up for the sake of his health—in toast to his late wife, hoping she'd been as happy in her relationship as he'd been in his, and then he toasted once again, in honor of his love.

A soft "ahem" from Bernard brought him out of his reverie.

"Yes?"

"Sir, perhaps it would be best if you retired now. You haven't been sleeping well, and tomorrow may prove stressful, to say the least."

Alfred slowly rose to his feet, only to discover one was asleep. Resting his hand on the back of his chair, he shook the offending limb to restore circulation. The return of sensation through opening blood vessels shot a sharp spike of pain through his leg. If only all the veins and arteries in his body could be so easily repaired, it would be well worth the momentary discomfort. Satisfied he might now walk without tripping, he followed Bernard from the room, taking little heed of the length of shadow following in his wake.

Once in his bedroom and seated in a far more comfortable

chair by a gas-log fire—a fixture more for show and psychological comfort than to ward off cold—Alfred allowed his butler to remove his shoes and gently massage his tired feet. "Would you like another brandy, sir?" Bernard inquired.

Alfred stared at his glass in surprise; he hadn't noticed he'd emptied it. "I believe I will. Thank you."

Warm and comfortable, he watched Bernard take the elegant snifter from his withered hand and quietly leave the room, only to return a moment later, the crystal balloon now sloshing with two fingers of amber liquid that sparkled in the firelight.

"Is there anything else you'd like before bed?"

After careful consideration, Alfred decided to confide in his friend and gain an ally for his plans. "What do you know of my nephew Alex?" he asked.

Bernard's heavily lined face gave no indication of his personal opinion, and, as usual, he selected his words carefully. "A most brilliant man, I believe, and very popular with the… ah… ladies. Why do you ask?"

Alfred stifled a laugh at how the incredibly straight, straight-laced butler phrased his answer. Yes, Alex was brilliant when he applied himself; however, applying himself didn't happen often. Bernard's perception of Alex's popularity with the ladies also held true, though it was no big secret he was more popular with men.

"No particular reason. You've arranged a room for him?" Even without asking, he trusted his dependable servant to have everything in order.

"Yes, sir, as requested. I placed him in the blue room. This meets with your approval?"

"Yes. Paul will have his normal room across from mine?"

"Yes, sir, as always."

Alfred considered the arrangement and then changed his mind. "If memory serves, Paul is also fond of the green room. He loves the view of the gardens. Why don't you put him there instead?"

Bernard peered at him quizzically from overtop a pair of round-rimmed glasses. Given their long association, and Bernard being equal parts servant and friend, questioning his employer's decisions had never been discouraged, provided he intended no disrespect. "Are you sure that's wise? Putting them across the hall from one another, so far from your own room? You know how your nephew values his privacy."

Alfred smiled indulgently. "Bernard, get a brandy for yourself and join me here by the fire. I'd like a chat."

Bernard shuffled from the room and returned a few minutes later, carefully avoiding Byron's favorite chair in favor of an overstuffed ottoman. He took a sip of his brandy, sighing in contentment and savoring every drop as was his habit whenever he indulged in spirits—a rare occurrence. "What would you like to discuss, sir?"

"First, tonight we're friends; drop the 'sir'. You can resume it again tomorrow if you need to, but no formalities tonight, please."

"Yes, si—Alfred. Now, what do you need me to do?" The suspicion in Bernard's voice bordered on comical.

"You don't have to commit murder, old man, relax." Reaching over to the table between his chair and Byron's, Alfred removed two of the many pictures crowding the polished marble surface, gazing fondly at the enormously different men in each. The first depicted a tall, big-boned, and ridiculously handsome man with sun-bronzed skin, penetrating blue eyes, and wavy hair resembling Alfred's own.

He handed the photograph to Bernard. "What do you see?" he asked.

"Your nephew Alex. Might I say he looks surprisingly like you when you were younger," the butler suggested, diplomatically latching onto a neutral topic. "It certainly appears he's taking advantage of those gym memberships too."

For the amount Alfred's accountant sent off each month for fitness clubs and personal trainers, the young man should be winning marathons, though Alfred doubted how much money actually made it to those gyms. Another on an ever-growing list of reasons to put his long-delayed plans into action. "Actually, Bernard, he's the spitting image of his late mother. It's a pity you never met her. My poor, accidental sister. How the country club ladies must have snickered behind Mother's back at this change-of-life child. I adored her, however. She was better than any pony or puppy in her simple wish to be loved. I'll forever kick myself for not being a proper brother and protecting her from that damned fortune hunter. What were my parents thinking to allow that marriage? They probably hoped for an heir, knowing by then I'd never give them one.

"How she endured their badgering is beyond me. In the end, she showed them. After her worthless husband left, she refused to hand Alex over to nannies, insisting on being a hands-on mother. My parents were horrified!" Alfred smiled fondly at the memory. Little Victoria hadn't stood up for herself often; however, no one prevailed against her when it came to her son's well-being. What a fight to remember, and the only one of his recollection she'd ever won.

"Alex adored his mother," Alfred continued. "Unfortunately, she didn't enjoy the same good health the rest of the Andersons did. She died at thirty-eight." He sighed, recalling unpleasant memories. "You know, I always considered the boy distant and cold after her passing. Don't get me wrong; I love him as my own, regardless of his faults. Sitting at Byron's bedside, holding his hand and watching him slip further away from me, I truly began to understand why my nephew is the way he is."

"What do you mean?" Bernard asked.

Alfred took a sip of his brandy and stared thoughtfully into the fire. "As painful as her illness was for me to endure as an adult, Alex was only nine years old when his mother lay dying. Oh, my parents tried to send him off to school, but he refused to leave, wanting to stay with her."

His eyes filled with tears, the memory still painful of finding Alex in his sister's bed the night she died, clinging to her cold hand. No doubt the poor child had been with her when she breathed her last. Alex had grown sullen and with-drawn afterward, never regaining his former youthful cheer.

"I wanted to adopt him, you know. You can imagine how the suggestion went over at the time. In the end my parents raised him, giving him everything money could buy, provided they didn't have to actually spend time with him. I never understood how his own flesh and blood considered him merely an heir to carry on the family line. Of course, they thought the same of me, once."

Alfred had barely survived such a frigid environment. How much worse had it been for someone as loving and caring as his nephew used to be? Taught to believe his only value lay in his name and in the blood running through his veins, which the elder Andersons insisted made them better than everyone else.

"When Byron fell ill, I couldn't comprehend why Alex never once came to visit him, even though he called several times each week. At first his lack of concern hurt me, and I believed him callous. I'd even planned a trip to Houston to give the boy a piece of my mind. Byron explained that, after watching his mother die horribly of the same disease, Alex simply couldn't bear to witness another loved one suffering, something I'd not taken into account. Alex adored his mother, and Byron, too, so I'm inclined to agree.

"There's also an advantage to footing my nephew's bills," Alfred said with a sly sidelong glance.

"And that is...."

"On several occasions he bought airline tickets from Houston to Los Angeles and later canceled, which I believe proved Byron's theory. Despite his avoidance, Alex truly loved Byron, of that I'm certain."

He took the picture from the butler and returned it to the table, bringing the other one close enough to see with his failing eyesight. This man had dark, straight hair, laughing eyes, and a slight build, as unlike the man in the first photo as day from night, in more ways than appearance.

"Take a look at this one," Alfred said, handing the frame to Bernard.

The butler smiled at the photo's subject. "Paul's such a like-able fellow," he said. "It's a pity he didn't have red hair like his father and uncles. He's very much like his mother, I believe."

"Yes, Paul is a nice young man, if a bit too trusting some-times. I wish I had his energy! Hiking, running, bicycling—he always seems to be in motion." Alfred remembered a time when he and Byron had enjoyed such activities. The weekend house in Bishop, California stood empty through the long months of his lover's illness, their outdoor toys gathering dust, never to be used again—at least not by him.

Pushing those thoughts aside, he leaned in, as if confiding a huge secret. "You know, I find it ironic that the only nephews of two gay men are gay as well."

Though hardly news to any of the household staff, his long-time butler gave him a questioning gaze. "What're you getting at, Alfred?"

Smiling like the fellow conspirator he hoped to be, he explained, "I promised Byron I'd do everything in my power to get those two together."

"Heaven help us!" Bernard exclaimed. "Alex and Paul? I'm sorry to say this, Alfred, I know you mean well, but do you honestly think you should? Alex Martin eats men like Paul Sinclair for breakfast and goes out hunting another for lunch! Those two are as different as can be. How do you propose to unite someone so worldly and, excuse my saying so, spoiled, with someone completely humble and guileless?"

"Well, I'm going to need your help. Here's the basic plan...."

CHAPTER TWO

ALEX turned the classic Mercedes-Benz 280SL Roadster into the parking lot of Club Inferno and accelerated up to the entrance, bypassing the other drivers dutifully waiting their turn. His pride and joy didn't deserve to wait in line with Hondas, Fords, and the occasional BMW. He climbed from his vehicle and tossed the keys to the waiting attendant, trusting his baby to be meticulously cared for. The tip he'd hand over later, a standard arrangement, guaranteed it. Those who afforded the price didn't have to wait in lines, and Alexander Martin could well afford it.

"Hey, Leo," he greeted the doorman, again bypassing the long line of people huddled in the unusual chill of the Houston evening, waiting to be admitted into the city's hottest new club. This time, the price of privilege wasn't paid in cash, but by toying with the club's owner. Alex was smart enough to realize that once Rico got what Rico wanted, the thrill would be gone, because he himself played similar games. After finding someone exciting enough to pursue, he promptly lost interest the moment he'd made the conquest. Without fail, he'd conquered all who'd caught his eye sooner or later. No one ever resisted Alex's model good looks, ample charms, and bottomless wallet, courtesy of an extraordinarily wealthy family of which he was the last, and destined to inherit the mother lode.

Leo nodded and waved him inside amid a chorus of complaints from those standing nearby. Alex smiled and winked, knowing his ass would be ogled as he sauntered into what he considered his own personal shopping mall of sex. From the corner of his eye, he watched Leo key a lapel mike, and knew from past experience the bouncer was telling Rico of his arrival.

As if on cue, the rather plain, very wealthy club owner appeared the moment Alex checked his jacket and started making his way to the bar, playing up his entrance for the crowd to see. They were seeing, all right. He sensed their eyes on him even with his back turned.

"Alex, how good to see you again," the portly entrepreneur gushed, rushing forward to kiss the object of his thwarted advances. At the last moment, Alex turned his head and thin, chapped lips connected with his stylishly unshaven cheek instead of their original target. Undeterred, Rico beamed, ordering the bartender, "Vince, get Alex his usual." He smiled coyly, running appreciative eyes up and down Alex's body, adding, as if it were a grand gesture, "On me."

Well, of course Rico sprang for the drink. If asked to pay for it himself, Alex wouldn't be allowing the garrulous man to fawn over him like some lovesick schoolboy. Rico was an annoyance Alex endured for the perks, such as his choice of the lovelies who frequented the club and never having to wait in line. Rico also wouldn't be too angry about being brushed aside for another. No, instead the opportunistic club owner would indulge his inner voyeur via the security cameras installed throughout the building, perpetuating the game of cat and mouse he'd played with Alex for the past few months.

Alex accepted his martini, gracing his host with a smile in lieu of thanks, and then brushed the barest tips of his fingers across Rico's lips, gratified at the shudder they inspired. "I know you're busy, baby, so I won't keep you," he said by way of dismissal, making his way to the crowded dance floor to pick out the lucky man, or woman, who'd share his bed tonight, or a corner of the back room. He actually preferred men, but he didn't want to discourage the holders of his purse strings, who hoped he'd provide a son to carry on the family name.

Artfully arranging himself against a shadowed wall, he watched with a predator's eyes the beautiful bodies writhing in time to the hard beat of a techno tune, provocatively dressed and parading themselves, waiting to be noticed.

He silently assessed the hopefuls, dismissing one after another for some flaw: too fat, too thin, hideous clothes, too much makeup, thinning hair, etcetera, until he selected a promising prospect and settled in to wait. Two young men, barely of legal age to be in such a club, were staring into each other's eyes, oblivious to all else around them. Alex's lips twitched into a devious smile. This was going to be fun.

He watched the couple kiss and caress each other to the point where he had to reach down and adjust the prominent bulge in his slacks. When they were nearly making love on the dance floor, he made his move.

Draining his martini, he discarded the empty glass on a nearby table, ignoring the indignant "Hey!" from its occupants. With precise timing, he eased onto the dance floor, neatly inserting himself between the two dancers. He turned his back to the attractive brunet, his true target, facing the less desirable member of the couple instead. Putting on his best predatory smile, Alex wrapped his arms around the man's slender shoulders, locking their mouths together, his tongue demanding entrance. After a moment's hesitation, access was granted. Alex winced at the taste of cigarettes and beer, which only proved him right in not pursuing this particular offering.

The man pulled back and exclaimed, with a fervor normally reserved for fans meeting their rock-star idols, "I know you! You're that rich guy, Alex Martin. Gawd, you're hot!"

Alex inwardly cringed at his entire existence being boiled down to "rich guy." Outwardly, he poured on the charm, enduring the blatant flirtation of his admirer. More than likely the guy thought he'd hit the pickup jackpot. The blond leaned in to resume the kiss, as Alex predicted he would, disregarding the incensed brunet, who loudly protested the turn of events.

Before either of the pair could react further, Alex pushed the guy away and trained his heated gaze on the bewildered eyes of the other dancer. Jilted lovers made such easy prey. He grabbed his intended target by the shoulders, pulling him into a tight embrace, and then reached down to clasp a gloriously tempting ass. "Why should I settle for him when I can have you?" Alex purred, nibbling a sensitive earlobe and eliciting a gasp.

Upset at being brushed carelessly aside by his partner, the brunet didn't even put up a token protest when Alex claimed his lips in a bruising kiss.

Yes, definitely the wiser choice. Apparently, this half of the couple liked rum and Coke and, thankfully, seemed to be a nonsmoker. Alex hated the inevitable whining when he refused a sex toy a postcoital cigarette, for he loathed the things and didn't allow smoking in his condo. He smiled, noticing that, judging from the hard length pressed against his thigh, the man boasted a cock to be proud of. Pulling back from the kiss and making his choice between bed or back room, he leaned in to be heard above the music. "What do you say to getting out of here?"

The guy nodded, and Alex couldn't keep the smirk from his face. The whole process had taken less than five minutes. Too easy. Wrapping an arm around the fuck *de nuit*, Alex led him away from the dance floor and the blond, who even now stuttered a protest. "James, you get your ass back here now, or it's over!"

"Anyone important?" Alex asked.

He received the exact reply he'd expected. "No."

Gazing down at the sleeping form tangled in the silk sheets of his bed, he experienced a twinge of something others might label "remorse." No, Alex didn't regret alienating the two lovers at the club or taking advantage of others' emotions. What disappointed him was how quickly the guy'd given in. Where was the thrill of the chase if you got anyone you wanted simply by asking? Faces and names (if he'd even known them to begin with) blurred together in an endless stream of willing mouths, asses, and pussies, freely offered because of who he was, what he looked like, or the advantages to be gained by sleeping with him. He knew it was a perverse desire, but for once he'd like to find someone who thought enough of themselves not to settle for the quick fuck-and-forget he offered— someone to tell him no or hold out for more.

Reaching down, he grasped a spray-tanned shoulder and shook the sleeping youth. "Hey, time to get up."

Sleepy, crystal-blue eyes slowly opened to gaze up at him in confusion—something Alex hadn't noticed last night in the heat of passion. What a pity; he'd always been partial to brown eyes. Oh, well, this one wasn't a keeper, anyway.

"Wha...?" the young man asked, clearly fighting off the remnants of sleep.

"You need to go," Alex said, catching a whiff of morning breath and deciding last night wasn't worth a thank-you after all.

"Why? I thought we could do it again," the naked man purred, obviously waking up enough to realize where he was and with whom.

"That's not possible; I have a plane to catch. Get dressed and let yourself out."

Generous lips formed into a pout. "You're kicking me out?"

"No, I'm telling you to leave. I have to pack and get to the airport." Inwardly Alex cringed. Apparently his one-night stand didn't catch on quickly. Why did he always end up with the beautiful but dumb ones?

"I thought...."

Alex narrowed his eyes, using the intimidating glare he'd perfected over the years in similar situations. "You thought what? That I wanted more than a fuck? Whatever did I do to give you that idea?"

The disbelief on the guy's face might have been considered adorable if Alex were the kind of man who found things adorable, which he wasn't. Besides, he needed to hurry.

"Well, last night, when you made love to me—" the man whined.

Again Alex cut him off. Leaning down, nose to nose with a guy who'd worn out his welcome, he growled, "We did *not* make love, we *fucked*. It was passable, but losing points by the minute. Now, get up and get out." He turned his back in dismissal, entering his massive closet to begin choosing the necessary clothing for his trip.

Hmmm…. He'd worn that suit before; he'd have to buy a new one. Listening with half an ear, he heard the sounds of his guest dressing and hoped to hear his front door closing at any moment.

When the sound of slamming doors didn't reach his ears, he turned, only to find the lost-looking pickup, half-dressed, watching him with tear-filled eyes. "What now?" Alex huffed, his patience nearing an end.

The boy sniffled. "I don't know where to go. That was my boyfriend with me last night. I don't think he'll welcome me back with open arms now."

Alex allowed the nuisance to see every bit of the anger and impatience he could muster. "And that's my fault how? Did I hold a gun to your head and force you to reject him in favor of the first person who noticed you? Hmm? Did I? Did I make any promises other than to fuck you into the mattress? A promise I kept, by the way."

"No," the now not-so-sexy boy answered. One lone tear spilled down his cheek.

Not tears! Alex needed to act quickly or the annoying sympathy he'd never completely squashed in the name of being an Anderson would come into play, and he wouldn't make his flight in time. Thinking back to his cold, unfeeling grandparents and their self-righteous superiority, he used the lessons they'd taught him from birth and hardened his heart. Channeling the spirit of his ice-cold grandmother, he snapped, "Would you please get out of here? I told you I have things to do!" He turned his back, gratified at the forceful slam of his front door seconds later. Hurriedly checking his security cameras to ensure his guest hadn't enacted some form of revenge, he promptly pushed the whole episode out of his mind, returning his attention to packing and what he'd be facing in the coming days.

How he hated funerals! His uncle controlled his allowance, though, making his appearance mandatory. He sighed. No, the obligatory trip to LA wasn't the reason for his bad mood; that was merely what he'd told his casual acquaintances when they'd asked. Truthfully, for all his projected indifference, Alex cared for Uncle Alfred and his uncle's partner, Byron, and even if he didn't visit them often, he'd always counted on a warm welcome when he did. Therein lay the problem. A certain amount of guilt, one of many emotions he avoided religiously, plagued him for not being with Byron at the end. The slight wasn't intentional, only every time he booked a flight, he'd later panicked and canceled. Though she'd passed away a painfully long time ago, images of his dying mother haunted him, and he couldn't bear to witness such a painful end to yet another person he cared about. A coward? Him? Absolutely. Now he had to face his uncle, knowing he'd let the man down.

He secretly envied the two men their close relationship and never once viewed his uncle's lover as the gold-digger his grandparents accused the man of being. No, the money had meant absolutely nothing to Byron Sinclair, and Uncle Alfred himself had been the center of the redhead's universe. Long ago, Alex gave up on the dream of one day meeting someone who saw beyond the face, body, expensive condo, and money. Someone who took the time see Alex, the man, lurking under the façade of Alex, the wealthy playboy. Someone who loved classical music and a good book, and who'd rather spend a quiet evening at home than out clubbing. Someone who would take him down a peg or two when Anderson arrogance inflated his ego, as Byron had done for his uncle. He'd come to terms with the fact that he'd never have what those two men shared, and, deep down, it broke his heart that his uncle no longer had it, either.

THE gray Bishop sky reflected the gloomy mood of the lone man sitting on the rooftop—his sanctuary in times of trouble. His much-loved uncle had died far too young, and Paul hadn't been there to offer comfort at the end. His uncle had rallied on Friday, and everyone concerned had deemed it safe for Paul to go home, check on his bookstore, and then return to Los Angeles the following week. The poor man hadn't lasted long after Paul's departure, and Alfred, Uncle Byron's partner, had called and broken the sad news scant moments after Paul arrived home.

The two older men had made a striking, if unusual couple, and regardless of the difference in age, status, and hereditary wealth, they'd created a lasting relationship strong enough to withstand numerous hardships, showing any detractors the error of their ways.

Despite his sorrow at his uncle's passing, Paul smiled, fondly recalling the two men who were like fathers to him, filling the void created when his own father died in a senseless mugging when Paul was a boy. The example they'd set would be hard to follow. Still, he hoped someday he, too, would have a loving, enduring relationship like theirs. He promised himself, and his uncle, not to settle for anything less.

Those generous-to-a-fault men would have spoiled him if he'd let them, but all Paul wanted was their time and their love. He neither needed nor wanted their money. He'd financed his education with money from his father's life insurance policy, and during college and after graduation he'd worked hard to save for the down payment on his store, once more refusing to accept handouts from the wealthy couple when they'd offered. Instead, he'd purchased an older building in need of repairs and lovingly refurbished the relic with his own hands—his proudest achievement.

He'd never be rich and didn't want to be. Even without the uncles' help, he lived comfortably, managing to tuck away a little for a rainy day. *Unlike that fool Alex Martin,* he thought bitterly. The worthless asshole had never done an honest day's work in his life and greedily accepted anything and everything offered, acting entitled to the money and never acknowledging Alfred and Byron's generosity for the gift it was. The ungrateful bastard repaid the kindness by never setting foot in his uncle's house, except to ask for a new car or a new condo, or some equally expensive status symbol. Why, Alfred's nephew never once, to Paul's knowledge, even called to ask about Byron's health in the months the poor man had been sick. Small wonder that in twenty-six years, Paul hadn't met the man, and he'd been content not to. It mystified him that both his uncle and Alfred truly adored the slacker, and the unconditional love extended beyond mere familial obligation. They turned a blind eye to Alex's faults or excused them with a chuckled, "Oh, that's Alex being Alex."

Paul stared out over the hazy skyline, huge, fluffy snowflakes starting to fall, making him pull the homemade quilt tighter around his slender frame. Yes, he'd make his way back to Los Angeles and support the man who meant the world to him, and woe be to the spoiled Alex Martin if the bastard chose to show his arrogant face!

CHAPTER THREE

WHEN the announcement came for first class, Alex boarded the plane and was already seated and sipping a feeble excuse for a gin and tonic by the time the poor schlubs began migrating toward coach. With any luck, he'd catch a brief nap once airborne, something he desperately needed after his late night.

Thinking back to the one-nighter he'd picked up at the club, he couldn't help but feel a deep sense of disappointment. Even while insinuating himself between the obvious couple, he'd held out the hope that they'd merely laugh at his interruption and continue with each other or even confront him in righteous indignation for daring to intrude. It hadn't happened. Instead, one had recognized Alex and taken the bait, prompting his lover to retaliate. No matter how many times he used the same tired old ploy, it always ended the same way. Was anyone in a committed relationship anymore?

Closing his eyes, Alex contemplated the answer to his question. Uncle Alfred and Byron had had such a relationship. Alex seriously doubted anyone ever stood a chance of coming between those two. He wondered what would happen now. Would his uncle be able to move on and find someone new, or was he destined to mourn for the rest of his days?

Making a quick decision, Alex decided to stay for a while, spend time with the man who'd filled the father figure role in his life, and attempt to help ease the pain Alfred certainly must be feeling. Yes, he'd play consoler, and once convinced his uncle would be okay, he'd get back to his life. It shouldn't take more than a few weeks, right? At the very least, he owed an extended visit to the beautiful men of Los Angeles, to sample what the city offered. Satisfied with his plan, he smiled and relaxed into his seat, falling asleep before the plane left the ground.

THE hastily packed car idled in gridlock, on a slow approach to the choking haze encircling Los Angeles. Paul loved his visits, but only because of his uncles and Alfred and not the city itself, which he hated. He loved clean air and the great outdoors—things not found in the city. One more reason he hadn't objected when his mother moved them back to Bishop, California, following his father's brutal murder. Plus, hearing his mother go on about how his poor father would still be alive if he hadn't followed his brothers to the big city had further influenced Paul's decision of where to live.

Sighing in frustration, he flipped through his collection of compact disks in search of something calming to help shake off painful remembrances best left in the past. Locating a CD he'd forgotten, a leftover from a former lover, he inserted the disk into the player of his older-model Ford, smiling as the familiar strains of a classical guitar filled the car. Jordan had excellent taste in music. What a pity he hadn't had the same goals in life, or the morals, Paul did. The lack of moral fiber eventually ended their relationship. Regardless of Jordan's lack of fidelity, Paul had truly loved the man, and the betrayal hurt deeply. The bitter memories didn't stop him from enjoying the CD, for he cherished the reminder of happier times. Besides, his uncle and Alfred loved it.

Thanks to his Uncle Byron and the man's de facto spouse, Paul knew what kind of relationship he wanted, even if he'd failed miserably thus far in creating one. He was realist enough to know he might never find the life partner he longed for, and dreamer enough not to quit looking. He was just taking a "temporary hiatus." A long temporary hiatus. Uncle Byron had been twenty-four when he'd found the one destined to share his life; at the time, Alfred had been forty-six. Paul sincerely hoped it wouldn't take him twenty more years—too long a time to be lonely.

By the time the third music track ended, traffic began moving again, albeit slowly: another reason he hadn't moved back to the city when his uncles begged him to. He also maintained a staunch belief that whatever he achieved in life he'd do on his own, and sweethearts that they were, the two benevolent men wouldn't have been able to keep themselves from meddling. He'd even warned them long ago to stop fixing him up with rich, eligible men and allow things to happen naturally, being a firm believer in fate.

When he finally pulled into the gated drive of the house he considered a second home, Paul was exhausted. A few sleepless nights while forced to stay in Bishop and arrange for the management of his store—before taking an extended leave of absence—didn't help matters. Tired and unfocused, the last thing he needed was entering the gates in the back of Alfred's

black Escalade and pulling to a stop before the front entrance—
the man he'd spent much of his life avoiding.

With suspicious eyes, Paul watched the tall blond unfold
long legs and stand beside the vehicle, scanning the surroundings like a master surveying his territory before settling a sky-
blue gaze on his observer. Paul supposed the man meant the
gesture to appear accidental, and anyone else might have
believed that.

Thanks to his uncle and Alfred, Paul's exposure to Hollywood types left him able to recognize the calculating, assessing
perusal for what it surely was: he was being measured, and he
hoped the arrogant beast liked the view, because an eyeful was
all the asshole would ever get. Enough pictures lay scattered
around the house for Paul to identify Alexander Martin in the
flesh. Even if there weren't, the stranger bore an unmistakable
resemblance to Alfred.

While pretending to ignore the new arrival, Paul couldn't
help noticing the man was just as good-looking, and probably
every bit as arrogant, as he'd imagined. He forced his eyes
away, listening in on instructions to the driver of the Escalade,
Isaac, about luggage, as if Alex wasn't capable of carrying his
bags for himself with his gym-rat body.

Eyes carefully averted, Paul removed his own bag from the
trunk of his car, not wanting to bother the staff with something
easily handled by himself. Resolve holding until the man's back
turned, Paul gave in to his curiosity and scrutinized the well-
built body belonging to one of the last living members of a
prestigious "old money" family, and the heir to Alfred's
substantial fortune.

Born five years before Paul, pictures didn't do justice to the
flesh-and-blood man. Alex stood at least six feet tall, with
broad shoulders and a firm, nicely rounded backside, well

displayed in tailored pants. Paul definitely understood how such a man acquired the reputation of a heartbreaker. Blessed with the killer combination of looks and money, Alex Martin would be a hit in the club back in Bishop. Although Paul received numerous offers during his infrequent visits, he usually left the club alone. He suspected the gorgeous Alex wouldn't be as picky.

Paul reminded himself that Alex Martin was a waste and a loser, holding firmly to his belief that money didn't make a man a good person—the opposite holding true in many cases. Judging from the gossip he'd heard over the years, Alex was far from a good man, even if Alfred and Uncle Byron casually discounted his transgressions. All the man was good for, in Paul's eyes, was holding out a hand and living the good life, with nary a thought for anyone else.

Duffel in hand, Paul bustled down the walk leading to the rear entrance of the house, closer to his room. As he'd done for most of his life, he pretended to ignore Alex Martin's existence even while hoping the presence of three large suitcases didn't mean the bastard intended to stay long.

THE shadow that had in life been Byron Sinclair would have sighed if still capable of breath. Focus as he might, the best he accomplished was a mere trembling of the picture frames. About to give up his futile endeavors, Bernard's timely arrival inspired a new plan.

Although the normally logical butler kept any personal interests carefully hidden, Byron knew Bernard held a keen fascination for the paranormal, and hoped to use his influence to prod the man into accomplishing his goals for him. Positioning himself behind the fastidious servant, he shouted, "Bernard? Bernard!" only to be frustrated when the man didn't hear him. He usually got a response before the name was out of his mouth the first time! The ostrich feather duster never faltered, brushing back and forth over the leather desktop as Bernard bent to the task of cleaning Alfred's already spotless office.

"Please, Bernard! This is important!" Byron implored.

He was about to give up hope when a blue-veined hand tentatively rose and wiped at an ear, as though brushing away an annoying fly. Encouraged, Byron focused every bit of his energy into communication, pouring out his intentions and praying for a response. "Bernard, this is what I need you to do...."

His efforts finally paid off. The butler straightened, features scrunched into a puzzled frown as he studied his employer's desk. "Now, what're those doing here?" he muttered, removing two of the three photos sitting on the surface, leaving only the picture of Paul. He placed the other two on the mantel above the fireplace.

Task accomplished, the unnoticed shadow pumped its fist in the air in triumph and hastily fled the room, anxious to see his nephew who, although Paul didn't know it yet, had just come home.

FEELING a bit disoriented, Bernard left the ground-floor office, quickly forgetting his confusion when he spotted Paul standing in the hallway.

"Bernard!" the young man exclaimed, dropping an overloaded bag to the floor and then gripping him in an enthusiastic hug.

Bernard returned the heartfelt greeting, gasping when the intense embrace knocked the wind from him. "Hello, Paul. How wonderful to see you! How was the drive down?"

He stepped back and attempted to take the duffel out of habit, only to be stopped by a firm hand on his arm. "I can get my own bag, thanks," Paul said, slinging the loaded duffel over his shoulder. "Traffic was a bear, as always. It's good to be back." The bright smile disappeared, the happy expression turning grave. "Tell me, how's Alfred holding up? I know this is a terrible blow. We both thought Uncle Byron was getting better."

"He's holding up, though I fear he's still in denial. Come, let's get you settled into your room, and then I'll take you to see him." Leading the way to the sweeping staircase that led to the upper floors, Bernard paused on the first step, suddenly forgetting his destination. Why in heaven's name was he taking Paul to the green room? He turned to the man at his side, who wore an equally puzzled expression, and bowed his head in embarrassment. "I'm afraid the mind is the first thing to go," he muttered. "Of course you'll want your usual room across from Byr... I mean, across from Alfred's."

Paul clapped him on the shoulder affectionately. "That's okay, Bernard. I can find my room by myself." He jokingly added, "Unless you've moved it while I was away."

Bernard shook his head and smiled weakly at the attempted humor. "No, we haven't moved it. Although...." He struggled to remember what he'd been about to say. When the thought didn't return, he settled for, "How wonderful to have you back where you belong."

"Thank you," Paul replied, turning down the east wing

hallway to the room he'd stayed in, whenever visiting, since boyhood. Bernard watched him go, wondering why an extra shadow trailed behind him.

THE spirit of Byron Sinclair celebrated another little victory. Alfred meant well by his direct approach of putting the two men close together. However, experience and careful observation had taught Byron that standoffish Alex resented intrusions and intruders, effectively nipping any matchmaking plans in the bud.

No, dealing with temperaments like Paul's and Alex's required subtlety and finesse. Byron had years of practice at both.

CHAPTER FOUR

"WILL that be all, sir?" The driver deposited Alex's belongings in the blue room, his admiring gaze clearly conveying hopes that the answer might be no.

Alfred employed Isaac as a groundskeeper, handyman, and, when the occasion warranted it, driver. While Alex knew some of his peers might think it low class to seduce the help, Isaac's ebony skin and wanton willingness had tempted him before, and he'd succumbed. Who could blame him? Isaac obsessed about his body, and worked hard on his appearance. The efforts paid off spectacularly.

Alex actually preferred men with a slighter build, but for a casual fuck, his only prerequisites were "attractive" and "exciting." The bulging muscles and shoulder-length dreadlocks also served to set Isaac apart from dime-a-dozen club boys. He was near Alex's age, too, and mature enough to understand that one fuck did not a commitment make. Sadly, regardless of his exoticism and availability, Alex had had him—and simply wasn't interested anymore. Besides, someone new lurked in the house to provide a worthy distraction if things worked in Alex's favor, and they usually did.

After dismissing the disappointed servant, Alex left his room in search of his uncle. He'd been afraid to visit during the last few months of Byron's illness, though he'd called frequently, hoping they'd understand his absences didn't indicate a lack of caring. Caring was never the problem. He loved Alfred and Byron both wholeheartedly. The problem lay in Alex's massive case of cowardice.

Too late now to turn back the clock and own up to his responsibilities in regards to Byron, but better late than never with Alfred. Alex was here now and would do his best to assist his uncle through this time of sorrow. Regardless of the numerous times Alfred had repeated the sentiment, Alex wasn't entirely convinced of the old man's sincerity when he said, "I'm fine."

Midway down the marble staircase, Alex stopped in his tracks, spotting his aged uncle, eyes closed and smiling broadly, embracing the attractive stranger who'd caught his attention outside. A vague sense of familiarity swept over him, but where he'd seen the man before he couldn't say. Boy-next-door handsome as opposed to drop-dead gorgeous, despite his small stature the newcomer possessed a casual elegance one didn't soon forget—not to mention a killer ass.

With narrowed eyes, Alex watched the two kiss each other on the cheek, and when Alfred wrapped an arm around slim shoulders and led the way down the hall, it appeared more a fatherly gesture than the affection of a lover. Still, due to his uncle's strict upbringing, even with Alfred's longtime love, public displays of affection were kept to a minimum. And they'd shared a genuine love, which no one could deny.

However, Byron had been ill for an awfully long time before he died, and having been over twenty years younger proved age differences weren't a problem for Alfred.

Could Alfred have already found a replacement for the man who, at this exact moment, lay in a casket at the funeral parlor? Even without proof, the possibility disappointed Alex. The older couple presented a shining example of men in a monogamous, committed relationship. To discover he'd been mistaken about the depth of what they'd shared—well, it nearly toppled Alex's idols from their pedestals.

For a moment he considered retreating to his room and waiting until the stranger left, but immediately discarded the idea. This was his uncle's house, and no interloper was going to come in and take Byron's place easily. About to follow the pair down the hall, he heard the *snick* of a closing door, followed by retreating footsteps. Perhaps Uncle Alfred was alone now and he could get some answers.

His soft knock on the office door was answered by the familiar gruff baritone of his mother's only sibling, bidding him to come in. The smile lighting the still handsome face of his uncle as he entered did Alex's heart good. No matter what happened in life, Uncle Alfred remained a constant, someone to depend on. When Alfred struggled unsteadily to his feet, icy fear clutched Alex's heart. Gone was the robust gentleman of memory who could take on the world single-handedly, replaced by a frail, silver-haired senior in the waning years of life.

"Uncle, are you not well?" Alex asked in genuine concern. Though he stood to inherit more money than any one man might need in a lifetime upon Alfred's death, he had no wish for that to happen anytime soon.

The old man winced, rummaging in his desk with one hand

while clutching his chest with the other. Alex instinctively jumped into action, hurrying to his uncle's side and finding a prescription bottle hidden under a stack of papers. Alfred's eyes squeezed shut in pain while Alex fumbled open the cap and shook the pills into his open palm.

"How many?" he demanded.

Alfred plucked a single pill and placed it under his tongue, slowly sinking back into his chair.

That the great Alfred Anderson could be ill was unimaginable, and Alex stood paralyzed, watching helplessly. He breathed a sigh of relief when the color seeped back into Alfred's ashen face.

"Terribly sorry, Alex. Unfortunate side effect of getting so damned old, I'm afraid." When Alfred met Alex's eyes, the frailties of his body were noticeably absent from his intense gaze, his mind still as sharp as ever. "Thank you for coming. I've missed you," he murmured quietly.

"It's good to be here." Returning the pill bottle to the desk drawer, Alex awkwardly added, "I'm sorry about Byron."

"Thank you. Though I miss him terribly, at least now he's free from pain."

Not knowing what else to say, Alex leaned down and wrapped his uncle in an affectionate, if cautious, hug.

"I'm old, damn it, not fragile," his uncle growled into his ear, as arms, softening with age, wrapped Alex in a welcoming embrace. After a moment Alfred sat back and studied Alex intently. "You're looking good, as always."

"And you're looking…." Alex couldn't find the proper words to use in this circumstance.

His uncle gave a soft bark of derisive laughter. "Admit it. I look like what I am—a relic with very little time left."

"You'll outlive us all and well you know it," Alex replied, fervent in his denials. His uncle would live forever. He had to, if for no other reason than Alex wanted him to.

Alfred sighed and ran his wrinkled, aged-spotted fingers through his still full and wavy hair. The family's trademark golden locks had faded to silver. "I'm glad you came. We need to talk. May I offer you a drink?"

How like the man to skip the social niceties when they were alone and cut straight to the chase. Assessing his host's physical condition, Alex feared what he was about to hear. "I don't suppose you have any vermouth handy, do you?"

Alfred chuckled. "You know where the bar is. Would you be so kind as to refill my water glass while you're there?"

"Of course." Alex took the empty glass and refilled it before mixing himself a martini, his uncle's words convincing him he'd need a little liquid courage.

When he neared the desk, he couldn't help noticing the lone portrait displayed there—clearly the man from the hallway. What was the photo doing where a picture of Alfred and Byron normally stood? Scanning the meticulously decorated office, he finally located the familiar image—on the mantel next to a picture of himself. Barely suppressed anger bubbled to the surface. There must be a logical explanation, although from what he'd witnessed in the hallway, he believed he knew what was going on and didn't like the implications one bit. Still, due to his uncle's illness, he needed to handle the situation delicately.

"Alex?" His uncle called his attention back where it belonged. "Please have a seat. As I said before, we need to talk."

Alex noticed how tired the man sounded, and little wonder,

with the stress he'd dealt with over the last few days. Taking a fortifying sip of his drink, Alex deposited the water glass on the desk and sank into the leather chair across from Alfred. "What is it?"

"I'll come right out and say this because you have the right to know: I have a heart condition, and it's serious."

"What do the doctors say?" Fear gripped Alex like an iron fist. At seventy-six, the man was hardly young, though healthy for his age.

"They found out a few weeks ago and wanted to do surgery immediately, though with Byron...." Nothing more needed to be said. Alex knew how much Alfred had doted on his partner, and he would have put his lover's needs before his own, even risking his own health.

"What about now?" Alex asked.

"That's what I wanted to talk to you about. I've tried never to be a burden or ask anything of you; however, the time has finally come when I need your help."

Alex responded without thought. "I'll do anything you need me to."

The corners of Alfred's mouth lifted slightly in a weak smile. "Three weeks from today, they'll perform a procedure to open a blockage in my heart and insert a stent. I'll be in the hospital no longer than three days and able to resume my work in a week. Until then, I need to teach you to run this estate, as a precaution. An estate that will be yours soon, I'm afraid."

"Uncle, don't talk like that!" Alex pleaded, tendrils of panic curling into his belly. "You're going to be fine. Of course I'll learn what I need to know, but only so you won't be burdened while you recover."

"There's more." Alfred's sigh sounded ominous.

"Oh?"

"Even if I do recover, Alex, it's time to pass the torch." Alfred paused to take a sip of water, staring at the glass in his hand. "I'd like you to consider moving in and managing the day-to-day operations of the Anderson empire and the businesses I'm invested in. I find I'm quite ready to retire."

Oh. Alex certainly hadn't expected that. He loved his life, going where he wanted and doing what he pleased with only himself to answer to. Nevertheless, Alfred had been generous and never once asked for anything in return. But Alex couldn't even manage his own checkbook—that was why Andersons kept accountants on the payroll—let alone manage his uncle's affairs. He paused a moment to consider, finally deciding he could possibly survive a few changes to his normal routine. He'd miss his freedom, but surely he wouldn't have to give up his nightlife completely if he moved in. On second thought, though, he could hardly bring casual fucks to his uncle's house. Maybe he could split his time between his condo in Houston and possibly find another here in LA. "I don't see how I could possibly say no," he replied, surprising himself with his sincerity. He'd work out the details later.

The relief on his uncle's face was well worth any sacrifices he'd have to make. "Good, that's settled, and I cannot tell you how glad I am that you're going to do this for me. I had no idea what I'd do if you'd said no."

The innocent comment, that the man who'd always been so giving even considered such a possibility, stung like a slap in the face. Sure, Alex loved his carefree life. Did enjoying his independence make him so selfish that his uncle thought him capable of turning his back on a loved one in need? He'd opened his mouth to respond when a soft knock interrupted them.

"Come in," called Alfred.

"Excuse me, sir; it's time for your medicine." Bernard's eyes widened when he noticed Alex. "I didn't know you'd arrived. Why didn't you tell me?" he asked, his lips turning up in a genuine smile.

Alex rose from the chair to be enveloped in a hug, and he awkwardly patted the butler's bony back. Except with his uncle, Byron, and numerous flings, physical displays of affection made him uncomfortable. *"Andersons do not engage in public displays,"* he'd been told often enough while growing up, like "Anderson" equaled a noble title.

Finally, Bernard relinquished his hold, smoothly returning to the role of restrained butler. "I take it you've settled in and will let me know if you have need of anything?"

Alex beamed fondly at his uncle's right-hand man. "You know I will."

"Very good, sir. Now if you'll excuse us, your uncle needs his medicine and a nap." A sharp glower from the steely-eyed butler ended Alfred's weak protests.

"I'm sorry, Alex. We'll talk more, later. I have to do what he says… or else."

Alex didn't stop to question what "or else" entailed, bidding them a good afternoon. He decided to forego his room in favor of visiting the kitchen to see if Martha, his uncle's housekeeper, had any of those wonderful oatmeal cookies he loved. He strolled down the hall, realizing his uncle's health concerns and Bernard's untimely arrival had made him completely forget about the stranger. Maybe later.

"Martha?" Alex called as he opened the kitchen door, expecting to find the gray-haired matron fussing about the brightly lit room. He stopped in the doorway, speechless at the sight greeting him. Instead of a plump, elderly housekeeper, he found the dark-haired man who'd puzzled him earlier, standing on a ladder, replacing the light bulbs in an overhead fixture. That explained a lot, in his opinion. It seemed his uncle wasn't above amusing himself with the handyman. Ordinarily, Alex applauded such—flaunting convention fit right in with his own methods of operation. In this case, however, the lack of propriety cheapened the memory of the partner who'd shared thirty years of his uncle's life, a partner who hadn't even been given a proper burial yet. Besides, wasn't changing light bulbs part of Isaac's job?

The stranger froze, gazing down warily, and Alex realized he'd been right in his earlier assessment. Although the man could very well be a money-grubbing gold-digger intent on taking a feeble old man for every available cent, the slightly built brunet made for attractive scenery, in a bookish, intellectual kind of way. A fall of dark-brown hair brushed his forehead, straight and thick. Auburn highlights shimmered under the light of the newly changed bulbs. Well-defined cheekbones and angular features lent him an exotic air, and judging his height against the six-foot ladder, he only reached about five and a half feet tall.

Sinewy muscles rippled under his snug T-shirt, compact and appearing more the product of work than a gym, and low-riding jeans hugged his slim hips, displaying a good view of flat belly when he raised his arms over his head. His lower lip, slightly fuller than the top, gave him a pouting expression, and even the librarian-type glasses perched on his nose did nothing to lessen his appeal. In short, he was exactly the kind of man Alex liked. He even had light-brown eyes!

Forcing himself to recall who the guy was and what he was doing there, Alex scowled. Attractive or not, it was time to put the upstart in his place. "I know what you're trying to do and I won't allow it," he announced, folding his arms across his chest.

The man laughed, his voice much deeper than Alex would have imagined coming from someone so small. "I'm changing a light bulb. Do you have something against me being able to see while I make dinner?"

A cook? The guy was a cook? Well, it made sense. Due to his uncle's illness, hiring a chef would be logical. However, that didn't give the man the right to take advantage of the situation. And where was Martha? Surely the woman who'd been employed at the house for ages hadn't been tossed aside for the sake of a boy toy.

"No, I have no objection to you *cooking*," Alex answered coolly. "What I object to is your crossing the lines with my uncle. You wouldn't be the first to see dollar signs when they looked at him, and likely not the last. None succeeded in parting him from his cash, and let me tell you, he's been conned by the best."

Furious amber eyes burned into Alex's as the man climbed down from the ladder. "I see. Well, rest assured there's only one person in this room after Alfred's money, and it sure as hell isn't me!"

Alfred? The cook addressed his superior by first name? He'd also kissed Alfred in the hallway. Martha was the only servant in the house allowed to kiss her employer. Furthermore, what was that crack about money? The Anderson legacy belonged to Alex by right, or soon would. Who the hell did this man think he was? "Let's cut to the chase, shall we? My uncle just lost his partner and he's vulnerable. Whatever game you're playing with him, I want it stopped."

A ferocious glare answered him.

"If it's money you're after, name your price. I'll pay, you go away. Deal?"

Alex had to hand it to him. The guy played his role well, burning with righteous indignation so realistic Alex nearly believed it himself.

"You're the asshole nephew, Alex," the man growled through clenched teeth.

"Yes, and you're the gold-digger who thinks he can flaunt his tight ass in front of a grieving old man and get himself a tidy bit of cash. Now that we're properly introduced, why don't you run along and find yourself another sugar daddy." Alex couldn't control the anger seeping into his words.

A reddened face and sharp gasp were Alex's only warnings before the stranger loosed his wrath. "Look, Alex, while you've been out thinking only of yourself, screwing anything that'd drop its pants, I've been here when your uncle needed me!" He smacked his hand onto the countertop. "When his lover lay dying, I was here. The night Byron died, Alfred called for hours and only got your stupid voice mail. Me, he got on the first ring! Now I'm minding my own business, trying to cook one of his favorite meals, one of the few pleasures Alfred has left, and you stroll in here flinging accusations!"

The agitated hornet of a man marched across the room and yanked a phone book from a shelf beneath a wall-mounted phone. "Why don't you take your overinflated ego out to a club somewhere and start fucking your way through greater Los Angeles, while me and my 'tight ass' get dinner on the table?" He flipped opened the directory to "Restaurants and Clubs" and flung the book at Alex, pages flapping. "There's plenty of skanks at the local nightclubs. Only don't bring them here. That would be disrespectful."

He hoisted the ladder to his shoulder and then stormed out the back door, muttering under his breath.

Alex stood clutching the open phone book, speechless, something that didn't happen often. Well, he certainly understood what his uncle saw in the feisty handyman/cook. Regardless of a deceptively unassuming appearance, the man exhibited the same spirit and fire of Alfred's late lover. Feisty or not, Alex wasn't going to give up with so much at stake. The usurper wasn't going to take advantage of the situation, and Alex would see to it if it was the last thing he did.

OH DEAR. First impressions certainly hadn't gone well, yet Byron remained convinced that his and Alfred's nephews belonged together, each being similar to their uncles in temperament and personality. Their first meeting, while explosive, hadn't been explosive in the way he'd hoped. He loved his nephew, but the boy did have a temper, especially when under attack, though Byron could hardly fault the apple for falling close to the tree. The Sinclair temper did little to dispel the myth of fiery redheads, and his and Douglas's arguments had been legendary. If his plan failed, he had only himself to blame, since he'd planted the seeds of jealousy to begin with.

Regardless of the failure of the initial meeting, he stood by the belief that placing forbidden fruit before Alex's nose was the only way to truly capture the boy's attention. If Byron had learned one thing about the man over the years, it was Alex's penchant for winning at all costs, and believing he couldn't have something made the prize much more enticing, eventually pushing him toward the edge. Yes, Byron suffered a twinge of guilt for involving Alfred, but was sure he'd be forgiven. After all, Alfred often quoted, "Sometimes the end justifies the means."

The one shining moment in the whole encounter had been the growing bulge in Alex's slacks as he'd verbally sparred with Paul. The spark had lit; Byron simply needed to fan the flames until they blazed. *The end justifies the means, indeed.*

CHAPTER FIVE

Murmured conversation greeted Alex, and he hesitated before the closed dining room door. Despite his best intentions, he couldn't help eavesdropping, especially when one of the voices was deep and rich, totally unlike Alfred's. The words made his blood boil.

"Alfred, you know I love you with all my heart. Still, I don't think this is right. I know he's your nephew, but I don't trust him. He's never here and hasn't done anything for anyone in this family outside himself."

"In this family?" How dare the meddler consider himself a relative? Adding insult to injury, even now the two-bit con man tried to turn the tables before Alex had a chance to expose the manipulative bastard for what he was.

"Now, Paul…," his uncle said in tones once used to placate Alex's stern grandparents.

Paul? Why did the name sound familiar? Frantically searching his mind for some reference to a servant or business associate named Paul, Alex strained to catch the words while his uncle continued, "While it's true he's not been here, I've never asked him to be. I'm sure if I'd told him...."

"Told me what?" Alex demanded, bursting into the dining room.

Paul regarded him from a position kneeling on the floor by Alfred's chair, the tilt of his chin haughty and unapologetic. "His napkin fell, I was picking it up," he offered as explanation for his compromising position. With fluid, graceful motions, he rose and obtained a new napkin from the adjacent buffet before seating himself to the old man's left, eyes clearly challenging Alex to question him.

"Uh-huh," Alex replied. An eyebrow rose in mocking disbelief. How dare this mere servant presume to sit at the same table with the family? His grandparents were probably rolling in their graves!

The butler chose that moment to enter the room. "Excuse me, sir, might I have a word?

As Bernard conversed in hushed tones with Alfred, Paul muttered under his breath, *"Honi soit qui mal y pense."*

Shame be to him who thinks evil of it? Well, now, what a shocker. Apparently, boy toy learned a little French somewhere down the line—or read a book or two.

When Bernard left, Alfred, oblivious to the byplay, indicated the chair to his right, directly across from Alex's nemesis. "Sit down, Alex. You're in for a real treat tonight." He gave an indulgent smile. "Paul prepared beef brisket with all the trimmings—my favorite!" With a crafty gaze, he added, "I believe it's one of your favorites as well, isn't it?"

Alex wouldn't give the man the satisfaction of the correct answer, which would have been "yes!" Instead he feigned indifference. "What happened to Martha?" He silently fought the urge to grind his teeth in frustration over the fact that what-ever "Paul" offered, his uncle seemed to be buying.

"Martha? Oh, we gave her the night off, didn't we, Paul?" The affectionate overtones turned on the handyman/cook/fuck toy made Alex's stomach churn. "Oh, forgive me," Alfred said. "You have met Paul, haven't you?"

"We've met," Alex confirmed, barely restraining an impulse to punch something.

Clearly mistaking Alex's meaning, Alfred beamed. "Oh, good. You know, I'm amazed the two of you never crossed paths before. Not once in all these years."

Years? "Years, Uncle? Exactly how long have you known *Paul?*" Alex spit the name like something vile.

His uncle appeared confused. "How long? Well, his whole life, naturally. He was born a few years after Byron and I built this house. Don't you remember? I'm sure I sent Victoria pictures."

"Pictures?" Alex's harsh gaze cut over to the subject of those pictures, who defiantly ignored him by serving Alfred from the numerous bowls on the table.

Suddenly, he recalled his mother showing him pictures of a chubby, bald baby before she died. "Paul Sinclair? P.J.?"

"The one and only," his adversary retorted from across the table. "Only no one's called me P.J. since I was twelve."

Alex searched for signs of his adversary's having won the first round. Instead of gloating, Paul appeared tired as he placed a filled plate before Alfred. Then the stress momentarily lifted from his features, replaced by a fond smile. "I hope it's as good as you've been building it up to be." Paul loaded his own plate and sat quietly, eyes downcast.

Realizing with a start that they were waiting for him to begin, and seeing no graceful way out, Alex ladled small amounts from each bowl onto his plate before serving himself a modest portion of brisket, fully expecting a barely palatable meal. In his experience, beautiful men belonged in the bedroom, not the kitchen. That was what cooks were for.

He reluctantly sampled everything, pleasantly surprised to discover the meal was, in fact, delicious. So the mystery man was Byron's nephew. You couldn't tell it by looking at him; the man bore no resemblance to any Sinclairs he'd ever met, which was why he hadn't recognized the guy. Didn't all Sinclairs have flaming red hair and milk-white skin? And being Byron's kin didn't prove Paul wasn't after Alfred's money. Byron and Alfred had never married, even during the brief period of legal gay marriage in California, but they'd been together a very long time. Perhaps Paul expected a share of the Anderson inheritance? *He'll get it over my dead body.*

Dinner proved a quiet affair, with Paul and Alex answering Alfred's questions while never speaking directly to each other. If the old man noticed their suspicious glances, he gave no indication. After a dessert of fresh fruit, Alfred made his apologies and retired for the evening, leaving "you young folk" alone to get better acquainted. Alex silently glared at Paul for a full minute before pushing his chair back and stalking from the room without a backward glance.

He knew his uncle wouldn't mind him borrowing the BMW, and even if Paul's suggestion had been made facetiously, Alex took advantage of the information and drove to the first club to catch his eye, searching for a distraction. He ordered his usual martini and leaned against the bar, already drawing curious glances from the sparse early-evening crowd.

If he were being honest with himself, he wasn't really in the mood for playing; he merely needed a release for his pent-up frustration. P.J. Sinclair. How Alex had tried to forget the name over the years, envying Paul a living mother and a father with the decency to die instead of walking away, never to look back except in a feeble attempt to make a profit from his late wife's death.

Through an endless stream of lawyers and deliberations, Alex's poor excuse for a father never once asked to see him, even while seeking full custody—primarily for the money to be gained for Alex's upbringing. Alfred fought tooth and nail, and in the end, the courts awarded Alex to his maternal grandparents. He knew Alfred cared for him, and he'd seen his uncle regularly, but usually when Alfred visited Boston or they vacationed together. His grandparents discouraged visits to the West Coast for fear Alex would be corrupted by "those Hollywood types" and his uncle's sexuality, and when old enough to do as he pleased, his visits were brief and infrequent, at best.

His thoughts were interrupted by a lean club boy in too tight jeans and a mesh shirt that revealed barbell-impaled nipples. He winked and sauntered over to pose provocatively against the bar. "Hey, handsome. I haven't seen you in here before. New in town?"

The guy was unoriginal and flaming, which wasn't Alex's type. In his favor, he was available and passably attractive—particularly as, with pale skin and bleached-blond hair, he bore no resemblance whatsoever to the olive-skinned, dark-haired nuisance back at Uncle Alfred's.

With a pronounced sway to his hips, the man drew closer, licking glossed lips and trailing his fingertips along the edge of the bar. Batting his lashes and grinning wickedly, he ran his eyes suggestively up and down Alex's body. "I'd be happy to show you... around."

Well, things couldn't get any less complicated. "Let's go," Alex replied.

JUST a little more…. After hours of intense concentration, Byron finally managed to move the book resting on the nightstand. Slowly and surely, he worked the heavy, leather-bound volume to the edge, waiting for the right moment, and once more….

The book fell to the floor with a resounding thud. Byron smiled and counted the seconds until he heard hurried footsteps and the opening and closing of doors. Alfred, who slept like the dead, didn't even flinch.

"Alfred? Are you all right?" Paul hissed into the darkened room. Light spilled through the door from the well-lit hallway.

Though he knew he couldn't be viewed by human eyes, Byron instinctively pulled back into the shadows. With a relieved-sounding sigh, his nephew retrieved and returned the book to the nightstand. He paused for a moment, gazing down at the old man lying cocooned in blankets and pillows. Alfred settled himself more comfortably into his soft nest with a satisfied sigh.

Placing a kiss on a crown of silvery hair, Paul whispered, "Good night, Alfred, sleep well."

A gentle smile played upon Alfred's lips, and Byron watched his nephew's mouth turn up in response. Apparently assured everything was fine, Paul turned and left the bedroom, easing the door closed behind him.

The poor child. He'd lost his father and his uncle, the only two family members who truly understood him. His strict, Catholic mother cared for him in her own way, never quite grasping the significance of her son's sexual orientation and choosing denial over attempting to fully accept her firstborn.

Douglas, while he loved Paul, was married to his job. When Alfred passed, the boy would be very much alone.

On several occasions Paul had brought home someone reasonably suitable. Unfortunately, most of his lovers quickly grew bored with his quiet lifestyle and unassuming ways. Then he'd met a colossal failure named Jordan, a highly unstable individual who'd ultimately broken Paul's heart. Since their breakup, Byron knew his own illness had kept his nephew from pursuing an active social life, and Paul spent any free time in an effort to ease a dying man's suffering and comfort a grieving Alfred.

Since Paul didn't know how to look after his own interests, it was up to Byron as uncle to ensure "old and lonely" never happened to him, and the wheels of phase two were now in motion.

TWENTY minutes after his encounter with the willing stranger, Alex left the club, following a less than memorable servicing in the men's room. It wasn't skill the man lacked—his mincing mannerisms left Alex cold. Alex liked men, with a definite preference for men who were *men*. His most recent conquest bordered on too feminine for his tastes. Regardless, the lackluster blowjob beat sitting around pretending to be one big, happy family at his uncle's... but not by much.

The antique grandfather clock in the foyer announced the arrival of midnight as Alex quietly entered the seemingly deserted manse. Making his way toward the staircase, a hushed voice caught his attention. He stealthily eased down the hall toward his uncle's bedroom. In the middle of the night, Uncle

Alfred should be sleeping. Why would anyone be down there to possibly disturb him? Was something wrong?

Sensing movement, Alex stilled and waited. It took a moment before it dawned on him that the voice he'd heard belonged to his uncle's nephew-by-partnership, Paul. Why was he not surprised? He realized the time and narrowed his eyes, contemplating why the man might be leaving Uncle Alfred's bedroom so late, clad in a pair of royal blue boxer shorts and nothing else. Even more disturbing was the sincere smile pasted to Paul's face.

Alex's heart nearly stopped. Yes, he'd already figured the guy was taking advantage of Uncle Alfred, but to desecrate his own uncle's memory—and Byron not even buried! Alex didn't believe his opinion of Paul Sinclair capable of sinking any lower, and he vowed to get the opportunist out of the house without delay and keep him out.

Returning to his room, he tried unsuccessfully to remove the vision of a seminaked Paul from his mind. Without the "librarian" glasses, Byron's nephew appeared far less bookish than during their earlier encounters, and far more sensual. Add to that the tousled hair and scanty attire and the guy practically screamed, "Come fuck me!"

And that smile! When Paul smiled, it transformed him into a young, carefree creature, someone even a connoisseur like Alex found tempting.

In his mind, that lithe body stood naked before him, Paul smiling for him. As much as he hated to, he understood the attraction. Perhaps Paul's relationship to Byron tore down the boundaries that propriety should have built. Alex considered the danger Paul presented, his devious mind forming a plan. He'd seriously regret any pain his schemes might cause his uncle, but Alex needed to expose the usurper's true nature, and the only way to do that was seduce Paul and prove he was nothing more than a fickle gold-digger.

Lying in bed, Alex mulled over his plan, liking the strategy more with each passing moment. He conveniently pushed aside images of his uncle's disappointed eyes and focused instead on the smooth skin and toned body of his target. Yes, like the slut from the club earlier, and many back in Houston, he considered this seduction already a done deal. Alex would lure Paul to bed, fuck his brains out, expose his duplicity, and slam the front door once Uncle Alfred tossed the whore out on his well-used ass.

Satisfied with his plotting, Alex yawned and began to drift off to sleep. As consciousness slipped away, phantom fingers brushed an errant strand of hair from his forehead. In his dreams, he was nine years old again, Byron sitting by his bedside, comforting him after yet another dream about his mother under the discreet guise of "men talk," as Andersons never admitted to weaknesses such as nightmares. Into the darkness, he whispered, "I'm sorry, Byron. I should have been here. I miss you."

In his dreams he heard a barely audible, "I know."

WORDS! He'd actually spoken words! And the book! Byron was gaining influence in the corporeal world beyond his greatest imaginings. Now, he lay on the bed next to his beloved, frantically repeating the things he'd wanted to say before the end. Though asleep, Alfred's lips curved upward in response to Byron's chants of "I love you."

CHAPTER SIX

How disappointing. Last night miracles had happened, and now? Nothing. Not the first wiggle or twitch. Even if someone had been present, they couldn't have heard Byron's disheartened sigh. He knew this because no one came running during his earlier scream of frustration.

He stared down into his nephew's laundry hamper, sweeping his transparent fingers once more through the object of his intention with nary a movement to show for his efforts. Replaying the past few hours, he reached the conclusion that, as a creature of shadow, his strength increased during the night and peaked around midnight. It seemed the rising sun chased away more than darkness.

It appeared he possessed one single power no matter what the hour, and with that thought in mind, his shadowy spirit passed through the closed bedroom door in search of Bernard, his unwitting helper.

"GOOD morning, sir, I trust you slept well?"

Bernard settled a breakfast tray on the nightstand and fussed about the room, opening the blinds and performing his normal morning rituals. A glance at the clock showed precisely 8:00 a.m. Byron often boasted you could set your watch by the punctual butler. He'd never once been late in his numerous years of service. No, not once in…. "Bernard, when were you born?" Alfred asked abruptly.

The butler in stopped in his tracks. "Sir?" he questioned in mid-pull of a drapery cord.

"You've been a part of my household since before Byron and I built this house, yet I don't know your age. How old are you?"

"Don't you know? I'm sure it's in my resume."

The evasion surprised Alfred, who was used to prompt, forthright answers. "I didn't personally review your resume. The former Mrs. Anderson hired you, if I recall."

Bernard resumed his tasks with his back turned, his shaking hands causing the window blinds to rattle when he reached to straighten them.

"Bernard? Is something wrong?"

"No, sir. Why would anything be wrong?" His trembling voice belied his words.

Alarmed at the unexpected reaction, Alfred did something he'd seldom done before—he gave a direct order. "Bernard, come here and sit down."

"As you wish," Bernard murmured, shoulders slumped in defeat. He struggled to move an armchair closer to the bedside, and Alfred suddenly noticed, for the first time, what familiarity and daily contact blinded him to. The hands fiercely gripping the padded leather armrests were as wrinkled and age-spotted as his own, the hair on the man's head just as silver. There was also far less of it.

Bernard's thin lips were trapped between teeth that Alfred knew soaked in a glass at night on the bedside table, and eyes once capable of spotting a speck of dust from across the room studied the patterns in the carpet through the thick lenses of bifocals.

When Alfred reached out his own weathered hand and covered the long fingers fiercely gripping the chair, his butler finally peeked up. "What the matter, old friend?" Alfred asked. "Why does the question bother you? I was merely wondering if and when you planned to retire, and if I'll need to find a replacement. Not that there's a hope in hell of replacing you," he hurried to add.

Cloudy gray eyes filled with tears, and the thin lips trembled. Fearing the worst, Alfred demanded, "Bernard, what's wrong? How have I upset you?"

Barely intelligible words escaped between choking sobs. "I don't want to leave! Got... no place to go!"

Surprising himself with his own strength, Alfred pulled the frail man from the chair and onto the bed. He enfolded Bernard in his arms and rubbed lulling circles on a bony back. "Shh. Why do you think you'd have to leave?"

Again he listened carefully to hear the words through the force of pitiful crying. "I'm too old! I can't... can't do my job anymore. I've outlived my usefulness, and I... I have no family left with time for me, save one great-niece, and you and your nephews."

"What do you mean, you can't do your job? I'm not questioning your work performance," Alfred assured the distraught man. "I merely wondered if you'd like to retire and do what you want to for a change."

"I... I've been doing strange things. I find myself in places... I don't know how I got there, or why I'm there." The wracking sobs eventually began to subside, though still frightening, particularly as Bernard never exhibited such behavior before. "You clearly told me to put Paul upstairs, but I forgot. I... I've moved things around and I don't know why." With a final wail for good measure, he added, "And I *am* doing what I want to, sir!"

Alfred chuckled softly and crooned, "It's all right, Bernard. Memory loss and misplacing things comes with getting older. The same things happen to me all the time. In fact, I'd be totally lost without you to keep my life organized."

His attempts at comfort only inspired louder sobs. Realizing Bernard needed to get the stress out of his system, Alfred held him close and rocked him, patiently waiting out the storm. When the heartbreaking cries reduced to weak hiccups, he resumed the conversation. "Bernard, I'd like to offer you a new position."

Watery, suspicious eyes rose to meet his. "A new... position?"

"Yes. Think of yourself as butler emeritus, if you will. It's come to my attention that I need to hire new domestics." He quickly held his hand up to discourage more tears. "No, hear me out. You're the best butler and the best friend a man could ever ask for, and I speak for Byron as well as for myself. What we'd have done without you, I shudder to think. However, we need to be totally honest with each other. My time is coming to an end." Again Alfred raised a hand to cut off protests. "Deny the facts all you want; you know it's the truth as well as I do. My only regret is that I couldn't live to the end of my days with Byron at my side." A bittersweet smile crept across his face. "I suspect we won't be separated long."

Holding Bernard's gaze, he explained what he had in mind. "I want you to train new staff and prepare them for the day when this house will have new masters."

"Masters?" From behind lined lenses, Bernard watched him closely, expression wary.

"Yes, Bernard: masters. This house will be the joint property of Alexander Martin and Paul Sinclair upon my death. I've added a stipulation that you continue to live here for as long as you like—as a retired family member, not a servant. I've been putting aside a fund for your retirement, and for the other employees of this house. It's quite a tidy sum, even by my standards."

"Why?" Bernard's eyes widened with surprise.

"Because you're as much a part of this family as anyone and...." He winked conspiratorially. "I want you to keep an eye on the boys. Would you do that for me?"

Bernard replied without hesitation, "Anything for you, Alfred."

"I was hoping you'd agree." Alfred smiled and kissed his old friend's balding head. "What say the two of us go out to breakfast and hash out the details, shall we?"

A faint tinge of pink crept up Bernard's cheeks. "I'm sorry, sir! Your breakfast is ruined."

"I'm sure Martha made me a lovely breakfast, too, and entirely healthy, as usual. This morning, I'm craving bacon and eggs for a change. Here, take this back to the kitchen while I shower and dress. Have Isaac bring the car around. We'll leave in half an hour." Alfred reluctantly untangled himself from his friend's embrace. Even if they weren't Byron's arms, the physical closeness of another body had been nice... while it lasted.

BERNARD immediately missed the warmth and comfort of being held close, something he'd rarely experienced in his life, and never from his gay employer, who'd always taken meticulous care to avoid intimidating his heterosexual employees.

He rose from the bed and gathered the now cold breakfast tray, realizing he still hadn't answered Alfred's question. In light of their conversation, revealing his age seemed unnecessary. Alfred's houses were all he remembered of his life, all he wanted to remember. The time before hadn't been happy. Now, he'd get his wish to live the remainder of his life where he felt needed, where he felt he belonged. What a tremendous relief not to be dismissed out of hand for the inability to perform his duties with the efficiency he'd once prided himself on.

Suddenly, an overwhelming urge to go to Paul's room consumed him, though he knew Paul was currently at the funeral parlor visiting with his uncle. Returning the tray to the nightstand, Bernard listened closely for the sound of running water. He couldn't say why it felt important that his employer not discover his plans. Relieved to hear a rumbling baritone emanating from the shower, singing the familiar strains of an old love song, he crossed the hall and quickly retrieved the item he sought.

Once he'd arranged the article on the bed, he returned the tray to the kitchen, humming along with Alfred's tune.

"UNCLE Alfred?" Alex rapped his knuckles lightly against the door before entering his uncle's bedroom. Singing from the bathroom inspired a chuckle; he recalled times he'd heard that particular ditty before, sometimes blended with Byron's tenor. They'd sung together like they'd lived together—in perfect harmony for the most part, with enough sour notes to keep things interesting.

Apparently, now wasn't a good time for a visit. As Alex turned to leave, a splash of bright color caught his attention. Sparing a glance to the closed bathroom door, he crossed the room to investigate the scrap of blue cotton contrasting starkly with the pristine white sheets of the unmade bed. He squinted before reaching out to pick it up, recognizing the offending garment as too small to belong to his uncle. He'd seen it before, and not long ago.

Anger burned through him, and he flung the damning evidence back where he'd found it. So his suspicious were true. Far from being upset about Byron's demise, Paul had taken full advantage of the situation, wasting no time in taking his uncle's place in the man's own bed.

The flames of rage were further fanned when Alex's active imagination supplied images of two bodies, one old and withered, that he tried to block, the other young, firm, and wanton, writhing together on the sheets. While he'd been out, leaving his uncle unattended, the conniving opportunist had made a move. Well, it certainly wouldn't happen again. Until he managed to convince his uncle to kick Paul out on his manipulative ass, Alex needed to stand guard.

An unbidden image appeared in his mind of that same ass wearing the thin covering now lying rumpled on the bed. Alex frowned. It had been past midnight when he'd seen Paul dressed in these, leaving the room. He must have returned later. What was he trying to do, give the old man a heart attack?

After a moment, clarity dawned. Yes, that was exactly what the young slut wanted to do. As open as Alfred was, Paul undoubtedly knew about the heart condition and planned to use the knowledge to his advantage. Well, he wouldn't get away with it.

The sudden quiet alerted Alex that his uncle's shower had ended and he was about to be caught snooping. He gently closed the door behind him, hastily retreating to the privacy of his own quarters to fume and plot against the man most certainly using his considerable charms to secure a hefty chunk of Alex's family's fortune.

While he dressed for Byron's funeral, his resentment for Paul grew.

CHAPTER SEVEN

THOUGH Paul knew his uncle had been well known and liked, he wasn't prepared for the massive crowd gathered to bid their final farewells.

Entering the sanctuary, Uncle Douglas at his side, he spotted several familiar faces, and many more he recognized from magazines. Some met him with sympathetic eyes while others turned away as if not knowing what to say. He greeted everyone warmly, hoping to put them at ease, unlike the man walking ahead of him, escorting the grieving Alfred.

Alex stared straight ahead, pointedly ignoring the crowd while the four of them strode down the aisle to the front of the cathedral and the pews reserved for their use—conspicuously empty save for Isaac, Martha, and Bernard. What was Alex's problem? He could at least acknowledge those who'd come to pay their last respects.

Maybe the man's just a dick. A definite possibility considering he'd avoided the house during Uncle Byron's illness and hadn't been a frequent visitor before then. *Be civil and get through today; maybe he'll go back to whatever hole he crawled out of.* Paul, recalling the circumstances, restrained a snort. "Hole" about covered it. The man was nothing but a slut—a gorgeous, totally worthless slut. *Probably never worked a day in his life.*

It didn't matter what kind of prestigious family he'd descended from, Alex Martin behaved like a common whore, uncaring that the one handing over money had lived a monogamous lifestyle for nearly as long as the arrogant asshole had been on the planet.

Paul subtly manipulated the seating arrangements, knowing Alex dared not challenge him in public, placing Alfred between the two of them. He fully expected to earn an evil glare, but didn't rightly care. Surprisingly, when he chanced to catch Alex gazing at him, his expression was far from hostile. Paul decided not to dwell on the change right now, for Alfred was the important one, and Uncle Douglas, seated on Paul's other side. Any pissing contests would have to wait.

Hoping the absence of evil glares meant an unspoken truce for the duration of the service, Paul turned his attention to the presiding minister. As he listened to the eloquently prepared eulogy, the reality sank in that his uncle was truly gone and not merely away at some business function, as he'd like to believe.

Silent tears tracked Paul's face, and he shyly glimpsed Alfred from the corner of his eye, trying his best to be strong. The worst of his mourning had occurred privately, on the rooftop of his store. It hadn't been pretty. He definitely didn't want Alfred to witness his pain, adding another thing for the poor old soul to worry about.

Although equally quiet in his grief, tears streaked Alfred's weathered face, occasionally wiped away with a handkerchief, only to be replaced by more. Paul gently squeezed his arm, fully believing no comfort would be offered from the man on Alfred's other side.

Chancing a quick peek, Paul's mouth dropped open as Alex divided rapt attention between the minister's words and comforting Alfred. Paul's surprise turned to shock when he noticed the tears staining the man's face. My God! If he hadn't known better, he'd swear Alex Martin had miraculously grown a heart!

Teary blue eyes roved upward and locked with Paul's. No words were spoken. He and Alex reached a silent agreement, at least temporarily, for the sake of the occasion. Throughout the service and at the graveside, they dealt politely with each other, even if the interaction was noticeably devoid of warmth.

After the final prayer, Douglas approached and hugged Alfred. "If you ever need anything...."

Alfred managed a weak smile. "I know, Douglas, I know."

Prayers said and mourners departing, Paul, Alfred, and Alex rode in a long black limousine back to the house. The day had taken its toll, and Alfred's head bobbed. Paul gently pulled Alfred onto his shoulder, earning a raised eyebrow from Alex. What was with him? If Paul didn't know better, he'd swear the guy was jealous. He quickly shook the notion off as ridiculous. He'd been around Alfred since birth and considered him a father, especially after the death of his own.

Alex couldn't possibly think.... Nah, no way. Regardless of what he'd said in the kitchen the first day, he'd soon learned Paul was Byron's nephew. No, he was simply being Alex: aloof and untouchable. Then again, he'd shed genuine tears at the funeral.

Paul stood no hope of ever figuring the man out, and hopefully, Alex would soon be on his way back to wherever he went to ignore his family. Paul knew those thoughts were hardhearted and uncharitable, but in truth Alex hadn't made himself available to offer comfort or attend matters as he should have.

When they arrived back at the house, Paul, out of long habit, moved to help Alfred to his room. A hasty "I can take care of it" from Alex had him stepping back, ready for battle.

Bernard averted the conflict by assuming control. "It's time for his medicine and a nap," he informed them, effectively ending the fight before it started.

All eyes turned to Alfred, who shook his head and chuckled. "I believe I must do as Bernard says. I'm a little tired and some rest might do me good. In fact, if you two don't mind, I think I'll have dinner in my room tonight and turn in early."

Of Paul, he asked, "Could I trouble you with showing Alex around a bit? I daresay he's not nearly as familiar with the area as you are. Perhaps you can make a reservation at Berkley's. I'm sure you'd both enjoy getting out after the day you've had, especially since I won't be joining you for dinner."

Paul expected an argument, and was oddly disappointed when one didn't come. Alex merely nodded, hugged his uncle, and wished him a good night. He turned and raised an expectant eyebrow.

With no diplomatic way out, Paul bid Alfred and Bernard a pleasant evening, then prepared to lay a few ground rules for the time he and Alex were apparently going to spend together.

Before he managed to say anything, Alex stopped him. "Look, Paul, I know we got off on the wrong foot; how about we start again?"

Paul didn't trust the sincere expression for a minute. "Start again how?" The smug smile blossoming to life on the handsome devil's face seemed familiar—Paul had encountered its like before on the faces of used car salesmen and former lovers.

"Well, I don't know about you," Alex drawled, a gentle

reminder of the years he'd spent living in Texas, "but I'm starving. What do you say we do like the man said and go to the restaurant he suggested: Buckeyes?"

"Berkley's," Paul corrected.

"Whatever. How about a nice, quiet meal and then maybe you can show me some of the sights?"

Either Alex was sincere or a damned fine actor, and if not for prior experience with Alex's kind, Paul might have been taken in by the apparent change of heart. Even so, he thought long and hard before deciding that since Alfred had suggested dinner out—and he'd do anything to make Alfred happy—maybe he should accept the offer. What could possibly go wrong? Worst-case scenario, if the asshole picked a fight and ditched him, he'd simply call a cab.

"Okay," Paul finally answered. "Give me a few minutes to change."

"What's the dress code?"

"Not too dressy, not too casual. I guess you could say business casual, as this is a weeknight."

"Okay." Alex glanced at a watch probably worth more than Paul's car. "I'll meet you at the door in fifteen minutes."

"That would be fine." Sudden inspiration hit, and Paul fought a laugh at the scheme unfolding in his mind. "I'll bring the car around."

Unfortunately for Alex, with his back turned, he missed Paul's evil smirk.

A QUARTER of an hour later Alex stood with his hands on his hips, glaring. "What the hell is this?"

Paul donned his best "cat that ate the canary" grin. "This is my car. I told you I'd pull it around, didn't I?"

"This isn't a car; this is a rusted-out piece of shit."

"Yeah, you're probably right. However, it's my piece of shit, and if we're going to make our reservation, you'd best get in." Paul enjoyed every minute of Alex's discomfort.

"There's a whole fleet of cars in the garage. Why not take one of those?"

"Because they're not mine," Paul explained logically.

Alex huffed and glowered at the vehicle, as though he hoped the rust bucket might go away. In the end he opened the passenger door and squeezed his large body into the tiny car. "Could you have possibly found a more uncomfortable vehicle?"

"Well, there's one smaller model I seriously considered. I ended up picking this one because it got better gas mileage." Who knew taking Alex out could be so much fun? If Paul had to spend an evening with his worst nightmare, well, he'd make the most of his misery, scoring a few points for the home team whenever possible.

A disgruntled "Harrumph" was all the response he got.

His passenger remained silent and brooding while they wound their way through the less frequently used roads and alleys that helped them beat downtown traffic, finally arriving at their destination with minutes to spare.

When Paul reached Berkley's, Alex swiveled his head, checking out the parking lot. "No valet parking?"

"No," Paul replied simply, keeping to himself the "spoiled brat" comment aching to spring off his tongue.

"And you say this was Uncle Alfred and Byron's favorite restaurant?"

"That's right." Paul shut off the engine. It knocked a few times before finally dying. "Alex, just because they had money didn't mean they flaunted it. In fact, Alfred once told me that if all you experienced of the world was first class and room service, you'd miss out on the other 99 percent of what life has to offer."

Having gotten the last word in, he climbed from his ancient vehicle, invoking the righteous anger of the driver's door, which shrilly protested. Momentary embarrassment shallowed his victory. He tried to keep his car in good condition, a near impossible task given the frequent trips he'd made over the past few months. Excessive mileage and years took their toll, not to mention the road salt and damp weather the old girl endured in Bishop. With a sigh, he acknowledged that, like it or not, the time had come to consider a replacement.

The two men crossed the parking lot silently and then entered the quaintly decorated restaurant. The maître d' rushed forward. "Good evening, Mr. Sinclair. I'm sorry to hear about the loss of your uncle. Such a wonderful man."

"Thanks, Henri."

Snapping his fingers at a lounging busboy, Henri murmured, "Go tell Thierry an important guest is here."

An imposing man in chef's garb hurried out from the kitchen a moment later, embracing Paul in a breath-stealing bear hug and planting a loud kiss on both cheeks. "Paul Sinclair, how are you doing, darling?"

Paul fought the embrace enough to choke out, "I'm fine, Thierry, and you?'

"Tsk, tsk, tsk. Don't lie to me, sweetie, I know better." Stepping back and grasping both of Paul's slender hands in his own beefy ones, the stocky Frenchman bent to peer into Paul's eyes. "You have my condolences. I'm truly sorry about your uncle's passing. So sad, he was a sweet, sweet man. Lovely funeral, by the way. How's dear Alfred holding up?"

Paul shook his head. "I can't say for certain. He tells me he's fine, and you know Alfred."

"Yes, Alfred could be on fire and he'd tell you he's fine." Finally noticing Alex, Thierry's eyes lit up. "Oh my; who's this stunning creature, Pauly? Have you been holding out on your Uncle Thierry? I didn't know you had a boyfriend."

Heat crept up Paul's cheeks. "I don't!" he blurted, earning raised eyebrows from both men. Even the maître d', discreetly pretending to ignore them, cast furtive glances their way.

Attempting to draw attention away from his hotly flaming face, Paul managed introductions. "Thierry, this is Alexander Martin, Alfred's nephew. Alex, Thierry Guillaume, owner of Berkley's."

"Alexander? Of course! The resemblance is unmistakable. You look like a younger version of your uncle." Ignoring Alex's obvious impatience, Thierry continued his ebullient rambling, "I've known him a long time, you know. He and Byron, so much in love. I'm very sorry for your loss." Even while offering sympathies, he cast suggestive peeks at Alex.

Sensing an imminent meltdown as Alex's hostile glares escalated to growling, Paul intervened. "Thierry, we've had a long day and we're starving. Can you send over some appetizers and a bottle of the merlot Uncle Byron liked? My usual table, please."

Thierry sighed, apparently conceding defeat. "I hope you enjoy your dinner. If you need anything, you have only to ask."

Paul dipped his head in acknowledgement before he and Alex followed the maître d' to a table near the back of the restaurant. "I thought you'd appreciate some privacy." Noticing Alex's stony expression, he ensured Thierry was out of hearing and then explained, "He means well, he truly does. He just comes on a bit strong sometimes."

Alex emitted a weary sigh. "Is he always like that?"

"Friendly?"

"No, looking at his customers like they were pieces of meat."

Paul considered Thierry's behavior. "Truthfully? I've never seen him act so unprofessional before. I know he ended a lengthy relationship recently; maybe he's a bit on the prowl." What was the problem? Didn't Alex live to be fawned over?

The arrival of the waiter with their appetizers and wine kept the conversation light. Alex surprised him by saying, "The same for me, thanks," when Paul placed his order.

"Uh, no offense or anything; you do realize what I ordered, right?" he ventured.

"Saltimbocca? Of course, it's one of my favorite dishes, although I prefer the veal version. I'm sure the pork will be acceptable."

They shared something in common? More than just Alfred and Uncle Byron? Paul might be setting himself up, but he had to ask, though he knew the question would seem absurd coming out the blue. "What's your favorite book?"

Without missing a beat, Alex answered, "Which genre?"

Paul's wasn't quick enough to hide his surprise. "You read?"

Alex's eyes crinkled at the corners, and he appeared to be fighting a laugh. "Well, I may not use the darned thing, but I did earn a law degree. Last I heard, literacy was a basic requirement."

For the second time that evening, Paul felt his face flame. "I... I'm sorry," he stammered, "what I meant was...."

"I know what you meant," Alex said, letting him off the

hook. "The truth is I love to read. I'm currently working on a mystery novel about a priest in eighteenth-century Italy."

"The Monk in the Shadows?"

When Alex nodded, Paul found himself babbling. "You're kidding, right? Wow, I finished that book a few days ago. It's one of my favorites. How far are you into it?"

"Brother Rupert has left for Sicily."

Hmmm… about a quarter into the book. I wonder if he's found the clues yet. "Who do you think the killer is?"

The waiter brought their salad course. The greens sat ignored and slowly wilting, no match for scintillating conversation.

"How is it you've already read a book that hasn't yet been released?" Alex asked. "I had to pull a few strings to get my copy."

Paul smiled, warming up to one of his favorite subjects. "Owning a bookstore has its advantages. I get to preview upcoming releases."

"You own a bookstore?"

"Yup." Paul couldn't hide a pleased grin. "I worked at a chain during college for peanuts to learn the business. When I graduated, I found an old building in Bishop in need of major repairs and made a deal."

Alex opened his mouth and closed it again, staring at Paul with a quizzical expression. "Why didn't you buy into a franchise and build a new building? Wouldn't that have been easier?"

"Nothing worthwhile is easy," Paul replied. "Besides, buying land and building from the ground up cost more than my budget allowed. In the end, I did most of the work myself and saved a fortune."

Dinner went by quickly after they'd broken the ice, and

Paul found himself relaxing and enjoying both dinner and the company. From time to time, he reminded himself that this wasn't a friendly date and he needed to stay on guard.

After leaving the restaurant, they took their time driving home. It had been one of the most pleasant evenings Paul had experienced in a long time, all things considered. That is, until he parked his car and entered the house, intent on checking on Alfred, having a nightcap, and curling up with a good book.

The moment they were inside, Alex pinned Paul against the foyer wall, his insistent mouth descending in a savage kiss. "What the fuck?" Paul sputtered, attempting to fight off the sudden aggression.

"You know you want me, baby, why be coy?" Alex rumbled against his panting mouth.

"Alfred...."

"He doesn't have to know," the husky voice answered, too quickly.

"Stop it, Alex! I have to go check on Alfred!"

With unmistakable lust in his eyes, Alex commanded, "Meet me in my room later."

Paul hissed, "Oh, *hell* no!"

Alex's shocked dismay was gratifying. "What? What did you say?"

If looks could kill, Alex Martin would have gone up in flames. "Let me go, Alex. I need to go see about Alfred, and then I'm going to bed—alone."

Once Alex released his hold, Paul sprinted down the hall like the hounds of hell were nipping at his heels, embarrassed beyond belief, for though truly offended by Alex's actions, his traitorous body had other ideas. His sudden erection made a quick retreat awkward. He only hoped the arrogant bastard hadn't noticed; the last thing he needed was to fuel Alex's already raging ego.

THE evening went better than expected, and Alex didn't even have to pretend he'd had a good time. In different circumstances, he'd have enjoyed himself immensely. It was one of the best dates he'd ever had. *Wait a minute*, he reminded himself, *dinner with Paul Sinclair wasn't a date.*

Having forgotten his original intent in feigning friendship with Paul confused him, to say the least. The man was handsome, sincere, and passionate when he spoke of weekends spent sawing and hammering, slowly refurbishing a labor-of-love bookstore.

The image Byron's nephew presented to the world conflicted drastically with Alex's presumptions. On the one hand, Paul Sinclair seemed to live simply, driving a car long past its prime and working hard to build a business with his own hands. On the other hand, Paul had his own room at the mansion, across the hall from Uncle Alfred's. Why did he say he lived in Bishop?

Making his way to his own lonely room, Alex recalled those bright eyes, aglow with excitement for such mundane things as polished wood floors, the smell of old books, and plans to renovate the upper floor of the bookstore into a coffee shop. For a precious few moments, the brooding and serious façade had cracked, allowing them to share an unexpectedly enjoyable meal, discussing trivial aspects of their lives while meticulously steering clear of heavier topics. Like Alfred, or the man they'd recently laid to rest.

If Paul was, in fact, Alfred's lover, Alex could hardly blame the old man. Paul wasn't as polished as most kept men of his acquaintance; no, far from it. He obviously didn't spend hours perfecting his looks, and his appearance seemed unaltered by a surgeon's knife, a rare occurrence in the show-business circles of Los Angeles—the sources of Alfred's financial power.

While substantial money had passed down through the family, Alfred Anderson, attorney to the stars, had done well in his own right and could well afford to keep his boy toy very comfortably.

Alex loved his uncle and wanted him to be happy, but moving so quickly to a new lover seemed disrespectful to Byron, especially in light of Paul's age. Nearly fifty years separated the two, though rationally Alex knew age didn't matter. His uncle was an adult and not in the least bit senile. Alfred had the right to make his own decisions.

Finally, the real issue dawned on him. As much as he fought against the inappropriate attraction, he wanted Paul, and guilt rankled. Damn, the man was good. Not only had Paul enchanted Uncle Alfred, he'd managed to charm Alex as well, something no one else had ever done.

No, it wasn't going to happen. Alex intended to expose the manipulator, and once he was out of the picture, Alex would help his uncle find a more suitable partner—preferably someone closer to Alfred's own age. Afterward they could both put Paul Sinclair out of their minds for good.

CHAPTER EIGHT

THE days passed, and Alex's structured schedule rivaled his college days'. He rose early, spent much of the day learning from his uncle or other associates, and if he went to bed late, it wasn't due to clubbing. No, these days his free evenings found him sequestered in his uncle's office, researching. The Internet proved a valuable tool for learning pretty much anything, like the success rate of his uncle's upcoming surgery and the attending physician's stellar reputation. He also located a bookstore in Bishop, California, owned by Paul Sinclair, found that Paul had graduated college with honors and was highly active in charity work, both in Los Angeles and in Bishop.

Try as he might, he couldn't find one negative thing about the man anywhere. When questioned, his uncle's associates sung the man's praises—at length. Alex watched and waited for Paul to slip up, then watched some more. It didn't happen. On the contrary, with each new day he grew more and more impressed with Byron's nephew, almost willing to turn a blind eye on the evidence of Paul's being a little too close to Alfred. Almost.

Alex studied the man from across the dinner table, though Paul seemed oblivious, intent on his conversation with Alfred.

"There were seven interviews today for a butler and three for housekeeper." Paul sighed, placing his napkin on his empty plate. "We found some outstanding candidates. Thank goodness it's over and done with."

"Well, they should be the best," Alfred assured him. "They came from the finest agency in Los Angeles."

Paul scowled. "Well, except for…."

"Except for what?" Alex prompted, curious.

"Well…." Paul squirmed, twisting his fingers together. "The accounting firm keeps sending people, even though I told them we've made our decisions. To put it bluntly, those applicants were totally unsuitable."

Alex found it extremely telling that Alfred's accountant took such a personal interest in his client's affairs, above and beyond what the job description entailed. Unlike when he'd searched for information on Paul, the accountant's name and firm produced some pretty noteworthy results, and not all of them positive.

"Don't worry about it," Alex said, "I'll handle it. I've been meaning to give Maxwell a call, anyway."

Already rehearsing the conversation in his head, he nearly missed Paul's quietly murmured, "Thank you."

Alex merely inclined his head politely in acknowledgment. It'd been coming for some time, and he definitely needed to have a conversation with good ol' Maxwell. Sipping the last of his wine, he made a mental note to call first thing in the morning.

"THAT'S right," Alex said into the phone, most of his attention fixed on his laptop and his uncle's portfolio. One by one, he systematically updated user names and passwords. "We've already made our decisions. Bernard and Martha will train the new staff before retiring at full pay."

Alex's smile turned devious, though he knew the man on the other end of the line couldn't see him. "That's what Uncle Alfred wants." Sputtering indignation forced him to hold the phone away from his ear. He truly enjoyed dropping the next little bit of information too. "They'll both continue to live here. The guest house is being remodeled to include two apartments."

He listened quietly for a moment, or rather, pretended to. There was nothing his uncle's accountant could say that he wanted to hear. Digging the knife in deeper, he continued, "Paul conducted the initial interviews and background checks. The final decisions belonged to me, Bernard, and Martha." It should have been obvious at this point that the candidates suggested by the Turner, Turner, and Walden firm hadn't even been considered, nor would they be.

"Although we appreciate your concern, we don't need any more résumés at this time." Though his words were polite enough, he made sure his tone clearly conveyed, *"Don't send anyone else!"* Maybe the polite warning would get the man to stop harassing Paul with waste-of-time job seekers.

Of course the integrity-challenged bean counter protested the new arrangement. It kept him out of the loop he'd enjoyed for thirteen years. Questions had arisen when Alex assumed control of his uncle's investments, and it appeared Maxwell had used shady accounting practices with regard to his client's finances. Alex planned to ease him out slowly, and once his hands were prised free of Alfred's interests, the door would be slammed and locked. Planting informants in the household wasn't going to happen.

Turning a deaf ear to the protests while continuing to study his uncle's files, Alex bid the man an insincere "Good day," and then he ended the call.

Although he wasn't an accountant, Alex knew bill padding when he saw it, and Maxwell Turner had taken full advantage of Alfred's recent inattention to take what wasn't his. Three gym memberships and two personal trainers? Alex belonged to one fitness club and had never employed a trainer in his life. The duplicitous bastard must have trusted Alfred not to question any expenses submitted from Houston, and Alex asked an attorney friend to investigate the gyms Alex hadn't set foot in. The pilfering and mismanagement of Alfred's accounts might not be worth suing over, what with the negative publicity a lawsuit would bring, but definitely warranted a good firing. First, Alex needed to carefully extricate the man's greedy hands from any Anderson assets—Maxwell could still do a lot of damage.

Alex grinned, supposing, even now, that Maxwell was discovering that he no longer had access to Alfred's online accounts—and changing passwords were just the beginning.

Surprisingly, and proving he really was an Anderson at heart, one taste of business had left Alex wanting more, and he thrived on the challenges before him. His uncle invested with companies in fields of personal interest, which made the job even more enjoyable.

Equally amazing was how efficient Paul had turned out to be in assuming the role of secretary and household organizer, handling such mundane tasks as shopping and dealing with contractors about the planned changes to the guest house—tasks that, quite frankly, Alex found baffling. The cooperation left Alex free to focus on the financial and business matters, like monitoring spending on the project. Far from attempting to profit from his activities, Paul was a shrewd bargainer and watched every penny. The experience he'd gained during the renovations to his store proved invaluable.

With Isaac needed more around the house, Paul also escorted Alfred to his appointments. Unfortunately for Alfred, Paul talking directly to the doctor resulted in a severe reduction in his brandy consumption. When time for medication rolled around, now Paul appeared instead of Bernard, doling out pills and ordering Alfred to rest. Paul's every action declared his obvious affection for the old man.

Well, he has to behave like that, Alex rationalized. *He's a good actor, playing a role.*

He sighed, willing to admit, if only to himself, that it wasn't true. Paul Sinclair remained an enigma. When others were around, Alex maintained civility for Alfred's sake; however, the moment they were alone, he tried every trick in his vast repertoire to get into Paul's pants. Each and every time, Paul firmly declined the offers, carefully orchestrating the schedule to allow them little time alone.

Alex's stomach grumbled, and he rose and stretched, deciding to visit Alfred for a chat about Maxwell before breakfast. Tapping softly on the doorframe, he waited patiently before easing the door open and stepping inside when he received no answer.

"Uncle?" he called. A movement glimpsed from the corner of his eye drew his attention to the window. His uncle and Paul ambled along the garden path, occasionally touching or exchanging a casual glance. Things Alex's mind, eagerly seeking fault, blew out of proportion.

When they turned toward the house, he retreated lest he be

caught spying. About to leave, he recalled the morning not long ago and what he'd found on the bed. He couldn't help himself. Quickly scanning the sheets, he caught sight of a small, square package that had once held a condom lying on the comforter. Leaving the cellophane wrapper where it lay, he made a hurried exit, his blood pressure steadily rising with each step.

"WHAT'S on the agenda for today?" Alex asked, wiping the remnants of a tasty breakfast from his mouth. Martha's cooking would be sorely missed now that she'd announced her imminent retirement. At sixty-eight years old, she deserved to retire. However, he'd miss the cookies she used to bake for him. But she'd still be in the house and maybe up to the occasional request.

Paul, in the role of personal secretary, never looked up from pouring Alfred's tea. "You have a meeting with the attorney at ten and the broker at eleven thirty. I'll be taking Alfred to his doctor's appointment at ten thirty, and you'll be joining us for lunch at one at Berkley's."

Alex had to hand it to Paul; the man was efficient. "How about this afternoon?"

After a long pause, Paul murmured, "Have you forgotten? It's the reading of Uncle Byron's will."

Well, damn. Yes, he had forgotten.

Alfred placed a reassuring hand on Paul's. Between the gesture and the reminder that they'd soon be hearing Byron's final message, Alex suddenly found breakfast no longer agreeing with him. The warmth in Paul's eyes as he and the old man shared a quiet moment of silent communication quickly replaced any traces of remorse with something more familiar: suspicion.

Suddenly uncomfortable, Alex changed the subject. "You said the interviews were over?"

"Yes," Paul replied. "We narrowed the choices down to two possibilities for butlers, and Bernard decided on William McCord. He and the new housekeeper, Theresa Garcia, start today. They both came highly recommended."

Though Alex still harbored some resentment, he was a firm believer in giving credit where due. "I want to thank you for overseeing the hiring of the new staff. I've got my hands a bit full these days."

Alfred smirked, though prudently remaining quiet.

Eyes wide with surprise, Paul stammered his reply, "W... well, I know Bernard was worried. How considerate of you to let him choose his replacement."

They performed an awkward dance, working together for the greater good, which would have been a complete failure had they not both been sincere in their efforts to cooperate. It was becoming obvious to Alex that Paul was sincere in everything he said or did, casting doubts on his earlier assumptions about the man's character. There was still the matter of the evidence... like what he'd found before breakfast lying on his uncle's bed. He pushed the unpleasantness to the back of his mind for later thought. "Since he and Martha will continue live here and oversee things, they're actually doing us a huge favor." Besides, Alex was comfortable with them and didn't want them to leave.

Finally, Alfred added his sentiments, voicing Alex's feelings. "They've been with me so long; they're a part of the family. I'm rather embarrassed to admit I didn't know how old they were, and it's past time for them to relax a bit." His shrewd gaze focused on Alex. "How progresses 'Introduction to Business 101'?"

"I had no clue how much work there was to being you," Alex admitted. "I think I'm finally getting the hang of things, though. Um, I think you should know I intend to replace your accountant. Until I locate a suitable replacement, I'm going to be especially hands-on in that area."

"You do what you think is best," Alfred replied. His lack of reaction to the news spoke volumes. No doubt he knew everything and had merely given Maxwell enough rope to hang himself. Alex would've done the same. His uncle added, "If you need any help, I'm sure Paul could be of assistance."

"Paul?" Alex asked, suspicions and an eyebrow rising.

Alfred patted his mouth with a napkin. "He majored in business management with a minor in accounting."

Two smiles greeted Alex when he glanced up, Paul's bashful and Alfred's boastful.

"You don't say," he muttered.

"Oh, yes. Finished top of his class too!" the old man crowed, beaming like a proud parent.

Those smiles turned to each other, and Alex fought the temptation to make gagging noises. Was it his imagination, or had Paul walked with a slight limp this morning when he'd arrived at the breakfast table? Was Uncle Alfred more chipper than usual?

Thankfully, Bernard interrupted his thoughts. "Sir, Helena is on the phone from Boston. She claims it's urgent."

"It's always urgent with her," Alfred growled, rising from his chair. "Probably misplaced her pearl earrings again and wants me to come flog the maids until they confess. Excuse me, boys. I need to go see what the old dragon wants."

"Helena? Great-aunt Helena?" Alex asked.

"None other," Paul replied. Though outwardly calm, with no one around to ensure Alex played nice, he was probably ready to bolt and run. However, other than the nervous, side-long glances at the closed door, Paul hid his discomfort well.

Searching for a way to keep the conversation going, Alex offered, "She's still a harpy, I suppose. Always after me to 'get married and carry on the family name'. How quickly she's forgotten that my name is Martin, not Anderson." He cocked his head thoughtfully. "Although she did try to get me to change it a few years back."

Nearly choking on a mouthful of coffee, Paul spluttered indignantly, "Doesn't she know you like men?"

Alex snorted. "Makes no difference to her. Her second husband was gay as blazes, and they had two children, some-thing she likes to keep reminding me of. Even the very thought makes me shudder. Poor man. Her last name is no longer Anderson, either."

Quiet footsteps passed outside the door, and Paul, appar-ently reminded they were alone, set his cup down and pushed his chair back from the table with an apologetic frown. "Well, if you'll excuse me, I have work to do."

Alex rounded the table in an instant, effectively blocking Paul's retreat. "What's your hurry, Paul? You told me the schedule. There's still plenty of time before you need to be anywhere." As if on cue, the grandfather clock bonged the hour. Alex added suggestively, "Hmm... looks like I have time to spare too. I have a few suggestions of how we can fill the void."

"Alex." Paul huffed out an aggrieved sigh. "I'd hoped to get through one meal without having to deal with this. I've told you a million times: I am *not* taking advantage of Alfred."

"Prove it."

"Prove it? How?"

Alex's smile held no humor. "Sleep with me."

Anger flashed in Paul's eyes and he hissed between gritted teeth, "I don't have to prove anything to you, asshole."

"Because you can't," Alex murmured into his ear. "I *know* you fucked him. I found the condom wrapper on Uncle Alfred's bed this morning. You need to learn to be more discreet or you'll scandalize the servants." He turned and stalked away, leaving Paul openmouthed and staring.

A CONDOM wrapper? Alex found a condom wrapper? On Alfred's bed? Well, as far as Paul knew, the only person living in the house who'd had sex in the recent past was Alex himself. Well, Alex and possibly Isaac—and hopefully not together. But him sleeping with Alfred? Ridiculous! The man was like a father, for Pete's sake, and his own dear uncle's partner!

Paul fervently wished Alex would get over his irrational paranoia. They'd formed an uneasy alliance, yet whenever no one was around, the accusations began. As much as Paul hated them, he almost understood. He'd be the same way if someone attempted to take advantage of Alfred.

What a pity Alex didn't know how to trust, because, personality conflicts aside, they made a great team: Alex running the financial side of things and Paul handling domestic issues, including making sure Alfred made his appointments.

Then there were times when Alex forgot to hate him and spoke to him as an equal, though those were few and far between. Whenever Paul gained a measure of trust, some new, ludicrous, imagined evidence reignited Alex's suspicions anew.

Why couldn't the man simply accept that not everyone was out for all they could get, no matter who they hurt in the process?

Yes, dealing with Alex amounted to "one step forward and two steps back." How Paul hated the innuendo! Not for a minute did he believe the sexual offers to be real; it was as if Alex was testing him somehow. Try as he might, he couldn't think of the right answers, either. They seemed to change from minute to minute.

The longer he knew the man, the more Paul questioned his earlier opinions. Alex was nearly obsessive about hiding his true self from the world; however, little hints hid here and there if one knew where to hunt. Like certain books missing from the library shelves and Internet searches that hadn't been erased for websites dealing with heart disease and treatments. The attending physician and hospital where Alfred's procedure was scheduled had also been researched. Most telling was a bookmark for the closest paramedics.

Paul knew he shouldn't snoop, yet manners hadn't prevented him from picking up Alex's casually discarded phone one afternoon. A quick inspection revealed phone numbers for the doctor, hospital, and paramedics programmed into the device. Those weren't the actions of a cold and uncaring man.

Furthermore, Alex became oblivious to his surroundings when preoccupied, and on several nights, Paul quietly observed him in his quest for knowledge about Alfred's condition. When he wasn't actively trying to be an asshole, Alex could be a decent and caring man. And the decent and caring part of Alex's complex personality was starting to wear Paul down.

It had been a long time since he'd been with anyone, and Paul couldn't look at Alex Martin, sitting in his uncle's office avidly reading—glasses he didn't wear in public perched on his nose—without thinking of taking him to bed. Even now, the thought of how he looked, eyes lit with passion while reading some interesting passage, left Paul hard and aching for release.

Well, as Alex pointed out, Paul did have a while before he needed to be anywhere. Maybe he should take another shower —a cold one.

~

THE time finally arrived for the reading of Byron's will, and due to Alfred's condition, the event took place in Alfred's home office.

Richard Gentry, Alfred and Byron's legal counsel, ensured every designee attended: Alfred, Bernard, Martha, Paul, Douglas, Isaac, and Alex. The dour attorney read the preliminaries and then inserted a disk into a combination DVD player/television. The screen filled with a still image of Byron Sinclair, elegantly attired in a business suit and seated behind the desk of his downtown office, an indication that when the video was filmed, his condition hadn't yet kept him from public life or the job he'd loved. At the click of a button, the image came to life.

Paul's eyes filled with tears. His uncle looked like he had before falling ill. The video had obviously been made some months ago, as the man still sported a full head of hair and, for the most part, seemed healthy.

Quiet sniffles accompanied Byron's voice as he addressed those he'd loved in life. "Before we get to the details, I want to tell every one of you how much you mean to me. Alfred, words aren't enough. I have a special disk solely for you," he said with a saucy wink at the camera. "As much as I love these people, some things should be kept between the two of us, don't you agree, love?

"Paul and Alex," he continued. The two cast questioning glances at each other. "You are the sons I never had, and I regret the law was against our adopting and raising you as our own. Sadly, you don't know each other well yet. Suffice it to say that Alfred and I love you equally and hope you'll come to view each other as family, as we do.

"Bernard and Martha. You've been the most loyal friends a man could ask for and always did what's best for me and Alfred, regardless of the circumstances. Not a day goes by that I don't thank the heavens for you.

"Douglas, you old stick in the mud. We were quite the team in our younger days, and I'm going to miss our arguments, although you never win." Byron brattily stuck out his tongue, causing a few chuckles, particularly from Douglas himself. "You can argue with the best of them. Too bad you decided against a career in law. You might have given me a run for my money.

"Isaac, a man is measured by where he's going, not where he's been. You can't look back if you're looking forward."

Paul observed Isaac standing at the back of the room, silent tears trickling down his grief-stricken face. Those cryptic words obviously held great meaning for him. Paul narrowed his eyes as he saw… nah, couldn't be. A trick of the light made the weeping man appear to be enveloped in shadow.

On screen Byron continued, "I leave my entire estate to my partner, Alfred Anderson, with the exception of one item for each of you. I'm told my methods are highly irregular, but individual disks have been made, carrying a personal message from me to you, telling what the item is and why I want you to have it. Richard knows the details of my behest and will ensure my wishes are carried out. Know that I love you all, and if I'm able and aware, my love will continue long after my death."

The image faded to black. Each attendee received a disk and instructions to view Byron's video privately in their room, with Douglas using the vacant green room. Paul noticed that Isaac appeared much calmer, though he seemed reluctant to leave his corner. Finally, he took his disk, and with a sad smile, followed the others into the hallway.

After Richard's assurances that he'd attend to Alfred, Paul hurried down the hall to his room, putting the disk into the player and flopping onto the bed to watch. His uncle's image appeared on screen. Unlike in the earlier video, in this one Uncle Byron appeared more informally dressed. The disk had obviously been made at a later date, based on the noticeable absence of bright red hair and the defined hollows in his cheeks, signs of a battle being lost.

"Hey, P.J.," his uncle said quietly, invoking the childhood nickname Paul hadn't heard from him in years. Byron's voice was hoarse and raspy, a condition that plagued him during the final months of his life. "If you're watching this, it means I've lost the battle." With a wry smile he added, "Don't cry for me, because I won the war—big-time. I firmly believe the most important thing in life is who you hang with, and I was surrounded by the best people in the world. I also did what many fail to do: I built a lasting relationship with someone I loved more than life itself, who felt the same about me.

"It's always struck me as sad how few people ever know they're truly loved. I had that, and I want the same for you. I've noticed how you study me and Alfred, wistful expression on your face, and how hard you took the breakup when Jordan turned out not to be the one.

"Yes," the image confessed, "I knew more about him than you realized. I also recognized what you didn't. He wasn't the one for you, Paul, and you know it, though I can't fault you for taking your commitments seriously and being determined to make your relationship work. You're stubborn enough to try saving a lost cause.

"That's my fear—that you'll let your stubbornness keep you from the best things in life, like you've always done. This brings me to my next point: money. Every time we've offered, you've refused. Did it ever occur to you that we wanted you to have it? Or that it hurt us when you wouldn't accept our gifts?"

A knife ripped into Paul's heart. Had his uncle honestly mistaken his determination to be self-sufficient as ingratitude? His throat constricted and hot tears stung his eyes. What had he done?

His uncle's next words absolved his guilt. "I know that's not how you meant your refusals. You'd never hurt a fly. I want you to understand something: if we owned a candy story and offered you candy, we'd expect you to take it because we had plenty and wanted to share it with those we loved. In our case, we were blessed with money." Byron chuckled. "Perhaps candy would have been less bothersome."

Paul couldn't agree more.

"What I'm saying is: we love you and want to give you the good things we have; the same as any parent wants for their child. Although you refused what we offered, we put the money into an account." A frail hand rose, as if anticipating protest. "I know you worry about your half sisters and their future. The money will pay for their college, with enough left over for dorms, books, and a modest vehicle. It's the least I can do for my brother's widow and her children."

Though dying, his uncle's thoughts were still for those left behind. Paul vowed to be the kind of man his uncle had been: loving, thoughtful, considerate, and kind—traits further proven by his uncle's next words. "There's something I want you to have." A wholehearted smile eased the weariness from Byron's features, however temporarily. "Remember the last trip to the beach we made with Alfred and our artist friend, Eddie? The storm? Well, I remember you driving us down the coast, and later, driving us back, allowing me and Alfred to snuggle in the backseat. I want you to have the Jeep. Don't argue with me on this. I know good and well you won't replace your car until the damned thing dies on the side of the road, and I worry. I love you and don't want anything to happen to you. Besides, the Jeep's much better in snow than the car, and what happens if Alfred needs you in January? Will you be able to get there if it's snowing? If it helps, don't view my gift as me giving you a Jeep, consider it like I darned well expect you to be there for Alfred when he needs you, and I'm merely providing the means."

With a start, Paul realized how prophetic the words were— Byron died in the middle of January, with a snowstorm brewing in Bishop. If Paul had waited even an hour longer, the car wouldn't have made it past the city limits.

"One more thing," Byron said. "I know you won't accept money, so I've left stocks and certificates of deposit in your name. I'd never pressure you to do something you didn't want, though I hope someday you'll have the children of your own you've always talked about, and this is my present to them. With the exception of what I'm leaving the others, the remainder of my estate belongs to Alfred, as I know you wouldn't take it."

Though still afraid of being considered ungrateful, that his life wasn't about to change as drastically as Paul'd feared brought an enormous sense of relief. He liked things the way they were, only wishing his uncle were still alive to be a part of it and one day meet the children who'd be the recipients of such generosity.

The next statement came as no surprise; in fact, he'd expected it. "I have two favors I'd like to ask, though I know I don't even need to voice the first one. Take care of Alfred, will you? He's not well, and he's as stubborn as you are when it comes to admitting he needs help.

"The second thing is: keep your heart and mind open. You never know when you'll meet someone perfect for you, and always bear in mind that what you need and what you think you want are two entirely different things."

Tears were running down Paul's face as he watched his once vigorous uncle gasping for breath, the poor man's strength clearly at an end.

In a husky whisper, his uncle said, "Paul Jacob Sinclair, always remember that I love you. My name isn't on your birth certificate; that honor belonged to my brother. Not being your biological father didn't stop me from considering you mine from the day he died. You're the best son a man could wish for. Oh, don't cry for me, kiddo. More years would be nice, I won't deny it, but I can't complain. My life was good. Actually, better than good. I hate that I can't give you a hug right now, because I'm sure you need one. You always had a huge heart. How they got it in so small a body always amazed me."

One final wish concluded the message. "May your life be as wonderful as mine."

On the fifth replaying, Paul fell asleep to the comforting sounds of his uncle's voice. Being nearly asleep, he didn't realize it wasn't the recording quietly whispering, "I love you, P.J."

WHILE the others hurried to view their videos, Alex placed his disk in the player in his room and returned to the empty office to pour himself a gin and tonic. He'd neglected Byron, and guilt left him terrified of what the message might contain— well-deserved admonishments, no doubt, making them even more painful.

He returned to his room, drink in hand, where he paced, drank, and occasionally turned on the video player, only to turn the machine back off again, Byron's final message unheard. When the time came to rejoin the group for dinner, he freshened up and hurried downstairs. It didn't pay to be fashionably late in the Anderson household, a fact drummed into him from birth.

The others were arriving as he descended, wearing bittersweet smiles and red-rimmed eyes. They entered the dining room and took their places. No one commented on Paul's absence.

The new housekeeper served wine and appetizers before quietly departing, the model of a modern domestic servant. Alex found himself missing Martha and her acerbic wit already. Sitting at the end of the table, she kept unaccountably quiet. In spite of her eccentricities, she truly cared for both her employers and, on more than one occasion when Alex had called, she'd been at Byron's bedside, reading to him or playing cards. Even though the meal was elegant and delicious, the flavor lacked the seasoning of salty humor he'd become accustomed to when served by her hands.

The talk centered on Byron and his generosity, for the most part, and even the attorney joined in, sharing anecdotes about his former law partner. Byron's beneficiaries were open about what they'd received and what Byron's messages contained, though they probably kept certain details to themselves. Alex wondered what Paul inherited and if he'd foregone dinner to plan how fast he could spend his newfound wealth. Guilt immediately gripped him for his unkind thoughts, especially in light of the circumstances. The minutes ticked by with no sign of Paul; Alex began to worry.

Finally, he asked, "Do you suppose Paul's all right?"

His uncle appeared surprised at his question and clapped him affectionately on the shoulder. "Why, Alex, I didn't know you cared."

When Alex sputtered in indignation, Alfred said, more seriously, "He's fine, Alex. He was sleeping when I last checked, and I didn't want to wake him. Let him rest."

The conversation continued, and Alex tuned in to an amusing story, told at Douglas's expense, about how one of Byron's practical jokes had backfired horrifically. Even on such a solemn occasion, it did his heart good to know life went on and those left behind still found reasons to laugh.

Easing back in his chair, Alex observed the byplay surrounding him. As each person recalled their favorite memories of the deceased, he couldn't help admiring the beauty of Byron's gifts, each suited perfectly to the recipient and in some way connected to their stories.

The painting gracing the wall of Alfred's office was based on a photo taken during a long-ago beach trip, recalled fondly by Douglas. As such, the canvas now belonged to the last living child in the picture, who bore little resemblance to the ginger-haired youth remaining forever unchanged in the swirling oils of the canvas.

Even knowing the reason behind the gift didn't lessen Alex's sorrow. He'd always loved the painting. The brilliant blue sky and rolling whitecaps reminded him of summers spent with his mother at the family's ocean-side getaway, and later, of his trips to Aruba with his uncle and Byron. He'd never connected the three red-haired boys in the painting with Douglas, Byron, and Paul's father, Jacob, and he felt disconnected from the others who seemed to share an enormous family history. Some of the blame he could lay at the feet of his grandparents, for limiting his visits while he lived with them. Once he'd reached his majority, though, any slighting of family rested purely on his own shoulders. He had a lot of making up to do.

After dinner, Alex escorted Alfred to his room, pausing to listen at Paul's door. "Leave him be," Alfred scolded. "He's probably exhausted."

Prudently choosing not to comment, Alex noticed his uncle appeared to be sinking fast. He'd barely opened the bedroom door when the new butler appeared, pushing him aside to help Alfred get ready for bed. How was Alex going to make amends and bond with his family if he kept getting shoved out of the way? Sighing, he admitted that wasn't fair. The man was new to the job and more than likely trying to make a good impression. Alex stepped away and let William do what he'd been hired for.

As he watched, he realized that, like Theresa, William appeared respectful, speaking only when spoken to. Bernard always had something to say when he attended Alfred, and Martha chattered like a magpie. While the newly hired staff were quietly efficient, he wasn't sure the quiet part was a good thing, fearing the house would resemble a mausoleum in short order.

"Will you be all right, Uncle?" Alex asked.

"I'm fine, my boy. Maybe a bit tired." A wistful smile momentarily lifted the fatigue from Alfred's face. "If I didn't know before that Byron loved me, I do now, after hearing his final words."

Alarmed at the resignation in his uncle's voice, Alex asked again, "Are you sure you're all right?"

"When you get to be my age, Alex, you don't fear death. Now I have even less to dread—he'll be waiting for me. Quite frankly, though I'll miss all of you, I can't wait to see him again." Finally dressed for bed, Alfred allowed William to tuck him under the covers. "Good night, Alex," he said between yawns. "Pleasant dreams. And, Alex? I love you, son."

"Love you too," Alex mumbled, uncomfortable saying the words even though he meant them beyond the shadow of a doubt.

Quietly leaving the room, he stopped by Paul's door again before making his way to his uncle's office—the room in the house most comfortable to him. Mixing a drink, he stared sadly at the blank space where the painting had hung a few hours ago. He agonized over its loss and tried in vain to visualize other artwork occupying that space. None seemed as perfect as the one now in Douglas's possession. Sighing heavily, he turned his attention to his martini.

The grandfather clock had bonged eleven times and the house had quieted when soft footfalls announced someone's approach. Alex knew without checking who crept down the hall. Easing silently from the room, he followed the lone figure to the kitchen, waiting outside the door.

From the sounds of the muted clatters and the beep of the microwave, leftovers were being reheated. Alex slid to the floor, nursing his drink and biding his time. Finally, it appeared the raider was satisfied, and Alex rose to his feet, intercepting Paul when he stepped into the hallway. "Alone at last," Alex purred, alcohol and self-recriminations urging him to find a diversion. How kind of fate to generously supply one.

With far less fire than Alex anticipated, Paul asked, "What do you want?"

"Do you even have to ask?"

A weary sigh, followed by, "I suppose not."

"Come on," Alex urged, "what have you got to lose?"

"How about my dignity and self-respect?"

"Jeez, you're uptight, aren't you?" Alex only intended to goad Paul, nothing more, when he reached down to fondle the man's cock. He couldn't hide his shock upon discovering that not only was Paul generously endowed, but hard.

CHAPTER NINE

ALEX found himself in a most unusual position—for him—back pressed against the wall, pinned in place by Paul, who growled, "You have no intention of letting this drop, do you?"

Alex met Paul's hot glare, a mix of rage and something indefinable, and simply answered, "Nope," knowing he skated on thin ice.

"If I say yes, will you leave me the fuck alone?"

What? Paul said yes? The triumphant smile on Alex's face effectively hid his disappointment. Paul had been the only man, hell, only *person,* to ever refuse him, and now it seemed he'd given in like Alex's other conquests. The acquiescence felt strangely close to betrayal.

Faint puffs of breath ghosted over his face when his captor leaned in and delivered an ultimatum. "Fine. We do this my way. I'm calling the shots. You're only along for the ride, understand?"

Unprepared for this totally new side of the man, Alex's resolve disappeared and he nodded his agreement, never imagining Paul fully intended to assume control, or that so diminutive a man was even capable of dominance. Alex decided to play along, for now, and in time turn the tables, proving once and for all who was boss.

Smoldering eyes sparked like coals as Paul glared, and Alex feared being reduced to ashes under the power of the sizzling gaze alone. For the first time, he realized he'd underestimated his opponent, and a shiver of uncertainty crept up his spine, rendering him speechless. It had been so long since he'd experienced the pulse-quickening-breath-holding feeling that he almost didn't recognize the sensation for what it was: fear. Heady, delicious, overwhelmingly sensual fear.

Suddenly, the warmth disappeared when Paul stepped back and stood motionless a few feet away, watching. He turned, the heels of his brown loafers clicking across the marble tiles toward the staircase.

"Where are you going?" Alex asked, recovering from his shock enough to speak.

An arrogant sneer seemed out of place on a normally considerate and compassionate face, though it bore a vague familiarity too. Alex realized he'd frequently worn a similar expression himself.

"You hardly expect me to take you to my bed and risk disturbing Alfred, do you?" Paul's condescending tones once more reminded Alex of himself.

The mention of Alfred hardened Alex's heart, reminding him who, or rather what, he dealt with. No one conquered Alex Martin, especially not a two-bit gold-digger. Determined to win this game at any cost, he calmly replied, "What are we waiting for?"

Paul resumed his trek up the staircase. He topped the landing and gazed down at Alex, raising a haughty eyebrow. "Well?"

A business deal, not true desire. Alex was fully aware of the nature of their agreement. That still didn't keep his cock from hardening, his favorite fantasy image coming to mind. Lying naked against the comforter of the massive bed upstairs, his dream-Paul writhed provocatively against turquoise satin, a seductive smile playing across his generous lips. After a moment's hesitation, Alex followed, taking the stairs two at a time, justifying to himself that he wasn't betraying his uncle, merely protecting him.

They met on the landing and walked silently side by side. Paul opened the door to Alex's bedroom, and with a grand sweeping gesture, ushered Alex inside. Light spilling from the partially open bathroom door provided the only illumination. No sooner had they entered than Alex found his back pressed to the wall once again. He barely registered the predatory gleam in Paul's eyes before full lips took possession of his own. When he opened his mouth in surprise at the unexpected assault, his attacker took full advantage, plunging in and delivering a sizzling kiss, the likes of which Alex had often dealt but never before received.

Alex moaned in spite of his earlier plan to fuck the man, expose him for a money-grubbing slut, and walk away without a backward glance. Enjoyment had never figured into the picture—until now. Unexpectedly gentle hands caressed his chest through the sheer silk of his shirt, his traitorous nipples responding, forming stiff peaks against the gossamer fabric. A scant second later, those hands brutally grasped the lapels and jerked, ripping the shirt from neck to waist, mother-of-pearl buttons pinging against the walls and floor.

"Hey!" Alex protested, silenced when a hot mouth enveloped his nipple, tonguing and sucking the sensitive bit of flesh. Again he moaned, as skillful hands traced his chest, raising goose bumps with whisper-soft caresses.

Paul's mouth worked magic on the sensitive areas of Alex's neck while callused hands deftly unbuttoned and unzipped his straining fly, freeing the needy flesh within that, apparently, had no problem consorting with the enemy.

Paul soundlessly dropped to the floor, taking Alex's slacks with him. Cool air caressed newly exposed skin, followed by a warm wetness encasing his balls as first one, then the other was enveloped in an eager mouth. It required every ounce of Alex's fortitude to remain upright on trembling knees. One final lick to his sac, and then Paul's tongue lapped a wide swath up the underside of his cock. A contrasting coolness followed the warmth, Paul blowing against the damp skin, sending chills down his spine. A fervent tongue worshiped his cock and balls, alternating with cool puffs of air, leaving him gasping and begging for more. Finally, after much teasing, Paul's mouth engulfed his erection, and Alex thrust into the welcoming cavern.

Gaze locked with Paul's, Alex couldn't turn away. The sight of his nemesis, lips stretched wide while putting each and every previous blowjob to shame, took Alex's breath away. Alex reminded himself of their agreement, for nothing in Paul's actions indicated anything other than a passionate encounter between two willing men.

Alex braced himself against the wall, in real danger of falling. When he'd nearly reached his breaking point, Paul changed rhythm, taking Alex down his throat. Alex choked off a startled cry.

Lacing his long fingers into the silky darkness of Paul's hair, Alex surrendered to the pleasure, carefully avoiding thrusting too hard, no matter how badly he wanted to. Despite how he might have felt about them personally, Alex prided himself on being thoughtful with his lovers—until he'd fucked them, rather. Then he tried not to think of them at all.

Slowing his movements, Paul lifted each of Alex's feet and removed shoes, socks, and slacks before resuming his sucking with wild abandon, fingers brushing the sensitive skin where thigh met groin, then moving up to cradle Alex's tightening balls.

"Oh, God," Alex moaned. "Baby, you're good at that. Keep it up and I'm gonna blow."

The sinful mouth disappeared.

"Wha...?"

Alex suddenly found himself turned and pressed chest-to-wall, his legs spread by an invasive knee, lowering his height to give his diminutive conqueror better access. "You're still over-dressed," Paul hissed into Alex's ear. "It's time I took care of that."

Sliding his hands up Alex's chest to capture the lapels of the shredded shirt, Paul grasped the back in his teeth and pulled, ripping the luxurious material from Alex's body. The tattered remains slipped free, pooling in a silken puddle at their feet. Alex shivered, aroused by the aggressive display. Barriers now removed, Paul used teeth, lips, and tongue to explore the tender spots on Alex's neck, sucking and biting from ear to shoulder, paying special attention to areas that brought gasps of pleasure.

A firm grip guided Alex across the floor, Paul's mouth still exploring the spots that caused Alex to shudder. His moans rose to a fever pitch.

Too caught up in the moment to care why, Alex allowed himself to be manhandled toward the bed. Once there, he turned to face the dominating man wearing Paul Sinclair's body. Whoever this commanding stranger was, he might have the same thick, dark hair, light-brown eyes, and compact, well-built body, but he didn't act like the man who normally fled Alex's advances. Work-roughened hands shoved him, and Alex stumbled backward onto the soft fabric of the satin comforter.

Paul hovered above him, staring down like an investor assessing a purchase. *This shouldn't be happening.* Alex knew he should be the one taking possession, calling the shots. Never before had he been on the receiving end of such a skillful seduction, if Paul's actions could be called anything less than conquering. No, Alex always took control, and would again after conceiving a way to turn the tables without putting a stop to their odd agreement.

He observed, transfixed, as nimble fingers unfastened a belt, oh so slowly pulling the leather free, belt loop by belt loop, to drop it to the floor. Next, Paul grasped his tie and slipped it over his head, and then climbed onto the bed with the scrap of silk in hand to loom over Alex's prone body. Catching both of Alex's large hands in his smaller ones, Paul slipped them into the loop of the tie. Wrapping the free length of the supple material between them, he secured them tightly before tying off the ends to a spindle on the headboard.

Faintly trailing fingertips stroked his arms from wrist to shoulder, reminding Alex of his captivity. When Paul climbed from the bed, a moment of panic surged through Alex. Though tied loosely enough to easily free himself, abandonment didn't bode well. "Hey!" he shouted as Paul backed across the floor. "What the hell do you think you're doing?"

A lust-filled gaze was his only answer. His captor entered the adjoining bathroom, searching for something, judging by the sound. "Aha! Found it!" Paul exclaimed, reemerging a moment later.

With a knowing smirk etched upon his face, Paul stalked across the room like a big cat tracking easy prey. Alex's cock, already hard and aching, jumped at the thought of being prey, amazed that a born aggressor could get excited assuming such a passive role. No use trying to deny his arousal, which was becoming more and more pronounced with each passing moment.

Two soft thuds drew his attention to the items Paul dropped beside him on the bed, their implications clear. "I don't bottom—ever," he said, feebly attempting an authoritative tone.

Paul stared into Alex's eyes as he removed his glasses and placed them on the nightstand. With a smile of pure seduction, he eased his fully clothed body onto Alex's nude form, an unreadable expression on his face. What the look promised, Alex didn't know. He wholeheartedly believed it came with a guarantee, though: he wouldn't easily forget this night.

Still smiling, Paul bent his head down, five o'clock shadow abrading Alex's cheek. "My rules or nothing, remember?" Settling his weight more firmly, he locked his mouth to the sensitive flesh where neck met shoulder, biting hard enough to remind Alex who wielded the power.

Far from attempting to pull away, Alex arched up, wanting more. He bucked his hips, reveling in the friction of Paul's dress slacks against his bare flesh, knowing he was acting like a slut and too far gone to care. When Paul released his shoulder, in a brief moment of clarity he reminded himself that this was his adversary, not his lover. His body refused to listen to reason.

Paul rocked back on his knees and roughly rolled Alex over, causing the wrist bindings to tighten. Fear raced up Alex's spine. *What have I gotten myself into?* Paul carefully loosened the tie, though he didn't release Alex's hands.

"Is that better?" Soothing fingers stroked Alex's wrists where the tight material had chafed, and Paul murmured into his ear, "Relax, I'm not going to hurt you." He snickered. "I'm planning to do many things to you tonight. Hurting you isn't one of them."

Grunting affirmation, Alex willed his body to relax, reassured that Paul didn't intend to abuse him—at least, not tonight. Come morning, all bets were likely off. He decided not to think about tomorrow.

The popping of a bottle lid penetrated the silence, and Alex braced himself for the expected invasion, shocked when, instead of his ass, oil-slickened fingers found his knotted back muscles, working them with practiced ease.

At his breathy sigh, Paul chuckled. "I told you to relax, didn't I?"

Those talented hands worked outward from the center of Alex's back, easing tension with a thorough massage. He heard the sound of the bottle opening again, and this time his thighs and lower legs were rubbed and kneaded before Paul's surprisingly strong fingers found his glutes.

When his cheeks were gently parted, he tensed, though he knew from experience that doing so would only cause more pain. Far from the stabbing penetration he'd expected, a steady stream of cool air blew across his exposed pucker.

The soft tickle of facial stubble brushed against his ass as his thighs were forced wider apart. Once again, a hot tongue laved his balls before repeating the earlier swiping lick, this time moving from his balls to his hole. Alex hadn't been entirely truthful when he'd said he never bottomed, but he hadn't in a very long time. Casual fucks weren't allowed the privilege. Another puff of air tantalized his damp opening.

Suddenly, Paul altered the pattern of lick/blow, raising his head to bite Alex's cheek hard enough to shock, stopping shy of truly painful. The sensation shot straight through Alex's body and into his cock. *Oh, fuck, what was that?* Who knew being bitten could be erotic? Even more shocking, he found himself writhing, wanting more.

What came next was like nothing he'd ever dreamed of. Instead of gentle, controlled exploration, lips, tongue, and teeth launched a full attack, licking, sucking, and biting in an unabashed frenzy up and down Alex's back and buttocks.

Paul's moans created erotic vibrations to stoke Alex's already raging libido. Even without direct stimulation to his cock, Alex teetered on the edge of orgasm, every fiber of his being screaming for release. Far from fearing penetration, he now hovered on the verge of begging Paul to fuck him.

The mind-numbing sensations ceased abruptly, and he sobbed aloud in frustration, left hard and aching, denied completion.

Soft snickers accompanied the now familiar sound of the bottle top. Excited as he was, Alex no longer dreaded the fingers he knew were going to breach him. Thanks to Paul's attentions, he longed for them, arching back in an effort to speed up the process. After what seemed a small eternity, a well-oiled finger slid effortless inside, quickly joined by another. While they hovered at his entrance, preparing him, they never penetrated far enough to offer satisfaction or relief.

Alex groaned in disapproval when those fingers slipped from his body. The soft rustle of fabric against fabric announced Paul removing his clothes. The condom Alex spotted on the bed earlier offered reassurance, as he hadn't thought that far ahead himself—a stupid oversight he'd never made before. What was it about this man that aroused him to the point where he couldn't think? Or was it that, deep down, he'd never seriously thought Paul would ever take him up on his carnal offer?

The warmth of Paul's hand grazed Alex's hip as Paul patted the comforter, searching, the tearing sound a moment later proving he'd found what he sought. Paul shoved a pillow under Alex's hips, raising his ass and presenting it like a gift to the lover... no, the *man* who'd soon take it.

As Paul lowered himself, Alex longed to see the naked body about to claim him. He tried, unsuccessfully, unable to turn his head far enough. A slight weight covered his back, followed by an insistent nudging. Paul stopped. He inhaled sharply and then released the breath before murmuring, "Alex, do you want this? I don't care what we said before. I won't do this if it's not what you want."

In answer, Alex reared back, a bit too hard, resulting in an excruciating burn that caused him to cry out and pull away. Thanks to his bonds, he had nowhere to go, and his erection, full and hard before, quickly deflated. He panted through the discomfort.

The painful invasion stopped immediately, soft lips and hands tracing his shoulders. "Shh... easy, Alex. If you're not used to this, we need to go slow." Paul's husky voice lulled him. "Relax. Let me know when you're ready."

It humbled Alex that, though he'd ruthlessly taunted and insulted the man, Paul didn't plunge in brutally, mindless of any pain he caused. They were adversaries, right? Why did Paul take such care to be a tender and thoughtful lover, when by rights he should be cold and unfeeling?

The pain lessened gradually, and Alex's breathing returned

to normal. "Better?" Paul whispered, lips gently sweeping the back of Alex's neck again.

Alex nodded, not trusting himself to speak.

Paul tentatively maneuvered back and out of Alex's body. The pop top snapped and more lube dripped on Alex's opening, worked in by slick fingers. Paul repositioned himself, and this time, when he breached the tight ring of muscle, the burn was far less intense. Paul took his time, carefully working himself into the tight, seldom penetrated passage, stopping frequently to allow Alex time to adjust.

At long last, Paul's balls rested against his ass, cock buried completely inside. As slowly as it had entered, the cock that felt enormous eased out of Alex's stretched passage. The slow, unhurried motions continued until Alex grew achingly hard again and ready for more. Raising his ass to meet Paul's next controlled thrust, he silently pleaded for a more aggressive coupling. Paul gave him what he asked for.

Paul rode him, varying speed and depth, angling his hips to ensure Alex received the maximum amount of pleasure with each forceful penetration. When Alex moaned, a thrust was repeated, until Paul knew exactly what excited him most, giving it in good measure.

Once again hovering on the edge, Alex groaned his disappointment when Paul slowed and eventually stopped, sliding out once more. Paul turned Alex and gazed down with an expression far removed from the open hostility or sneering triumph Alex expected. Wasn't there supposed to be humiliation and getting even for the snide comments and ill treatment? Instead, Paul painstakingly saw to his comfort, ensuring the bonds weren't pinching before leaning down and capturing his mouth in another searing kiss. If Alex hadn't known better, he would have sworn Paul meant the passionate gesture.

Their lips parted, and Paul used his knee to separate Alex's legs, repositioning the pillow under him. He kneeled between those splayed legs, gazing down appreciatively, like a craftsman admiring his handiwork. Alex caught his first glimpse of his captor fully naked, surprised to see a completely hairless chest, abdomen, and groin. Paul sported a full and heavy cock, as long as Alex had believed, and much thicker. He felt a rush of gratitude for Paul's careful preparations; thoughtlessness might have caused serious injury.

"Like what you see?" Paul whispered in a voice gone husky.

Alex saw no use in lying. "Yes."

Paul's beamed a guileless smile as he positioned himself again, his weight braced on one wiry, muscled arm. He bent one of Alex's legs out of the way and guided himself back to Alex's stretched opening, leaning in and sinking his teeth into a muscled shoulder. He slowly worked his way in and then out, driving Alex insane with impatience.

Hissing sharply through clenched teeth, Alex arched his back and pulled hard against his makeshift bonds, wrapping his legs around Paul's thighs, trying hard to hurry the wickedly slow pace.

Paul teased for a few minutes, then relented and gave him what he craved. Bringing Alex once again to the brink, Paul settled into a steady, driving tempo, his hand finding and stroking Alex's cock in a frantic rhythm.

Deepening his plunging thrusts, Paul pressed further into Alex's ass and stilled, his cock pulsing and spasming deep inside. His hand faltered as he groaned out his completion. Alex found release a split second later, rendered more intense by the repeated denials.

With a heady sigh, Paul collapsed in a tangle of arms and

legs, still firmly embedded in Alex's body. He mumbled incoherent words against Alex's chest.

Careful as Paul was, Alex still winced when the man's spent flesh slowly eased from his body. He suffered another brief moment of panic when Paul disappeared without a word. The sound of running water prompted a sigh of relief.

Bare feet padding across the floor announced Paul's return. He carefully released the tie, raising Alex's abraded wrists and examining them before bestowing a gentle kiss on each.

Paul's intense brown eyes locked with Alex's as he wiped away the evidence of their encounter with a damp cloth. Never had Alex witnessed such heated passion directed at him, and for a moment he imagined the pseudoadoration to be love instead of the mysterious, unknown emotion it actually was. Triumph, perhaps?

"I didn't hurt you, did I?" Paul tossed the soiled cloth to the floor to join their discarded clothes.

Alex shook his head, fully prepared to be abandoned now that they'd satisfied the terms of their agreement, the idea depressing beyond his reckoning.

Instead of leaving, Paul folded the comforter down and urged Alex to crawl beneath it, climbing in afterward to snuggle against Alex's side.

"Paul, I...," Alex began, without any real clue of what he intended to say.

"Shh.... We're still playing by my rules," Paul replied. "Let's not try to talk tonight." He kissed the sting out of the words, delivering another soul-searing kiss Alex feared might prove addictive. Burrowing into the covers, Paul yawned and said, "Good night." Soon steady, even breathing confirmed Paul was asleep. More sated than he ever remembered feeling, Alex wasn't far behind.

BYRON hovered outside in the hallway once Alex and Paul climbed the stairs, decorum dictating that he not spy on two of his favorite men. When the moans and guttural cries quieted, he couldn't help himself and chanced a peek into the blue room.

Gliding over to the bed, he fought the urge to crow in happiness. Observing the peaceful sleepers lying entwined, he exulted that they'd finally put aside their differences and given in to their mutual attraction. Oh, how Byron loved being right.

Satisfied his work there was done, the spirit of Byron Sinclair, now beginning to assume the shape he'd worn in life, sped away to keep watch over his own sleeping lover.

CHAPTER TEN

CONSCIOUSNESS slowly surfaced, and Paul registered deep, even breaths from across the bed. A hairy leg brushed his ass, inspiring a hopeful twitch from his cock. He jumped and rolled away, gazing through bleary eyes at his bedmate.

What have I done? After weeks of holding Alex at bay, he'd finally given in to temptation. The only thing truly stopping him before had been the reasons behind Alex's pursuit. In those piercing blue eyes he was damned anyway—might as well earn the title he'd been given. Despite Alex's opinions, Paul wasn't a one-night stand kind of guy and should've shown more control. Grieving was a poor excuse to seek comfort from the enemy.

Depressed, lonely, and missing his uncle, the offer, however facetiously made, had come at the worse possible moment. He told himself he'd merely needed the comfort of a willing body, and Alex had been available; it wasn't personal. Paul sighed. He'd never made a convincing liar, telling himself half-truths to justify doing what he'd wanted to do anyway. Now, in the cold light of morning, could he live with the consequences?

Warily watching Alex for movement, he patted the nightstand for his glasses, blinking hard to clear his vision once he'd put them on. His breath caught at the sight beside him—the man he'd come to realize he wanted and had never hoped to have. Last night had been a one-time deal, one he'd expected to satisfy his desire and banish it from his system. His night with Alex, in fact, had only added fuel to a fire already burning out of control. Jordan had certainly never inspired such deep cravings.

Deeply asleep, Alex appeared more innocent, more approachable than he did while awake, his eyes darting randomly behind closed lids, long, sweeping lashes brushing his high cheekbones. The silvery moonlight shining through the window added burnished gold highlights to the wavy blond hair, a feature handed down from past Andersons that Paul knew from going through aging photographs. Alex was the last. Oh, some second-cousins-eight-times-removed or something similar hung out in Boston, but other than Alex, Alfred, and Alfred's eighty-seven year old widowed aunt, the Anderson legacy was at an end.

What a shame the man's DNA wouldn't be preserved for posterity. Alex made a nearly perfect specimen, at least physically. Too bad he insisted on acting like such a prick.

It was hard to reconcile the conceited jerk Paul knew firsthand with the stories he'd heard from his uncles of the considerate and thoughtful young man Alex had been in his younger years. Where had that person gone? Was it possible to get him back? Every once in a while, Paul caught brief glimpses of a caring soul, normally kept hidden by a mask of indifference, and Paul had made love to that caring person last night. As much as he wanted to believe goodness lived within Alex, the finer parts of the man's personality were kept under lock and key by the paranoid creature who believed Paul capable of seducing Alfred for money. Paul nearly laughed aloud at the sheer absurdity.

He knew he was deluding himself that anything could come of his wanting, and yet he lingered a moment longer to indulge in the illusion of Alex as his lover. At last, with a sigh of resolution, he leaned over and touched his lips to the sleeping enigma's. One last kiss. Bidding farewell to bittersweet fantasy, he rose and hastily dressed, abandoning the comforting haven for his own lonely bed, after briefly checking in on Alfred.

EROTIC tenderness in a well-used part of his anatomy greeted Alex upon waking, and he lay still, feigning sleep and listening, until it became clear he slept alone. He sighed. Going against his normal policy of fuck 'em and leave, he'd hoped Paul would spend the night, allowing them a chance to talk, although he didn't know what he'd say. Reality hit him like a smack in the face. *No, too much risk of Alfred finding out if boy toy wasn't in his room at night.* Oh, shit! Uncle Alfred! What had he done?

Last night had been about conquest, Alex told himself, a onetime encounter rating less than a casual fuck, or at least that's how it started out. Only, instead of conquering, he'd been conquered. When given the upper hand, however, Paul had refused to exploit his dominance. Instead of forcing his will, he'd taken the time to be an exciting and attentive lover. For the first time, Alex believed he was dealing with an equal, despite Paul's lack of pedigree or old money. Also for the first time, once wasn't enough. Far from wanting to kick Paul out and forget him, Alex wanted Paul's exquisite cock inside his body again. The man he'd avoided for most of his life intrigued him more than anyone else ever had.

Reality returned, reminding Alex of his original purpose for seducing Paul. Any benevolent thoughts vanished, replaced by guilt and suspicion. Paul wasn't an equal. He was one more man willing to sleep his way up the social ladder. How easily the fickle gold-digger betrayed the hand feeding him, even if he'd given in to put an end to unwanted advances.

Something occurred to Alex. Now that he'd gained the hard evidence he'd sought, would running to Uncle Alfred do more harm than good? What if Alfred truly loved Paul? Would this betrayal, following on the heels of Byron's death, be too much to bear? For that matter, was Paul still after money now that his deceased uncle had undoubtedly left him comfortably financed? "One item" could translate into a sizeable bankroll.

Alex shifted in bed, his soreness a reminder of how he'd spent the evening, and an image appeared in his mind of Paul, poised above him, claiming him. Forcefully banishing those thoughts, he rose and entered his bathroom, where an opened drawer revealed the lubricants and condoms Paul had searched for the night before. Alfred kept the guest bath supplied? Well, this was the room chosen for him—it made sense. *Paul knew they were here.* Maybe Paul's bathroom was similarly stocked, something Alex didn't want to dwell on.

He tried in vain to push reminders of the man from his mind and focus on his shower. Steady streams of hot water beat against his back, renewing his strength. Memories of the sexy seducer kneeling before him wouldn't be denied. He'd wanted desperately to wrap his fingers in dark hair and fuck that talented mouth, but hadn't had the chance to indulge properly. Now, visualizing his erection sliding past those pouty lips, stretching them wide, he tightened his grip to nearly painful levels and thrust violently into his clenched fist.

Moaning and bucking his hips, he stifled a yell, his orgasm slamming into him like a tidal wave. In his mind, Paul's mouth filled and overflowed, a greedy tongue capturing every drop. Panting heavily and bracing against the slick shower walls, Alex watched the evidence of his fantasy circle the drain before disappearing in a whirlpool of water and soap. Oh, shit, was he ever in trouble. The only man he'd ever fucked and wanted more from was off-limits.

Later, toweling off, he stopped to stare in shock at his reflection. Purpled bites decorated his shoulders and chest, leading up to his neck, and he shivered at the unsubtle souvenirs from a night when he'd been well and truly owned.

BREAKFAST was a quiet affair, mostly because Alex ate alone. Alfred couldn't eat or drink before checking into the hospital at ten o'clock, and neither Bernard nor Martha had talked to Paul all morning. Maybe the conniving little schemer had conceded defeat and given up.

Alex supposed it shouldn't have surprised him to find the missing conundrum in his uncle's room, busily packing a suitcase, something the hired help should have been doing, in his opinion.

"Good morning, Uncle," Alex began cheerfully, pointedly ignoring Paul, who retreated into the walk-in closet without acknowledging him.

"Good morning, Alex," his uncle replied. "I trust you had a pleasant evening."

More loudly than actually necessary, he answered, "Why, yes, sir. Most memorable, indeed."

He was rewarded by a heavy thump and an "Ow!" from the closet.

"Paul, are you all right?" Alfred cried out. With his uncle's attention diverted, Alex didn't bother to hide his smirk.

Paul emerged from the closet rubbing his head, a large, leather-bound book in his free hand. "Yes, sir. I found the mystery you were missing on the top shelf."

"I wonder how the blasted thing got there," Alfred mused. "Ah, never mind. Set it on the dresser, if you don't mind. It'll give me added incentive to get home and find out who killed the ambassador. Meanwhile, would you please pack a few magazines for light reading?"

Their easy familiarity wiped the smirk from Alex's face. Paul's quiet efficiency left him feeling inadequate, a reminder of the true price of his neglect. He'd unintentionally distanced himself so thoroughly that he was now unaware of his uncle's likes and dislikes, like he hadn't known the story behind the painting. When had his pulling away happened? When had he stopped knowing his uncle?

Paul closed a Pullman case, securing the requested magazines in a zippered pocket. Alfred smiled and said, "Thank you, Paul. Would you please ask Isaac to bring the car around?"

Though wary eyes regarded Alex with suspicion, Paul mumbled, "Yes, sir," and then he retreated from the room. When he rushed past, Alex couldn't help noticing kiss-swollen lips and the bright blush coloring Paul's high cheekbones, and had to admit that freshly fucked looked good on the man.

Alfred's sigh brought him out of his reverie. "I think he's taking this pretty hard, Alex," he began. "He worries way too much, you know. I thought losing Byron might kill me, but I suspect his death actually hurt Paul more." His uncle slid from beneath the covers to stand beside the bed in his boxers and a plain white T-shirt.

Alex started to protest, only to be cut off. "Byron meant the world to me, and I to him. When he died, I knew I'd be alone, even if only for a little while. My loneliness will have a short life, I suspect."

"Don't talk like that, Uncle," Alex scolded, overlooking the "alone" and "loneliness" comments. "You're going to pull through and live to be a hundred." Only then did he notice the stooped shoulders and sagging flesh, how the boxers and shirt hung limply on his uncle's body. *When did he lose all that weight?*

"There's no denying the truth, Alex. I've lived a long, full life, blessed as few are. Then Byron died, and life isn't the same." Alfred turned his back, pulling on a pair of navy slacks he found lying on the end of the bed. Like the underwear, they were far roomier than tailored slacks had a right to be.

Alfred entered his closet, still talking, leaving Alex no choice but to follow. When he stepped inside the door, however, an iron fist seized his heart and squeezed. The closet was neatly divided down the middle, and Byron's clothes still hung where they always had, his shoes haphazardly lining the walls, mocking reminders of Alex's cowardice.

He skimmed tentative fingers over the sweater he'd sent for Christmas, the cardboard tag on the cuff a silent condemnation for making excuses rather than being a part of Byron's last Christmas. Byron died three short weeks later, never having worn the gift. Alex squeezed his eyes shut, fighting burning tears. Instead of creating a memory and providing some comfort, he'd gone skiing instead, each and every night taking a different man to his bed in an effort to bury his guilt. The diversionary tactic hadn't worked very well.

As painful as it was for him to be bombarded by the haunting memories, how much harder would it be for Paul, who'd been in this closet, surrounded by Byron's personal effects, only moments ago? "What about Paul?" he asked, suddenly feeling sorry for the young man who, by all appearances, played second fiddle, facing constant reminders that another owned Alfred's heart. What kind of financial gain made up for being with someone who loved—and forever would—a ghost?

Back turned, Alfred couldn't see the tears and misunderstood the question. "You're alone by choice, Alex. Paul is different. He was never meant to be a solitary creature. I'm afraid being around me and Byron made him want what we had."

Was that the reason Paul chased after a man old enough to be his grandfather? The desire for a solid relationship? "That's not a bad thing," Alex conceded, considering the situation in a new light. Paul's rejection finally made sense, especially if he wanted long-term. Until now, Alex hadn't believed in long-term, for himself, anyway, a well-known fact in this house. After a moment, he admitted, "If I could have what the two of you had, I wouldn't be alone, either."

"Really?" his uncle asked, glancing over his shoulder as he donned a light-blue shirt, eyes wide and a grin blooming across his face.

Alex dismissed such foolish ideas with a shake of his head. "It's not going to happen. No one can see past the money. No one sees me."

Alfred released a brief chuckle. "Oh, I don't know about that. I think if you let someone actually *see* the real you, you'd be amazed at their reaction." With a quick glance toward the door, Alfred lowered his voice and murmured, "I need to hurry and tell you this before Paul comes back."

Though curious, Alex remained silent. Was his uncle about to confess? The invisible fist gripped his heart once more.

Alfred winced, lowering himself onto a low stool, and Alex stepped forward, offering his arm for support. When had the man become so frail? Even more shocking, his staunchly independent uncle allowed his help, using the offered arm as leverage to ease himself down, taking deep, panting breaths. "Thank you, Alex. No matter what you might think, I'm not getting older. Unfortunately, my body is. It won't seem to do what I tell it to anymore. Anyway, I want to talk to you about Paul. Like I said, he's not used to being alone. Promise me, if something happens to me, will you watch out for him?"

Ah, a confession. After weeks of speculation, Alex expected a sense of justification at being proven right. Why, then, did he feel like he'd lost something valuable? "He seems perfectly capable of looking after himself," Alex said, remembering the seductive predator from the night before.

Alfred continued, not knowing that he was, in essence, asking the fox to guard the henhouse. "He's not as strong as you are, and has the tendency to believe the best about the wrong people. Someone could easily take advantage of him."

Prudently remaining silent, Alex wondered what Paul might have said about their night together. If his uncle knew, surely he'd come right out and say so, wouldn't he? Andersons weren't exactly known for subtlety, or for sharing what was theirs.

Instead of accusations, Alfred offered, "I love you both like sons and worry about you, but you're an Anderson at heart. Many have tried to take advantage of you, and failed. You'd never let it happen. Paul, on the other hand, has experienced firsthand how it feels to be used."

Words sparking possessive outrage, Alex growled, "Who? Who took advantage of him?" No matter what place he held, Paul was a part of the household, and Andersons took care of their own.

"I probably shouldn't be telling you this...." Once again, Alfred's eyes shifted toward the door. "About three years ago, before Byron fell ill, Paul met someone. He was young, witty and handsome." Eyes narrowing in annoyance, Alfred scoffed, "Unfortunately, he was exactly what you described, concerned only with the money."

Alfred pulled on his socks, wriggling his feet into a pair of loafers. "Jordan made a point of being available for parties, vacations, and social events, anything that allowed him to rub elbows with the rich. That part of Paul's life, he didn't mind sharing— the only part. He amazed even me by the creativity of his excuses not to visit Bishop. Eventually, he gave up the pretense of accepting Paul for himself and begged him to move here."

Alex didn't need to hear the rest of the story. Blessed with an active imagination and cursed with a possessive streak, he battled the image of "young, witty, and handsome" *in flagrante delicto* with Paul. He hated Jordan immediately.

"The problem," Alfred explained, "was that Paul didn't want to live the way Jordan wanted him to. He's happy with his life. Lord knows how many times Byron and I asked him to move here."

Misreading Alex's scowl, his uncle scolded, "Don't give me that look, young man! We begged you too, you know. Nothing would have made us happier than to have our two boys here with us."

Alex sighed, reining in his jealous streak and finally catching up to the conversation. No use arguing; he knew he should have agreed to move to LA when Alfred first broached the subject years ago. Instead of forcing the issue and pressuring him, as his grandparents would have done, his uncle allowed him his choice, never batting an eye at paying for an expensive condo in another state. If only there were a way for Alex to turn back the clock…. Desperate to change the subject, he asked, "What happened with Paul and Jordan?"

Once again taking Alex's arm, Alfred groaned as he rose from the bench, now fully dressed. A flash of pain crossed his face, and he paused a moment to recover.

"Uncle, are you all right?"

"I will be, give me a moment," Alfred replied, panting. Slowly he relaxed his hold, breathing easier. "Where was I? Oh, yes. *Jordan*"—he spat the name bitterly—"was pressuring Paul to buy a penthouse downtown, never believing when Paul said he didn't have money."

"Jordan broke up with him? Over money?"

Motioning Alex ahead of him, Alfred turned off the closet light and reentered the bedroom. "The little opportunist only wanted someone to support him. He'd prefer his easy money to come from someone youthful and handsome, but wasn't a stickler for details."

A gold-digger? Wasn't that what Paul was?

"He'd involved himself with some unsavory characters, and for Paul's sake, Byron and I ended the charade. Oh, we couldn't tell Paul the truth, of course. We let him believe Jordan had fidelity issues, which was true enough."

"What truth?"

Stoic Uncle Alfred, who'd spent the majority of his life

upholding the law and ensuring others did too, said, without a trace of remorse, "I paid him off."

"You did *what?*" Alex bellowed. Never in his life would he have believed his uncle capable of such if he hadn't heard with his own ears, and even then he wasn't entirely convinced.

Alfred confirmed it. "I paid Jordan to say he'd found someone else and disappear. All Paul knows is that he was unfaithful. Paul honestly and truly loved him, though I'll admit to never understanding why. The man possessed few good qualities.

"So you see, Alex, the two of you have something in common. Potential lovers look at you both the same way, fantasizing about wealth and power and expecting you to fulfill their delusions."

"Three years is a long time. He hasn't found someone new?" Alex prodded.

"The relationship only ended last year. They had two years together, more or less. I dare say poor Paul's a bit gun-shy now, all things considered."

"You want me to look after him?"

"Not exactly. I want you to look after each other."

Paul cut off whatever else Alfred might have said by reentering the room. "Are you ready to go, Alfred?"

"We'll talk more later," Alfred assured Alex.

THE patriarch of the Anderson household noticed the strained silence on the way to the hospital and chose not to comment. He knew the boys worried about him. Personally, he wasn't overly concerned with the outcome of his upcoming procedure, for death held little fear for him now. In fact, he'd invented every conceivable excuse to postpone the procedure, secretly hoping that, with Byron gone, nature would simply take its course. It hadn't happened, and he'd run out of excuses.

He knew his surrogate sons would take his passing hard, but he'd lived a glorious life and accomplished nearly everything he'd wanted to. Besides, without Byron, all the color had fled his world, and he was getting rather tired of gray.

He had one little promise to keep and then he'd be free to join his love. Surprisingly, "Operation Unite Our Nephews" showed signs of promise. Hiding a smile that would be out of place amidst the troubled faces surrounding him, Alfred recalled the early morning hours, barely suppressing his glee.

Since Byron's death, Paul had made a habit of checking on him before going to bed, and he'd scarcely returned from the bathroom when a soft tap had sounded on his door. Sliding swiftly beneath the covers, Alfred feigned sleep. A soft kiss brushed his forehead, then Paul whispered, "Good night."

When Paul left the room, reeking of sex, Alfred had stolen a glance at the clock: 4:00 a.m.

He'd little doubt of the identity of Paul's lover, and Alex's jealous and protective reaction to the story of Jordan confirmed his suspicions. Alex was an Anderson through and through, and Andersons were exceedingly possessive of what they considered theirs. Alfred's disclosures were true enough, but baiting his nephew had been fun. If he'd had more time, he'd have shown Alex the pictures of Jordan and Paul in Las Vegas, but pictures of the two men kissing in front of the Mirage might have proven too much. Andersons were a jealous bunch, with volatile tempers to match. One mustn't poke sleeping tigers.

Alfred kept himself entertained during the short trip, alternating his attention between a subdued Paul and a thoughtful

Alex, whose gaze shifted from Alfred to Paul and back again via the rearview mirror as he drove.

At the hospital, Paul settled Alfred into a wheelchair while Alex completed admission forms, each slipping easily into the role they were most comfortable with: Paul the consoler, Alex the businessman. Good boys. They'd learned their lessons well, even if they had yet to realize they'd been taught those roles almost from birth.

They both hugged Alfred and wished him well. An orderly wheeled him into the elevator on his way to surgery, and he smiled encouragement until the doors closed. *It won't be long now, my love,* he thought.

IN THE waiting room, Alex broke the silence first. "About last night...."

"It won't happen again." Paul snapped the words out from between clenched teeth.

"Why not?" Alex asked, surprised and disappointed even though he knew, for his uncle's sake, he couldn't continue an affair. Guilt hung like a heavy weight around his neck already. Nevertheless, it would be nice to be given a choice and not have Paul decide the matter for him.

Paul hissed, "Because I'm not one of your play toys! I'm not some fan boy to fall down and worship the great Alex Martin!"

This wasn't the way Alex envisioned the conversation taking place. "You were willing enough last night."

"You may have had my body, but you'll never have me!" Paul countered, eyes darting away.

Why won't he even look at me? "Listen...." Alex's words died when an elderly woman entered the room. He lowered his voice. "What makes you think I want you?"

Paul's mouth dropped open. "You mean you'll keep your promise not to bother me again?"

Alex sighed, visions of tossing Paul out on his ass replaced by visions of an eager lover lying tangled in turquoise sheets. "If that's what you want. Regardless of what you might think, I'm a man of my word."

A moment of silence was broken by a quietly murmured, "Thank you."

They settled in to wait, forced to sit next to each other in the crowded room. Visitors came and went, the clock ticking off the hours. Paul's head nodded despite the harsh fluorescent lighting. When Alex placed an arm around his shoulders, Paul jumped, shooting an accusing glare.

"Truce, okay?" Alex held up a defensive hand. "You can lay your head on me if you want. I promise I won't bite." The innocently spoken words conjured reminders of the marks Paul left on his body, causing an immediate reaction—one he was determined not to show. No matter how badly he wanted a repeat of last night, he'd given his word and intended to keep it.

After a few seconds of fidgeting, Paul leaned in, resting his head on the offered shoulder. "Thanks," he mumbled. Within minutes he'd fallen asleep.

Alex shifted in his chair to relieve his straining cock, pressed painfully against the front of his slacks, wondering why he hadn't lost interest, as he normally did after taking someone to bed. Perhaps the pull amounted to more than the sex. Whatever possessed him, it seemed to be what he'd needed all this time.

Relaxing as much as possible into the uncomfortable chair,

he replayed the morning's confusing conversation with his uncle, unable to understand why the man thought Paul needed taking care of. Paul Sinclair was definitely a force to be reckoned with. Hell, he could probably best any who stood up to him—if he'd a mind to. Why did he choose to serve rather than lead most of the time and give his trust to the wrong people?

Alex had lost track of time—enough passed for his arm to fall asleep—when the doctor finally entered the waiting room. The expectant eyes of roughly a dozen people latched onto the man in surgical scrubs. He nodded politely and made his way directly to Alex, who gently shook Paul awake.

"Mr. Martin?" the doctor inquired.

"That's me," Alex replied, standing with an arm still wrapped around a disoriented Paul.

"Hello, Paul," the doctor said, nodding curtly to Paul before turning his attention back to Alex.

The doctor explained the procedure and the prognosis without actually telling Alex anything, the brevity of the answer revealing far more than the words did. Basically, that there were things being kept from him by Alfred's decision. He let the omission slide for now, accepting the news at face value. Later, he intended to get the full story. "When will we be able to see him?" he asked, filing away questions for another time, knowing the doctor wouldn't disclose anything his patient instructed him not to.

"He'll remain in recovery for an hour of observation, and then be moved to a private room. You'll be able to visit once he's settled, but only for a few minutes. He needs his rest. If everything goes well, he'll be discharged the day after tomorrow."

Alex had serious doubts after witnessing his uncle's frail condition that morning and accepted whatever good news came his way, turning to hug Paul, who hesitated briefly before joining in the embrace.

"Hey, babe."

"Did you say something, Mr. Anderson?" the pretty blonde nurse asked as she wrapped a pressure cuff around Alfred's arm and began inflating the band.

Still groggy from sedation, Alfred waved a hand vaguely behind her. "I was talking to Byron."

Following the direction of his eyes, the nurse scowled. "There's no one there, sir."

Alfred studied the spot where his lover had been sitting only moments earlier. "He was right there a moment ago." Alfred searched the room, confused.

Smiling indulgently, the young woman patted his arm as she gathered her stethoscope and wrist cuff. "It's the anesthesia. It's only temporary."

"Damn, I was afraid of that," Alfred groused. For a moment, a young and healthy Byron had sat by his bedside, holding his hand and telling him everything was going to be all right. And for a moment, Alfred believed him.

CHAPTER ELEVEN

ONCE they'd settled his uncle into a room, Alex planned to spend his evening exploring the city's night life. When the moment arrived, however, he found he'd no desire for some nameless stranger. There'd be no repeat of last night with Paul, leaving him unaccountably saddened. More and more he questioned his previous beliefs, unable to reconcile that someone caring and thoughtful, someone who'd once been hurt by a fortune hunter, might possibly turn out to be one himself.

His previous plans for the evening now in shambles, Alex wandered into his uncle's office in search of booze and answers. Settling into his uncle's chair, he noticed that the picture of Paul on the desk had been joined by two more: one of himself, taken a few years ago, and another of Alfred and Byron. Thinking back, he remembered those pictures being on the desk during his last visit, and the image of the laughing, dark-haired man was why Paul had seemed familiar. Alex hadn't thought twice about it at the time.

He'd been taught not to snoop, but for the past few weeks he'd become enmeshed in his family's finances. Telling himself he merely wished to learn more about his uncle's businesses and investments, he opened the top drawer of the desk and peered inside.

At the front lay a stack of well-worn photographs, dog-eared from frequent handling. He picked them up and thumbed through them. Most of the later pictures were of Alfred and Byron, and Alex's eyes filled with tears at how ravaged Byron's formerly healthy body had become by the disease that ultimately claimed his life. Those photos he placed aside, unable to bear looking at them.

Next, he found a stack of older pictures featuring the two men and either himself or a dark-haired boy he assumed to be Paul. For a moment he wondered at never having met Byron's nephew growing up, before remembering why. For some reason, unfathomable now, he'd been jealous of the other child who'd shared his uncle's love. It wasn't that he lacked the old man's affection; he'd had Alfred's love in abundance. No, the problem was, after the death of his mother, Alex wanted someone to be his alone—sharing wasn't an option. Besides, Paul hadn't needed Alfred. Even after the death of his father, Paul had two uncles and a mother. All Alex had, besides his mother's brother, were obscure relatives and two elderly grand-parents whose idea of proper parenting equated to sending him to boarding school and shuttling him off to some tropical paradise during holiday breaks—in the company of anyone but themselves. They took the concept of "hands-off parenting" to new heights.

His vacations had always included Alfred and Byron, the only bright spot in an otherwise lonely life. Alex smiled and leafed through the pictures, remembering the good times they'd shared.

He came across an old, grainy photograph. A young boy,

perhaps nine years old, appeared lost and forlorn, dressed in a suit. At first, Alex thought the sad-looking youngster was himself at his mother's funeral. Upon closer inspection, he realized the boy was much smaller and sported a mop of unruly dark hair and glasses. As he studied the photo, drawn to the desolate image, it occurred to him that he and Paul had been around the same age when they each lost a parent.

Flipping through the rest of the stack, he found snapshots of a full life spent together by Alfred and Byron, and once again envied his uncle's partnership. Christmases, Easters, vacations, and time spent at home, captured for posterity. At the absolute bottom of the stack were two additional photos, obviously handled more than the others, judging from their disintegrating margins. The first depicted two men on a sailboat, one young, with flame-red hair, the other somewhat older, with blond hair beginning to gray. They gazed adoringly at each other, their love unmistakable.

Placing the picture face up on the desk, Alex removed the last photo. Without looking he knew who he'd find. There, before cancer disfigured her beauty, was Victoria Anderson Martin, the stunning blonde he remembered from his youth. Lovingly, he ran his fingers across the faded image, his heart constricting at memories of the vivacious woman who'd been his entire world. In the image she radiated happiness, smiling and playing with his six-year-old self at their summer cottage on Rhode Island.

He placed the picture next to the one of his uncles. They deserved to be framed and displayed. Further digging produced a stack of letters. Alex recognized his own nearly illegible scrawl immediately, and found other letters in the stack bearing writing he didn't recognize. He chose one at random to read.

· · ·

Dear Uncles,

Thanks for your gift, but I can't accept it. You know I love you both, and I know you have only the best of intentions for me. But if I'm to succeed in life, I have to do it on my own. I hope you understand.

Love,

Paul

What was that about? What kind of gift did Paul decline? Several more letters were variations of the same theme. Alex's questing hands found a stack of checks made out to Paul Sinclair. His blood boiled when he noted the amounts, until he noticed the dates. None of them had ever been endorsed.

The first bore Alex's college graduation date. His uncle had gifted him with money, which he'd used to buy his car. The check was written to Paul for the exact same amount. Only Paul had declined. Several more dates caught Alex's attention. The day he'd closed on his condo in Houston, also a gift from Alfred and Byron, there was a check made out for Paul, and again he'd returned the check, uncashed.

They treated us the same. What one received, the other was offered. Paul, apparently, hadn't allowed Alfred and Byron to buy the status symbols that he himself greedily coveted. Alex recalled the aging, barely functioning car he'd ridden in the night of Byron's funeral. Sitting in the drawer was a check for enough money to easily buy four new cars, yet Paul drove a barely functioning vehicle. It didn't make any sense.

His mind spun, seeking answers. Why didn't Paul take the money? Maybe he never received the checks. Alex ruled out the possibility of lost mail immediately, having read the letters of polite refusal. What was Paul's deal? Was he truly committed to Alfred, as Byron had been, not seeing the money but the man himself?

Guilt pressed down heavily as Alex reached the conclusion that everything he'd accused Paul of was a lie. Yes, the man might be having an affair with Alfred, the letters didn't disprove that. What they did show was that if Paul slept in Alfred's bed, it wasn't for the money. It appeared the only one in this equation in any way concerned with money was Alex himself.

He silently made his way to his room, knowing he couldn't stall forever—the time had come to listen to Byron's final message. He settled on the bed, watching with disbelieving eyes as the image of Byron appeared, totally bald, emaciated form propped up by pillows in a huge bed, making him appear even smaller. Though Alex had blocked it for years, a memory surfaced unbidden: his mother, golden ringlets falling by the handful, and his grandparents scolding him for hugging her in public and dislodging her wig. His mom simply smiled and kissed him, readjusted her hair, and scowled at her parents, telling them to leave him be. Later, as the disease progressed, Alex couldn't hug her for fear she'd bruise. The last fateful night, when he'd awakened screaming, he couldn't help himself. He'd waited until the nurse entered the bathroom and crept past to his mother's bed.

She'd stopped recognizing him days before, and he'd heard more than one whispered, "It won't be long now," among the household staff. When he climbed in bed beside her, those blue eyes, so much like his own, saw him, genuinely *saw* him, for the first time in more than two weeks. Her thin lips pulled back into a smile, and though her words were quietly spoken, she clearly said, "I love you, Alexander." He'd watched in horror as the light in her eyes dimmed and went out, her smile never fading. Alex was in college before he finally understood that he hadn't killed his mother, but had instead eased her passing.

"Alex," a raspy recorded voice began, drawing him back to the here and now. "I'm running out of time and I don't dare put this off any longer. First, I wanted to assure you that I know why you stayed away and I understand. Your calls and emails showed me how much you cared; I never doubted you for an instant." Byron stopped to sip from a water glass, the trembling in his hands impossible to miss. "I know you couldn't bear to watch me waste away, and I'd never ask you to. I regret you have to see me like this now. If it were in my power, no one else would witness my decline, either. For Alfred I fought, to be with him every possible moment. Now the time has come. I'm tired and have nothing left to fight with. Before I go, I want to take care of a few matters of business.

"Most of my estate goes to your uncle, as he is, for all intents and purposes, my husband. But there's something that means a lot to me that I'm entrusting to you, and I want you to think long and hard about what to do with it. The cold persona you work hard to project to the world can't fool me. You're a good man, Alex Martin, and I trust you to do the right thing.

"I'm leaving you the deed to a house in Bishop. You'll know why when you set foot in the door. I know without asking that you'll look out for Alfred. If he hasn't already asked you, I will. Please consider moving to Los Angeles. He loves you and misses you. Do this for him."

Byron's shaky tones fell to scarcely above a whisper. "I know you wanted to spend more time with us when you were growing up, and it's my deepest regret that Alfred and I didn't fight your grandparents harder for regular visitation.

"You're strong, capable of anything you set your mind to, and ruthless enough when necessary not to let anyone stand in your way. I've noticed you, how you watch me and your uncle. I've never told you before because plenty of others did, only in a less than productive way: you need someone, and not merely a warm body in your bed occasionally. I hate to picture you alone in the world, with me and Alfred gone. Promise me you'll open your heart, because if you don't, the right one will come and go and you'll never recognize him."

Though his voice faded as he tired, Byron managed a weak laugh. "That's right, I said 'him.' You think your uncle wants you to marry and have children to carry on the family name. I don't know where you got such a silly idea. All he wants is for you to be happy, and we know you well enough to accept that it's a man you truly want, not some flighty debutante.

"I have one final favor to ask of you. You don't know him personally, but you're aware I have a nephew named Paul. He's not as strong as you are, Alex, and I worry about what will happen to him. Promise me you'll take care of him?

"Finally, be happy, and know how much I love you."

Instead of the condemnation he'd deserved and expected, Byron's final words absolved Alex of blame. It lightened his heart that the man died knowing he hadn't intentionally been deserted; still, Alex couldn't forgive himself.

He huddled into a ball on his bed, more miserable than he'd been since his mother's death, barely noticing the shadow curling around him. Somehow, through his fog of pain, he sensed Byron's presence. Alex drifted off, dreaming of Byron's voice singing him to sleep.

AFTER the morning of Bernard's breakdown in the bedroom, Byron vowed not to use him again unless absolutely necessary, deeply regretting the consequences of his actions to the aging servant's already failing mind. Only, progress between the nephews stalled, forcing him to break his vow. Now he quietly congratulated himself on a stroke of genius for compelling Bernard to remove those pictures, letters, and checks from the safe and slip them into the top desk drawer. Alex was curious by nature, and Byron believed it would be only a matter of time before he found them, even if remorse ate him for using his old friend in such a manner. Once again the end justified the means, in his opinion, and the plan paid off as he'd hoped. Alex discovered the truth for himself, and Byron fully expected him to find Paul posthaste and apologize.

Instead, Alex chose to finally watch the video after everyone else had worn theirs out. Byron knew Alex loved him, and he loved Alex, although he'd never met anyone quite so stubborn. Well, yes, he had. Alfred could be like that at times. But he hadn't intended his words to hurt Alex. To his great relief, when he wrapped himself around the man's trembling form, his ghostly embrace afforded some measure of comfort for them both.

However, when Alex woke from his nap Byron stopped congratulating himself. That honeyed voice, so similar to Alfred's, booked a room at a local hotel. *What?* He had to stop Alex from leaving! Byron flitted frantically from room to room, futilely searching for a way to prevent the inevitable departure. Why was the man going now when he'd found out Paul wasn't after money?

Byron found his answer in Alex's hastily scribbled letter.

.   .   .

Dear Uncle Alfred,

I'm sorry I doubted your judgment and Paul's character. Even though it's a bit soon after Byron's death, I know his illness was long and drawn out, possibly allowing you time to reconcile yourself with his passing. Paul seems to be a decent person who truly loves you. I think perhaps it is him you should entrust with the running of your estate, not me. I've finally seen the light and realize I need to stop being a fifth wheel and let the two of you have some privacy. You've got my cell number, and I'm only a phone call away.

With your permission, I plan to sell my condo in Houston and find a place closer to you, something I should have done long ago. As far as Paul goes, you have my blessing.

Love,

Alex

Alex neatly folded the paper and tucked the letter into his shirt pocket.

Oh no! Alfred often accused Byron of going overboard on occasion, and it seemed he'd certainly done it this time. His scheming had backfired, and now Alex planned to do the one thing Byron had thought the man incapable of—be noble.

CHAPTER TWELVE

I'M A coward, Alex told himself for the tenth time, or maybe eleventh.

After spending a sleepless night in one of the city's premier hotels, battling his conscience, he found himself no closer to a solution to his problems than before. Alfred deserved better than a hastily written note and a stealthy departure in the middle of the night. He saw no other way but to face his uncle, and the sooner the better. However, due to his Alfred's delicate health, he'd have to be careful when and how much to confess. He took his frustrations out on the note he'd written, tearing the paper into tiny pieces before dropping them into a trash can.

A hot shower worked wonders for his headache and fatigue, leaving him cautiously optimistic about his upcoming conversation by the time he'd dressed. What a great relief the procedure had been a success, even if it did drive home the point that both he and Paul were needed to help Alfred recover from the double blow of losing a partner and treating a failing heart.

Alex vowed that, for the first time since his mother's illness, he'd put others' needs before his own.

The room service breakfast was palatable, if lonesome, accustomed as he was to company and conversation with his morning coffee and eggs. *If you get a condo....* Alex sighed, realizing freedom came with the price of solitude, something he'd valued only a few short weeks ago. Now, the thought of living alone, dining alone, sleeping alone, seemed so... lonely. A vision of Paul curled up on his bed crept into his mind. He slammed the door on the memory. No need to fantasize about what he couldn't have and shouldn't want.

With hospital visiting hours still an hour away, but tired of pacing in his hotel room, Alex drove to Mercy General to browse through the gift shop in search of a suitable present. Judging by the well-kept gardens behind the house, his uncle liked flowers. He perused the shop's display of cut arrangements, at a loss for what to buy. *Paul would know.*

Yes, Paul would know, like he knew Alfred's favorite meal or which magazines to pack. Alex sighed and selected carnations, trusting the clerk's advice that the arrangement was their best seller while pointedly ignoring the buxom redhead's blatant flirting. He'd come to visit a sick loved one and still found himself being hit on. Biting back an angry retort, he paid for his purchase with a platinum card, earning another thinly veiled come-on, and hastily departed before tossing manners to the winds and repaying rudeness with rudeness.

He soon remembered flattery and flirtation did have their place in the great scheme of things, artfully employing both to charm his way into his uncle's room thirty minutes early. Alfred answered his knock with a raspy, "Come in," and he entered the dimly lit room to find his uncle awake and smiling.

"Alex!" Alfred cried happily. "You're early. I hadn't expected to see you until later."

"I couldn't wait. How are you doing today?" Alex eased farther into the room, placing the flowers on an already laden cart, crowded with gladiolas in various pastel hues. His hastily chosen bouquet of yellow carnations appeared as out of place as he'd felt the night before, seated at the dining room table and listening to the others' shared memories—memories he'd cheated himself out of.

His uncle admired the offering as though the clueless purchase was the finest arrangement in the room instead of what it was—an afterthought. "I'm doing as well as can be expected, I suppose. Thank you for the flowers, Alex, they're lovely."

Alfred reached for his water glass, and Alex hurried to assist, stopped by a harsh glare and an admonishing, "I'm hardly helpless. The closet bench is one thing. This is a sip of water."

"I know, sir." Alex retreated, suddenly feeling extremely awkward.

"This type of surgery isn't what it used to be," his uncle explained. "They use lasers and balloons now. They still make an incision, only it's tiny." He held up fingers spaced approximately two inches apart. "No more 'stem to stern'. Why, they tell me the scar will hardly be visible. They even cut into my groin, not my chest." He added, with a wicked grin, "I always knew that was the true way to a man's heart. Do you think they listened to me?"

Reassured by his uncle's good mood and more optimistic about the chances of a full recovery, despite the lack of information from the surgeon, Alex pulled a chair closer to the bed and collapsed into it, his sleepless night taking its toll. "Did they feed you breakfast?" he asked, stifling a yawn and recalling his own lonely repast.

Alfred snorted. "If you can call it that. Juice and broth are hardly the breakfast of champions."

"Yeah? Well, I missed you this morning. I'm not used to eating alone anymore. I'm becoming a bit spoiled, I'm afraid."

"Alone? Where was Paul? Speaking of Paul, why isn't he with you?" Alfred perused the room as if he expected to find a stray brunet lurking unnoticed in a corner.

Okay, Alex hadn't planned to broach the subject this soon, but his faux pas opened the door. He hoped for the best and stepped through. "I… I didn't stay at the house last night, and incidentally, I'm borrowing your BMW."

Alfred appeared momentarily confused, and then a wry grin spread across his face. "Ah… and who is the lucky woman… or man?"

"No one," Alex blurted. "I moved to a hotel last night."

All traces of humor disappeared from his uncle's face. "Really? Whatever for? Is something wrong at the house?" Narrowed eyes accused him. "You and Paul didn't have a disagreement, did you?"

"Well…," Alex began, nervous about how to proceed, "not exactly."

Alfred trained the same disapproving gaze on him he'd used years ago when Alex got into trouble. "What's going on between you and Paul?"

"Nothing!" he responded, a little too defensively, perhaps. If Alfred's arms hadn't been strapped down and IV-filled, Alex knew they'd be folded across his chest. He sighed, admitting, "I haven't exactly been fair to him."

"Not fair? How?"

Too astute not to notice something wasn't quite right, and lawyer enough not to rest until he'd uncovered the truth, Alfred raised a questioning brow and waited. Alex took the opportunity to come clean. Carefully selecting his words, he tried hard not to upset his uncle. "When I first arrived, I didn't know who he was. He was hugging you, and, well, you seemed so familiar."

The old man snorted. "Of course we seemed familiar. He's the nephew of my partner! He practically grew up in our house."

Alex took a deep breath, braced himself, and then asked, "Is he your lover?"

Alfred sputtered, face coloring. "My lover? Alexander Anderson Martin! Are you out of your mind? He's like a son to me, as you are! How dare you think such a thing! He's Byron's nephew, for crying out loud!"

Alarmed, Alex placed his hand over the nurse call button. "Shh…. Uncle, calm down, calm down! I didn't mean to make you mad. I thought…."

"You thought what? That I'd replace the love of my life with his own nephew mere moments after his passing?" Alfred fixed Alex with the stare designed to back down agents and lesser lawyers. "Listen to me. There will never be another. Byron was my life!"

Alex hung his head, realizing how utterly ridiculous he sounded. "I'm sorry. It's just I found so many things that led me to believe—"

"What things?"

"For starters, I came home at midnight to find Paul leaving your room, wearing only his shorts." In spite of the circumstances, Alex's cock twitched at the memory.

"That hardly points to an affair."

"The next morning I came to your room while you were in the shower. I found those same boxers in your bed."

Alfred scowled in disbelief. "In my bed?"

"It wasn't only that." Alex cringed, reluctant to voice what now seemed ridiculously absurd.

"Oh, there's more?" Those thin arms did cross Alfred's chest then, or as much as the IV tubes and tape allowed.

No getting around it; he'd have to spill his guts about his blatant breach of privacy. Alex steeled his resolve, determined to clear the air and put everything out in the open as he should have from the start. "A few mornings later, I found an empty condom package on your bed."

Alfred's shocked gasp quickly changed to laughter, and then he winced, pulling a pillow against his body to brace his incision. After a moment, he calmed enough to say, "Oh, Alex. I was wondering why I found an unused condom in my trash can."

Alex was certain his uncle had lost his mind. "Sir?"

"It's Bernard, Alex. I'm afraid the old dear has gone a bit senile. In fact, his fears about his own senility prompted his semi-retirement."

"He put those things there?" Somehow, Alex couldn't image the steadfast butler doing something so inexplicable.

"He told me he's been doing odd things lately and doesn't know why. However, he's been such a good friend and loyal employee that I can't let him go. And for the record, I wasn't laughing at *him*. Good Lord, Alex, you should have seen your face!"

Well, he had to admit he deserved a little ribbing. "And you and Paul?"

"Heavens, no! As I said, he's like a son to me, as you are. I can't count the number of times Byron and I tried to get the two of you to meet when you were younger. Somehow my plans never seemed to work out."

Oh. That. "I'm afraid I have something else to confess."

His uncle's stern gaze and raised eyebrows once again brought back memories of childhood misdeeds and their consequences. "Go on."

"I never wanted to meet him," Alex mumbled.

"Why ever not? The two of you have a lot in common."

His reasons for avoidance seemed silly now, though at the time they'd made perfect sense. "The truth is, I was jealous of him. I got to go with you on vacations, but he got to come here or stay with you in Bishop. I went away to boarding school while he spent his weekends at the beach or hiking in the mountains with the two of you." Sadly, he recalled the postcards and letters, rambling ad nauseam about P.J. this and P.J. that. The love-starved child Alex saw it as betrayal, and the knife twisted in his heart with each new letter.

Alfred's expression softened. "Oh, Alex. I didn't know you felt so strongly. You never said anything. If you had, you know I would have...."

"Stood up to Grandmother? No, she wanted me to have a *proper* upbringing, which meant being raised by servants and teachers, and seeing my family only on holidays." Alex reached out to brush his fingers along Alfred's hand—once more resting on the bed—carefully avoiding meeting his uncle's eyes. Expressing his feelings to another was hard enough without being scrutinized. "I know you cared about me. Back when I was a kid, I used to hope one day you'd let me come live with you."

"You never knew, did you?" Alfred asked in amazement, as though realizing, too late, that he'd withheld critical information capable of clearing a client from a life behind bars.

"Knew what?"

"Alex, when your mother died I tried to adopt you. Back then a gay couple adopting wouldn't have been allowed."

"You did?" A burden carried on Alex's shoulders for twenty years suddenly lifted, his uncle confirming what he already knew deep down—he'd been wanted and loved. Byron had alluded to adoption, even if his uncle had never mentioned it before. To know Alfred hadn't intentionally left him in the care of two cold, unfeeling people because he couldn't be bothered with the responsibility of a child came as a tremendous relief.

Gazing off into space, lost in his own thoughts, Alfred finally answered, "Yes, I did. Until your father stepped up and demanded custody, and the best way to protect your interests was to award you to my parents. He didn't stand a chance against them."

Alex's heart hardened at the mention of his father— someone who, like many others, only wanted the money, not him. "I'm sorry I thought the worst about you and Paul."

Alfred offered a soft smile of reassurance, curling his fingers around Alex's hand. "As an attorney, I have to admit there was strong evidence to back your theory, but as your uncle, I need to say you should have spoken to me if something bothered you."

"It gets worse." This was Alex's opportunity to clear the air, and he needed to put the ugliness behind him, allowing the three of them to move forward.

"Worse?" Bushy gray brows knitted together over his uncle's eyes.

"I thought he was after your money."

Alfred sighed and shook his head in disbelief. "Alex, you may as well know, Byron and I always tried to treat you two boys as equals. Whatever we gave to one, we gave to the other

—or rather, we tried to. Paul never accepted a red cent from us."

"I know."

"You know? How?"

Choosing not to disclose his late-night prying, Alex offered instead, "Well, it's rather obvious. I've seen his car, how he dresses. Instead of hiring a contractor, he's refurbishing his store himself."

"Byron and I believed you and Paul to be the children we couldn't have. In all eyes but the law's, Byron was my husband, and Paul is his heir, as you are mine."

"Uncle, I know how close the two of you were, and it breaks my heart that Byron died so young." Releasing his uncle's hand and still carefully avoiding those too observant eyes, Alex added, "I hope one day to find something like that for myself. Someone who wants me and not the money, like Byron did you."

"Alex, look at me," his uncle commanded. Alex lifted his head and gazed into familiar blue eyes, warmth and compassion putting him at ease. "You will find someone someday, I promise you. One day, you'll turn around and there they'll be, right under your very nose."

"I certainly hope you're right." Regardless of Alfred's words to the contrary, Alex still had his doubts.

"There's something else you should know," Alfred murmured.

"Oh?"

"The Anderson estate, the properties and money, will be yours. However, my estate, or rather, mine and Byron's, will be divided between you and Paul. I'm sure he'll fight tooth and nail not to take it. That's the reason it wasn't left to him

outright. The disbursement is detailed in my own will, as
Byron and I agreed."

Far from being upset by this news Alex experienced a keen
sense of relief, the old adage about shared burdens being
lighter coming to mind. "And the house?"

"When we built the house we never intended the place to
be solely occupied by the two of us. We'd hoped to raise a
family, fill that big empty space with laughter. Sadly, it wasn't
to be. Laws weren't what they are today. We couldn't adopt
you or Paul, and contented ourselves with what time we could
spend with you. The house will belong to the two of you.
Perhaps the next generation will succeed where Byron and I
failed."

A moment of quiet understanding passed between them.
"Do you suppose Paul will agree to live there?" Alex finally
asked.

"I hope the two of us can convince him. Alex?"

"Yes?"

"Will you move in with me permanently?"

After watching the video and hearing Byron's words, he'd
had time to think things through. "Well, funny you should
mention that...." Alex smiled. "I'd already decided to sell the
Houston condo and find one here." At Alfred's disappointed
frown, he added, "I've suddenly come to the conclusion that I
absolutely hate dining alone. Since I now know I'm not inter-
rupting anything, I'd be delighted to stay."

"Wonderful!" Alfred exclaimed. "Now I have to convince
Paul." Easing back into his nest of pillows, he closed his eyes
and sighed contentedly, a thin smile playing about his lips.

Just when Alex thought he'd fallen asleep, one eye popped
open. "Alex? How do you feel about Paul?"

That was a good question, and one Alex hadn't yet figured

out. "Now that we've proven he's not some two-bit gold-digger, he's not a bad sort," he admitted with a shrug.

Alfred clutched his pillow tightly and sniggered. "I still can't believe you thought that handsome young man my paramour. At my age, I should be flattered."

"I owe you, and him, an apology."

"You do not. As I said before, it did my old ego good. I do know how you can make it up to me." His uncle winked.

"How?"

"By helping me convince him to stay."

A BRIEF search of the house turned up no sign of Alex. "Figures," Paul huffed over his morning coffee. The moment he started to think Alex a worthwhile human being, the man went out hunting ass. No, that wasn't entirely fair. Alex had every right to go out and find a willing partner. *At least he's giving me what I want and leaving me alone.* Paul wondered, if he'd truly gotten what he wanted, why he felt abandoned.

After breakfast he called the florist to ensure they'd delivered the gladiolas—Alfred's favorite flower—and hurried to the hospital, arriving seconds after visiting hours began. He knocked and then opened the door, grinning when he spotted Alfred sitting up and appearing little worse for the wear. His smile dimmed at the sight of Alex reclining in the chair next to the bed, looking smugly satisfied.

"Good morning, sunshine," Alex said, upping the wattage on his smile. He sat up, causing his shirt to gape open and revealing a vivid bite on his chest.

"Alex," Paul greeted coolly, concealing his red face in Alfred's neck with a hug. He'd actually slept with Alex! And left evidence for anyone to see! Ignoring his ill-advised one-night stand and the telltale love bites, Paul focused his full attention on Alfred. "How're you today? What's the doctor saying?" he blithered, hoping the dim lights hid his embarrassment.

Alfred grinned like a kid at Christmas. "The procedure went well, and if I'm careful and do what the doctor tells me, I'll be back on my feet in no time."

"Wonderful! The house seems empty without you." *And without Alex*, Paul added silently. No need to pad the man's already overinflated ego by telling him, though.

Alfred snorted. "The house would seem empty with a dozen of me in it. As much as I love the place and the memories it holds, sometimes it's too damned big."

"Well, I love staying there. It always felt like home to me," Paul replied, heartened by Alfred's improvement. After his uncle's illness, he'd developed a fear of hospitals, associating them with bad news. Particularly Mercy General Hospital, where he'd spent a good deal of time over the past year—and where his father had died. Despite the doctor's prognosis, he'd privately feared Alfred's trip a one-way ticket. He murmured an inaudible prayer of thanks.

A quiet "ahem" reminded him of Alex's presence. The man's twinkling baby blues gave a moment's warning before Alfred sprang the unexpected. "Paul, I know I've asked before, now I'm asking again. Please consider moving in, at least temporarily, until I'm back on my feet."

Paul's mouth dropped open, and he swept a panicked gaze back and forth between the two men, sensing collusion. Finding his voice, he squeaked, "How does Alex feel about me living under the same roof?"

"Alex?" Alfred raised a brow at his nephew, humor sparkling in his eyes.

"I think that would be an excellent idea," Alex replied with a grin.

"You're sure?" Paul went from surprised to wary at light speed. Alex had wanted him gone mere days ago; what happened since then to change his mind? Oh, yeah. Sex happened. Sadly, sex wouldn't be happening again.

Alex's answer sounded convincingly earnest. "Yeah, I'm sure. We've been talking, and I've decided to sell my place back in Houston. I'm moving here permanently."

"Here? Why?" Never in his wildest dreams would Paul have believed Alex would give up a glamorous, carefree lifestyle to move to LA and care for an aging relative. And if Alex relocated, Paul would have to watch the beautiful bastard fuck his way through the local population. That idea didn't appeal for more reasons than he cared to admit.

"Because Uncle Alfred asked me to," Alex replied simply.

"All in the same house?" Paul suddenly visualized himself as a mouse caught between two cats. No matter which way he turned, he'd find no escape.

"Well, we're still debating. I'd originally planned to find a condo downtown. However, it turns out Uncle Alfred wasn't a hot-shot California attorney for nothing." Alex cast a sly gaze at Paul. "He's kind of persuasive and likes having us both at the house."

So do I, Paul's heart said, frustration creeping in at the thought of seeing Alex every day, knowing he couldn't have more. They did say familiarity bred contempt. Maybe he'd lose interest after a few more weeks of daily exposure. His own reservations aside, the arrangement would make Alfred happy. It wasn't like Paul's store assistant couldn't handle things through the week, and he could always drive back to Bishop on weekends.

A nurse tapped on the door, saving him from having to make an immediate decision. "Excuse me, gentlemen. I need to change Mr. Anderson's dressings and remove his catheter. Would you mind stepping outside?"

"No problem," Alex answered. "We'll head down to the cafeteria and get some coffee." Grinning like a child with a new toy, he wrapped an arm around Paul, steering him from the room.

When the door closed behind them, Paul jerked away, hissing, "What the hell do you think you're doing?"

The wicked grin disappeared. "Look, I know what you're thinking, and I had nothing to do with the invitation. Uncle Alfred wants us with him—both of us." Alex's bold blue eyes held none of their usual mockery. "I know I haven't been there for him like I should, or for Byron, either, and there's nothing I can do about it now. I can't change the past, but I can try to do better in the future. Alfred's about all I have left, family-wise, and he wants me here. He also wants you here."

A warm hand cupped Paul's cheek, and the heady scent Alex had worn the night they'd spent together filled his senses, inspiring an immediate reaction. Paul jumped. Shit! One night in Alex's bed and he'd reverted to a hormonal teenager! No wonder the man was arrogant if he managed such an effect after a single night of sex.

Possibly misunderstanding the reason for Paul pulling away, Alex sighed, dropping his hand to his side. "I know I've said some things, done some things that I shouldn't have. I've made some pretty harsh accusations, and I'm sorry."

What? Alex apologizing? Paul opened his mouth to argue, but Alex cut him off. "No, just listen. I won't bother you again.

It's clear you love the old man in there as much as I do. I'm now coming to understand what kind of love that is, and I'm willing to admit I assumed wrong about a lot of things."

Again, Paul found himself wondering who this person was and what they'd done with the real Alex Martin—not that he'd pay the ransom if a note suddenly appeared. He liked this rational being much better, so he gave Alex the benefit of the doubt. "Go on."

Alex raked his fingers through his hair and stared at the floor. "I want you to understand how much I worry about my uncle. As misguided as I was, I only wanted to protect him. Knowing how you much you care about him, I believe you'd do the same."

Paul honestly couldn't argue the point. He had no idea what changed Alex's mind about him, but for Alfred's sake, he'd accept the cease-fire at face value—for now. He still didn't fully trust Alex, though he desperately wanted to. It would make working and living together a hell of a lot easier. Perhaps in time…. "I don't know what to say."

"Say you'll forgive me for being such an ass and come have coffee with me."

Sparing a quick glance at Alfred's closed door, Paul replied, "A quick one, maybe."

Together they made their way down the corridor, never noticing the shadow dancing triumphantly in the doorway.

CHAPTER THIRTEEN

"ARE you going out tonight, sir?"

A clean getaway came to a screeching halt at Bernard's sudden appearance in the hallway. Either he didn't know the house had been short one occupant the previous night, or his finely honed discretionary skills prevented him from saying so. Alex bet on the latter. Not much happened in the house that the ever-attentive butler didn't know about. His sudden arrival made an inconspicuous departure impossible.

Alex decided, in order to keep his promise and leave Paul unmolested, it might be better if he stayed in his hotel until his uncle returned home to act as chaperone. He fully intended to be a man of his word. Only, he'd never before faced a temptation as powerful as Paul Sinclair. It wouldn't do to push the issue at this juncture, so near to the breaking point. If he suddenly attacked the man across his uncle's desktop, it'd surely traumatize the servants, not to mention Paul's reaction —likely to be violent.

"You are staying for dinner, aren't you?" Bernard asked, as though standing in the midst of hastily packed suitcases making casual conversation happened every day. Alfred *had* mentioned recent strange behavior.

"Dinner?" Alex choked, nearly laughing at the ridiculousness of the situation. Here he was, sneaking out of the house like a rebellious teenager, and Bernard wanted to serve him dinner. Anyway, where was William? Wasn't Bernard supposed to be retiring? William wouldn't have stopped him. More than likely, he'd have offered to pull the car around or help pack. He'd also have done it without asking a single question. Actually, he'd have done it without saying a word, period. Alex sighed.

As inconvenient as the interruption was, Alex preferred dealing with Bernard over William. There was something to be said for employees bold enough to intervene if they thought it necessary.

"Martha gave Theresa the day off," Bernard explained. "She made manicotti, remembering your fondness for her Italian cooking." His voice dropped, as though fearful the nearly deaf woman might hear him. "You wouldn't want to disappoint her after she's gone to so much trouble, would you?" Piercing gray eyes peered over the top of Bernard's bifocals, daring Alex to decline.

What could he say? Alex sighed and placed his bags on the floor. "No, I suppose not." Besides, he remembered Martha's ill temper if she "slaved all day over a hot stove" and the resident males didn't worship her properly for her sacrifice. He didn't envy Theresa having to fill Martha's shoes.

Bernard's beaming smile grew nearly frightening. "Very good, sir. I'll take these bags back up to your room while you freshen up. You can join Mr. Sinclair in the dining room."

The mention of Paul's name nearly made Alex change his mind. He'd done Paul Sinclair a great disservice and owed him a tremendous apology, more than the feeble attempt at the hospital. How could he ever make amends for the harsh things he'd implied and said? At the very least, enjoying a nice Italian dinner and some light conversation before he left for his hotel wouldn't hurt. The table was wide. If he remained on his side, everything should be fine.

"Leave the suitcases, Bernard. I'll get them later," he said, knowing words were useless. The bags wouldn't be there after dinner. Bernard never allowed anything to remain out of place for more than the few minutes it took to tidy up. When Alex returned to his room later, every item would be in its rightful place and the suitcases banished to a closet, forcing him to repack—or not. He had little doubt that Bernard, now on alert, would bar any other attempts to leave. Time to admit defeat. "Fine, but get Isaac or William to help you."

"Are you quite sure? I don't mind."

Alex employed the considerable Anderson charm, much as he'd observed his uncle do over the years, to persuade Bernard without belittling his abilities or pointing out that the man was getting far too old to carry heavy baggage up a flight of stairs. "It's not like Uncle Alfred needs them both right now. Let the men earn their keep."

Bernard barely hid a gleeful smirk. "Very good, sir." He ambled off to the back of the house with a jaunty spring in his step. Was he whistling? Alex couldn't help but laugh, shaking his head in disbelief at having been so easily manipulated.

Returning to his room, he exchanged his club wear for comfortable slacks and a loose, lightweight sweater, then followed his nose to the dining room. The most glorious aroma rose from a large silver chafing dish on the table, and his stomach loudly grumbled its approval. Paul was already there, as he'd expected from Bernard's comment, leaning against the unlit hearth with a glass of wine in hand, staring at the pictures above the mantle with a wistful expression. "Good evening, Paul," Alex greeted him, determined to behave like a gentleman.

Paul jumped, eyes warily seeking the nearest exit. Alex sighed. Though they'd made remarkable progress recently, apparently he still had a long way to go to win Paul's trust.

Recovering his composure, Paul pointed to a bottle resting on the end of the table. "Would you care for some wine before dinner?"

"That would be nice." Damn, what a sight! Simply dressed in tight jeans and a black T-shirt, Paul wore a pair of worn loafers on his otherwise bare feet. His hair, still damp from a recent shower and sleeked back in a thick mass, had darkened to a soft black. The shirt clung to Paul's well-defined chest, and Alex fought the urge to run his hands beneath the thin material.

"Martha outdid herself tonight," Paul boasted. "I've always loved her Italian cooking, and I think you'll find the wine goes quite well with the meal." He poured another glass from the nearly full bottle and crossed the dining room to hand the goblet to Alex.

Paul hid his awkwardness admirably, and if Alex hadn't known what to look for, he might have missed the signs himself. Over the past few weeks, Alex had noticed Paul worrying his lower lip with his teeth when nervous, like now, and whereas Alex once would have taken advantage, he no longer wanted to make the man uncomfortable, especially not here in what was to be their shared home.

"Thanks." Alex accepted the glass and sniffed appreciatively before taking a tentative sip of the lightly tinged beverage, the semisweet wine rolling slowly over his tongue. "This is extraordinary," he exclaimed. "Your choice?"

Paul nodded. "It's my favorite domestic."

"A local winery?"

"Nah, Rhode Island, believe it or not. A friend of mine sent a case for my birthday, and I've been ordering from them ever since."

The garden-variety boy next door knew wines, did he? Byron had been renowned for his discerning palate when it came to fine vintages, despite a humble upbringing. Maybe he'd passed some knowledge to his nephew. "Well, you have excellent taste," Alex admitted, once again giving credit where it was due. "What say we see how well *your favorite domestic* goes with manicotti?"

Though Paul tensed and appeared ready to run, he gamely replied, "I thought you'd never ask. I'm starving."

Once they were seated, Martha bustled into the room, muttering absentmindedly to herself. For as long as Alex could remember, she'd served their plates personally, an unnecessary gesture, in his opinion. He bit his tongue and remained silent, having learned not to argue with her skewed logic. Better to go ahead and agree with whatever she said or did and get it over with. She'd win eventually, anyway.

"Evenin', boys," she rasped, voice rough from too many years of cigarettes. Alex detested the things, blaming them for his mother's untimely death. Unfortunately, he'd never been able to convince the formidable Martha of the error of her ways, and though she reeked of her favorite vice, he didn't pull away when she wrapped her arms around him and kissed him soundly on the cheek.

"Good evening, Martha," Paul and Alex replied in unison.

The true master, or rather, mistress, of the Anderson abode

rounded the table to kiss and hug Paul before uncovering the fragrant dishes and serving their plates.

"Mmm… it smells wonderful. Tell me, Martha, what's the special occasion?" Paul asked.

"Mr. Anderson told me you boys liked my manicotti and asked me if I'd fix it tonight." No matter how many years she'd worked for Alfred, she still insisted on calling him "Mr. Anderson" and often reprimanded Bernard for referring to their employer by his first name in her presence.

Kissing and hugging her employers was acceptable in her world, as was rapping a knuckle with a wooden spoon if proper manners weren't observed by the younger members of the household. However, calling them by their given names amounted to a taboo in her book, a concept thoroughly confusing to Alex. He chose not to comment, merely smiling at her playful teasing. "I always do what I'm told to do… except when I don't." She chortled at her own joke.

Ignoring her behavior, as they'd all learned to do, Paul asked, "That's pretty thoughtful of him, but why would he ask when he couldn't be here to enjoy it too?"

"Beats me," the housekeeper said. "He asks, I say 'yes, sir!'" Even Alex, a seldom visitor, knew her claim to obedience to be stretching the facts a bit. Alfred loved Martha's cooking and she had reminded Byron of his Great-aunt Lucille, so the household either politely ignored her little quirks or quietly accepted her eccentricities for their entertainment value.

After she'd filled their plates, Martha stepped back from the table, wiping her hands on her apron. "Is there anything else I can be gettin' ya before I leave ya to your meals?"

"No, Martha, that will be all." Alex smirked, noticing the wooden spoon peeking from the pocket of her apron. Some things never changed. Beneath the table he rubbed knuckles that still recalled the punishment for hands straying onto the bread platter without waiting to be properly served, though it'd been a good fifteen years since he'd last been reminded.

A sidelong glance caught Paul rubbing his own knuckles, and Alex bit his cheek to keep from laughing. Apparently he wasn't the only one who'd occasionally forgotten his manners.

The moment the woman's ample body disappeared through the kitchen door, the chandelier dimmed and then went out entirely, plunging the room into darkness. Before he had a chance to react, Alex heard retreating footsteps and, a moment later, the strike of a match. A brief flare highlighted Paul's features as he lit a candle.

The hall door opened and Bernard stepped in, flashlight in hand. "Forgive me, sirs, it seems there's an isolated power outage. I sent Isaac out to the fuse box to correct the problem. Would you like me to move your meals into the kitchen? It wasn't affected."

It didn't escape Alex's attention that Bernard arrived a split second after the lights went out. The butler must have been waiting outside the door until the proper moment. Keeping his observations to himself, Alex waited to see how the obviously staged scene played out.

Paul held the candle in one hand while shielding the flame with the other, slowly working his way around the room, igniting wicks, until the soft glow of a dozen tapers washed the walls in warm light. The flickering glow created an interesting play of shadows and light over Paul's features, painting auburn highlights across his damp hair. A captivated Alex murmured, "No, Bernard, that's all right. Evidently, we're to dine by candlelight tonight."

"If there's anything further you need, please let me know," Bernard replied with a stiff bow. He retreated into the hallway, pulling the door closed, not quite succeeding in hiding his satisfied smile from Alex's watchful eyes.

Now, how did that happen? It would have been ingenious to manipulate an intimate, candlelit dinner between the nephews, but as much as he'd like to take credit, Byron couldn't.

He found Bernard in the kitchen, dining with Martha. If Byron could have drawn breath, he would have sighed. Those wonderful meals, lovingly prepared by the peculiar old cook. How many times had he and Alfred dined at the same table where the boys were now seated, enjoying culinary master-pieces crafted by her skilled hands? Ah, to be young again. *Or to be alive again.* Byron frowned, though no one could see him to notice.

He was passing through the kitchen, literally, when a snippet of conversation caught his attention.

"I must arrange for an electrician tomorrow." Bernard spoke dramatically, gracing his dinner companion with a conspirato-rial wink. "I certainly hope there's nothing seriously wrong with the wiring."

"Ah, don't get your shorts in a twist, Bernie. It's nothing a flick of the finger won't cure," the cook replied with a lopsided smile.

"I beg your pardon?" Had Bernard always sounded so stuffy? *Must get his fusty airs from Alfred,* Byron commented to himself, snickering. As much as he loved the man, Alfred's high-brow Boston raising had provided plenty of opportunities for teasing over the years, especially in light of Byron's own small-town upbringing.

Martha cocked her head to the side. "Did you hear something?"

Bernard failed to hide his annoyance. "No, and neither do you, you deaf old crone. Now, don't change the subject. What did you mean?"

"Jeez, there ya go again, getting bent out of shape over nothin'."

"Martha, sometime within this decade, please."

The housekeeper snorted. "And they wonder why you never married."

Byron hovered nearby, floating weightlessly in the shadows. He loved a good argument, and the servants' squabbling provided quality entertainment.

"As God is my witness, woman! Cough it up before I strangle you, killing you from asphyxiation and me from a massive coronary as I attempt to wring the life out of that thick neck of yours."

"Touchy, touchy," Martha groused. "If'n ya really must know, I was only doin' what I was told."

Byron snickered again at the woman's guttural dialect, knowing she affected backward ways intentionally to goad the prim and proper butler, for he'd heard her on numerous occasions conversing as though to the manor born—when it suited her purposes. His attention switching back and forth between the two as though watching a tennis match, he eagerly awaited Bernard's next volley.

"What were you told, and by whom?"

Bernard's face turned an alarming shade of purple. In his fifty-four years, Byron had never acquired much medical knowledge, but it didn't take a license to practice medicine to tell him "purple face" wasn't a good thing.

"Mr. Anderson told me if a breaker marked 'Dining Room'

was to be accidentally switched off, certain young men could have themselves a cozy dinner. I had Isaac take care of it."

"Well, Alfred certainly gave you those instructions," Bernard sniffed.

"Why ya say that? How many times 'ave I told you not to be callin' Mr. Anderson by his first name? It's not right." Martha wrung her hands as if some great evil would befall them for his impropriety.

Bernard rolled his eyes, as did Byron. "I shudder to think of so massive a number. However, your efforts were quite unnecessary, I assure you." The normally stoic butler smirked. "The hutch has been against the wall for years, and few remember a dimmer switch hidden behind it. I turned it off while you had their attention."

It seemed the two seniors had independently worked toward the same goal. They began arguing over who'd actually succeeded, and Byron left them to their bickering, reminded wistfully of Douglas. He dearly missed their lively debates.

Despite his own health worries, it seemed Alfred intended to keep his promise to unite the boys, even involving the help. *Speaking of Alfred, time to check in on him at the hospital.* But first, Byron wanted one more quick peek at the nephews before he went....

"Now, isn't this cozy?" Alex gazed at his dinner companion from across the table. Paul's glasses reflected the candlelight, eyes appearing to flame. Alex's breath caught in his throat as he recalled the scene from his bedroom such a short time ago: Paul's profile, partially hidden in shadow, before he locked their lips together, like kissing Alex was the most important thing he'd ever done. A few short days ago, Alex's arrogance would have said, *"It was the most important thing he'd ever done."* Ironically, the part of him that sneered at lesser beings remained quiet. Maybe because there were no lesser beings present.

"Yes, it is," Paul replied, and Alex had to think hard to recall the question. "You know," Paul confided a moment later, "I've always loved Martha's cooking, but I'm also a bit afraid of her."

Alex chuckled. "When I was a child I thought my grand-mother was the most intimidating woman on earth, until I met Martha. I never knew a wooden spoon could be wielded so lethally."

Paul threw his head back with a hearty laugh.

Well, damn. For all his quiet intensity, he was capable of genuine laughter. Such a charming laugh, too! Alex didn't know whether to blame Paul's lack of wariness on the wine, the dinner, or the earlier apology, but during the course of the meal, Paul slowly unwound, and no longer appeared coiled to spring and run.

"How often did you visit?" Paul asked, refilling their glasses, a gesture not wasted on Alex. Far from being the spoiled plaything of a wealthy lover, Paul behaved in a thoughtful and kind manner, serving others without a second thought. Not as a servant, more as a polite host—as Byron had been.

When Alex thought about the question, his smile fell.

"S-s-sorry, didn't mean to be nosy," Paul stammered.

"No, it's all right." Alex had nothing to lose by being candid and answered honestly, "I didn't visit nearly as often as I would have liked."

"Why not? They both adored you. I'm sure they were thrilled whenever they had the chance to see you."

Alex sighed, wondering how much the man truthfully knew about his life. "You know my grandparents raised me, right?"

"Yes," Paul answered. After a moment's consideration he blushed and added, "Oh."

"Yeah, 'oh.' My grandparents didn't disown Alfred when his orientation became public knowledge. They didn't dare, even if they weren't exactly thrilled with their only son 'flaunting his perversion' in polite society."

His grandparents' treatment of Alfred was a sore subject for Alex, who idolized his uncle, considering him incapable of wrong. "They only allowed me see him on vacation or when he visited Boston. They did everything in their power to keep me from coming here, fearing too much exposure to his 'proclivities' and the 'LA lifestyle' would taint me." His gloomy expression turned into a self-satisfied smile, and he raised his glass in toast. "If they could only see me now.

"The rest of the family back in Boston, a useless bunch of hangers-on, gossiped and backbit, but none dared speak ill to Uncle Alfred's face. He's too powerful, even for them." Alex shuddered to think what the wolves might have done if Alfred possessed his partner's easy demeanor, recalling his self-righteous grandmother's scathing remarks about Byron Sinclair.

Voice subdued, Paul ventured, "You don't have to answer this if you don't want to, it's none of my business, but I'm curious because of what I've heard about them. Were they hard on you when you came out?"

"I didn't come out," Alex admitted, his words laced with bitterness at yet another example of cowardice. "They went to their graves thinking it a matter of time before I found the right stuck-up debutante, settled down, and gave them a great-grand-child to ignore." While he hadn't intended to demean his family publicly, keeping his feelings bottled up for years took its toll. The floodgate now stood open; he might never be able to close it again.

"It's different with Alfred and Uncle Byron...," Paul began.

Alex cut him off. "As far as Uncle Alfred knows, I'm bi. He's never discouraged my relationships with men, even though he's reminded me often enough that I'm the last of the Andersons." Byron correctly said Alfred never voiced such a thing; Alex read between the lines, completing the thought with words of his own. "He wants me to father children and continue the family line."

Paul's outrage, on his behalf, warmed Alex more than he cared to admit. "Surely you've spoken with him?"

Alex shrugged, staring into the depths of his wine glass. "You know the man and love him as much as I do. Could you tell him no?"

Paul's reply caught Alex by surprise. "Actually, I have no intention of saying no."

"What?"

"I don't intend to disappoint him or Uncle Byron. Like you, I'm the last. The last Sinclair." Paul leaned back in his chair and laughed. "Gawd, that sounds dramatic! Like *The Last of the Mohicans.*"

Even in the semidarkness, when Paul grinned, Alex noticed a crooked front tooth. Rather than detracting from his appeal, it added a certain "mischievous little boy" quality that Alex found endearing, particularly in comparison to his normal "perfect at any price" lovers, with their nips, tucks, and overly bright, bleached teeth. Lately Alex had come to appreciate Paul's natural appearance and attitude.

"What do you intend to do about it? The children thing, I

mean?" he asked. "Forgive me for being blunt, but I can't imagine you settling down with a woman." Again, a wonderful belly laugh washed over Alex's senses.

"Heavens, no!" Paul exclaimed. "I mean, there will be a mother of my children, God willing. We're just not planning on stripping down and doing the nasty." He visibly shuddered. "Besides," he added with a cheeky grin, "Lee could kick my ass to hell and back if she had a mind to."

"Lee?"

Leaning in, Paul asked, "Did you ever meet Bernard's great-niece, Cecelia?"

"That's Lee? It's been a long time; I haven't seen her in years. Didn't she grow up to be…?"

"A stereotype?" Paul supplied.

"I was going to say 'tattoo artist'. I suppose 'stereotype' works too. How's she doing?" A faded image came to mind of a pudgy little girl with brown hair and freckles who hated dresses and ribbons and who held her own in any kind of competition, from chess to fistfights.

"Let's say that 'Lee' suits her better than 'Cecelia' these days." Paul winked.

Alex deadpanned, "That explains a lot."

"Yeah, it does. Anyway, Lee's agreed that when I finally—" Paul rolled his eyes and mimicked the throaty voice Alex remembered from his youth, "—'find the man worth the grief', she'll carry my child as a surrogate—artificially inseminated, of course."

"Of course." Alex snickered. Chances were Cecelia Landers had surprised absolutely no one when she made her big announcement, if her outing even required an announcement at all, for as Paul had pointed out, she had prided herself on living up to stereotypes even in her teens. The more Alex deliberated, the more he admired Paul's having hit on the perfect solution. Lee was practically family, but not incestuously so, and if memory served, good people. Paul planned for fatherhood someday. For a moment, the old envy returned.

Alex never even considered the possibility of having children the way Paul intended to, resigning himself to a brief, loveless relationship followed by a slew of lawyers and custody battles. He'd win, of course, because he held all the cards, not to mention the money. It would still be costly and painful, particularly for the child. For that reason alone, Alex hesitated to consider such a possibility. However, with a friend, someone willing to help out of the goodness of her heart.... "Wait a minute," he asked, voicing his suspicion, "what's in your arrangement for her?"

Paul's smile broadened. "Well, she'd still be a part of the child's life, only not a traditional one. We're old friends, and she says she'll do this for me and our uncles. The thing she says she wants most from this is"—again with a spot-on Cecelia impersonation—"she wants 'to show all those skinny bitches in the minivans they got nothing on the dyke on the Harley.'"

Alex laughed at the image of a heavily tattooed and pierced, noticeably pregnant biker flipping off a soccer mom in a minivan.

The two men, caught up in their conversation, barely noticed the time, or that they supposedly didn't like each other.

After dessert, Paul took Alex on a brief walk through the garden, discussing a few planned additions and then, astonishingly, asking for opinions. Although Alex didn't know much about gardening, that didn't prevent him from being fascinated by his companion's animated explanations and plans, reminiscent of their earlier conversation about the renovations to Paul's old store building.

Evening fell, pleasantly cool without being frigid, and the full moon hung low in the sky, augmenting the pathway lighting lining the walkways through the garden. Paul yawned, and Alex suggested they call it a night.

As they entered the house, Alex couldn't help himself. "Paul," he breathed softly, brushing his lips lightly over Paul's, the briefest of caresses. "Good night, sleep well." He spun and strode purposefully from the room. If Paul chose to remind him of his promise, he didn't want to hear it. It took every bit of his willpower to limit himself to one kiss, and if he didn't get upstairs soon and away from temptation, he might do something that genuinely would horrify the servants.

He wasn't surprised to find his suitcases from downstairs had been brought up and unpacked, but everything he'd taken to the hotel the previous night had been returned as well.

CHAPTER FOURTEEN

A FEW days later, hard at work in the office, paying bills and arranging for the running of three separate households, plus vacation homes, an epiphany struck Alex. The house in Boston stood empty most of the year, requiring staff and utilities even when unused. If he truly meant to relocate his life to LA, he wouldn't need another full-time residence. Besides, the stately mansion held bad memories, and he'd avoided staying there whenever possible. Technically, the decision fell to Alfred, but Alex felt certain his uncle would probably agree to sell or capitalize on the house's historical value and earn a tidy tax write-off by donating the monstrous money pit to some preservation society. The house in Rhode Island, he'd keep.

Preparing the Houston condo for the market, he acknowledged that he'd never truly considered the glass and chrome showplace home, always referring to his dwelling as "the condo." He mused on what it meant to finally have a real home, until a soft tapping caught his attention. "Come in," he called.

The door eased open, and Paul stepped into the room

wearing a snug T-shirt and a pair of loose-fitting shorts. From the looks of it, he'd recently returned from his morning run and taken a shower, for his hair fell in a riot of wet strands around his face. And he was barefoot. Alex couldn't stop staring at those pale feet, toes curling into the plush carpeting.

"Are you all right?"

Glancing up guiltily to find Paul studying him, Alex stammered, "I'm a bit tired, I guess."

"Well, maybe you should take a break." Paul placed a stack of envelopes and periodicals on the desk. "I brought in the mail."

Alex sighed, contemplating the new arrivals. The last thing he needed—more bills. Normally the accountant handled the brunt of it; unfortunately, since the accountant had proved untrustworthy, the chore became Alex's. Also, Alfred insisted that Alex become intimately familiar with all aspects of the Anderson empire, including little windowed envelopes arriving like clockwork to demand money. In retrospect, Alex appreciated Alfred's insistence, for he'd never have known of the accountant's duplicity otherwise.

He rolled his gaze upward again. Sympathetic eyes studied him. "You do look tired," Paul said. "Would you care for a cup of tea?"

Alex didn't feel quite right treating the man like a servant, but a cup of tea sounded good. "Please."

"I'll be right back." Paul hurried from the room, faint traces of a smile crinkling the corners of his eyes. He seemed to find pleasure in doing for others, an alien concept to Alex, and one requiring further study.

Thumbing through the stack of mail, Alex began triaging: stacking items requiring his immediate attention in one pile, interesting magazines in another, and items he couldn't figure

EDEN WINTERS

out in yet another. He knew without asking that Paul had already thrown junk mail, fliers, and sales ads into the recycling bin.

A small, square envelope caught his eye, hand-addressed in calligraphy to Mr. Alfred Anderson, from Edmond Strickland. If Alex wasn't mistaken, it appeared to be an invitation of some kind. Well, no point in opening the gold-embossed envelope. His uncle was in no condition to attend a party. About to drop it in the trash, he paused mid motion when Paul returned, bearing a tray.

"What have you got there?" Paul asked, placing the tray on the desk and then pouring two cups of tea before adding precisely the right amount of sugar to Alex's.

"An invitation," Alex replied, turning the envelope over in his hands.

"Hmm... I didn't notice earlier." Paul took the envelope, opening it to peek at the card within. A smile of pure delight lit his face. "Edmond's finally opening his new gallery and is having an open house," he announced.

"I hate to rain on your parade, Paul, but you know there's no way Uncle Alfred will be able to attend."

"Well, he'll want to know; they've been friends for years. As a matter of fact, I'll show him over dinner. Knowing him, he'll still want to go." Setting the card aside, Paul sank into a chair and picked up his own cup.

Alex took a tentative sip. A single taste brought a smile to his face. Paul had added a touch of brandy, the way he liked it. He peered up into the smug face of his former adversary, who merely tipped his cup in a toast.

No denying the man made life easier, reminding Alex to eat, taking care of the household, every little gesture saying how much he cared. Paul also no longer avoided him, which would have made it more difficult to get anything accomplished. A more pleasant atmosphere existed in the house when they cooperated, like now.

Considering the invitation and Alfred's recovery, Alex put his foot down. "Out of the question. He just left the hospital, there's no way he can attend."

"No way I can attend what?" Both men were startled to discover Alfred standing in the doorway, dressed in robe and slippers. They'd managed to keep him in bed for nearly twenty-four hours before he'd demanded access to his own house. Since then he'd cheerfully checked in on everyone repeatedly to ask what they were doing, obviously bored out of his mind. Retirement didn't agree with him.

"Eddie's gallery opening," Paul said, jumping to his feet to help Alfred to a chair.

The old man rolled his eyes. "How many times do I have to tell you boys I'm not helpless?"

Paul dropped his gaze to the floor, muttering a quiet, "I know." Expression brightening, he asked, "Would you like some tea? I'm afraid tea is all you're allowed to have, though. No brandy. Doctor's orders."

"I believe I might," Alfred replied, frowning at the "no brandy" comment.

Paul nearly raced from the room. He literally lived to do for others, and appeared happiest when preparing tea or cooking a meal for his loved ones. Alex remembered Paul's cheerful smile when he arrived with the tea a short while ago. Was Alex himself now included on the list of loved ones? Though he hadn't tried again, Paul also hadn't taken him to task for the kiss in the garden. Interesting.

"Such a helpful young man, isn't he? So efficient," Alfred said. "He's right, you know."

Alex turned abruptly at his uncle's comments, embarrassed at being caught staring at the door through which Paul had long since departed. "Right about what?" Many things fit under the heading of "right" when it came to the diminutive Sinclair.

"Right in saying I'd like to attend Edmond's opening. He's worked hard for this, and I regret I'll have to miss his big night." Alfred sighed. Suddenly, he fixed twinkling eyes on Alex, his face lighting up.

Alex froze, instantly aware the old man had hatched a plan. A plan involving him somehow.

"Alex, when was the last time you attended a gala?"

Thinking hard, Alex replayed the past few months and finally latched onto something that might be stretching the truth a little bit. "I did attend a club opening a few months back. The owner is a friend of mine."

Scowling, Alfred shot back, "Club Inferno doesn't count."

Alex's jaw dropped. "Club Infer—how did you know about the club?"

"I wasn't a premier attorney in the scandal capital of the world for nothing, my dear boy. I have my sources."

Oh shit. If Alfred knew about Club Inferno, he knew....

"Yes, Alex. I know what the club is and I know why you go there. Let me also congratulate you on your decision to avoid Rico Vespucci. I've nothing against the *nouveau riche*, providing the *riche* is honestly acquired. Vespucci's wasn't." Those piercing eyes, so alive and alert, stared at him as though they lay open Alex's deepest, darkest secrets. "If and when you get back to Houston, you'll find your favorite cruising spot gone. The club fronted drugs and prostitution, Alex. The doors were closed and locked last week."

"Uncle?" Alex voice wavered. It struck him that the only

weakness and frailty in Alfred was in his body. His mind remained sharp, his sphere of influence equally vast.

Alex's ever-indulgent uncle finally, for the very first time, laid down the law. "For years I've watched you paint the town and have a high old time of it. I smiled and turned a blind eye, knowing that's what youth is for. You're thirty now. It's time to settle down and act like a man."

Immediately on the defensive, Alex challenged, "You want me to get married." He'd always known this day was coming and, as he'd told Paul, he couldn't find it in him to say no.

With a rueful smile and a shake of his head, Alfred quietly responded, "No, Alex. I could no more ask you to live a lie than I could stop loving you for who you are. How can you even think that of me? Would you put me in the same class as my parents, who expected such of me? Never! What I'm asking is for you take responsibility for your life and grow up a little. The world can still be your playground. You simply need to follow the rules, or"—one bushy eyebrow lifted—"make new ones. Anderson blood flows in your veins, after all. What you need is structure, Alex. Establish high standards of conduct for yourself and stick to them."

Alex nodded numbly, knowing he should have done this on his own without waiting for his uncle to make demands. "You're absolutely right."

Alfred's nod of approval had the same effect now as years ago, instilling a sense of pride that he'd pleased the only father he'd ever known. "I have a favor to ask," his uncle continued. "You're right in saying that I can't attend the showing of Edmond's work. Instead, I'd like for you to go instead and find a new painting to hang on the wall of my office."

Oh, was that all? For a moment Alex expected something truly horrendous to be asked of him, like visiting Aunt Helena.

He breathed a sigh of relief. "Is there anything in particular you'd like?" Though he'd never admit a fondness for culture publicly, as it might tarnish the shallow image he'd slaved to create, he'd frequently attended gallery openings for the sake of the art, not merely for the social whirl or out of a sense of familial obligation. Andersons, even half Andersons, tended to get lots of invitations. He hadn't attended any lately and was shocked to realize that, instead of attending cultural events and gallery showings, he'd been focusing solely on clubbing instead. How had that happened?

"You'll know it when you see it," came the enigmatic reply.

"Knock, knock," Paul called from the hallway, warning them of his arrival. "Tea's here!"

"One more thing, Alex," Alfred added with a meaningful gaze. "I want you to take Paul with you."

ALEX'S power of speech fled. Paul appeared attractive when scruffy, but cleaned up? Amazing. And the absolute best part? Paul didn't have a clue how gorgeous he was, and that, in Alex's opinion, was possibly his best feature.

A thick, coffee-colored mane contrasted starkly with the crisp white collar of Paul's shirt, and the black contemporary tuxedo jacket, cut to frame his crotch rather than cover it, accentuated Paul's compact build. Alex would bet he had no idea who'd designed his attire or how much Alfred had paid for the suit. Knowing might surely ruin the evening for Paul.

Paul smiled shyly, traipsing down the hall toward the foyer, and Alex considered any price well worth the results. The man made a fine sight in the tux, and Alex began to mentally devise ways to get him out of it. With a sigh, he recalled his solemn promise to stop making unwanted advances. When he'd started trying to lure Paul to bed he'd had ulterior motives; now the game had grown serious. The more he learned, the more he admired the open honesty of Paul Sinclair. The man represented all anyone dared ask for, rolled up into one convenient, sexy-as-hell package.

Was appreciation for his own appearance reflected in Paul's eyes?

"Are you ready to go?" Alex asked offhandedly, as though he hadn't been watching the clock for the past ten minutes, fearing Paul might change his mind. "I had Isaac pull the car around." He chuckled. "Not yours—the Benz."

Although Alfred lived well, he didn't flaunt his wealth in his daily living, and his garage contained fairly modest vehicles for their neighborhood: an Escalade, a Town Car, a Jeep, and a sporty BMW. Down at the far end, reserved for special occasions, sat Alfred and Byron's pride and joy: a 1958 Mercedes-Benz Type W180 220S Ponton sedan. Alfred insisted Alex and Paul "take his baby out for a little fresh air" for the gallery opening, which suited Alex. He loved making a grand entrance, and the Benz certainly guaranteed they'd be noticed.

"Why ever not?" Paul asked, lower lip stuck out in a pout. "Don't you think a bit of dirt would be the perfect touch for our monkey suits? And wouldn't we make quite the fashion statement when Old Betsy backfired? Not many vehicles come equipped with their own twenty-one gun salute."

"Did they charge extra, or are military honors a standard feature?" Alex asked, enjoying Paul's good-natured teasing. It wasn't often he found himself in a position to flirt, normally too poised and intent on being "The Great Alex Martin, Rich Guy." He found flirting surprisingly entertaining. Paul joining in the fun made it priceless.

Paul's smile had an immediate effect on Alex's libido, much deprived as it had been since their one night together. Recent abstinence must be the reason why he acted like a hormonal teen whenever his former rival came within a few feet. No one had ever inspired such instant lust in him before.

Grateful his own tux boasted a more generous cut and hid his body's reaction, Alex opened the door and ushered Paul through. "After you," he said, watching with keen fascination. The back of the man's tux appeared equally flattering.

He shot a warning scowl at Isaac when he noticed the driver also enjoying the view. It looked like he'd have to keep a close eye on his companion tonight. They hadn't even left the house, and already he'd met competition. Not that he expected any *serious* competition—he was Alex Martin, after all.

Climbing in, he settled himself in the car, a little closer to Paul than absolutely necessary. Paul didn't move away.

"So," Paul began, relaxing into the seat, hands clasped loosely in his lap. "Have you ever been to a showing of Edmond's work before?"

"Actually, until the invitation arrived, I'd never heard of Edmond," Alex confessed.

"Not much of an art fan, huh?"

"I wouldn't say that. I may not know much about art, but I can point and say, 'Oh… pretty!'" The comment earned Alex a laugh. He chose his words carefully. This newfound camaraderie might end in a minute if Paul thought him bragging. Alex opted to downplay any true interest in the subject and gave a modest portion of the truth. Now wasn't the time to flaunt wealth and privilege. "I took art history in college," he offered.

With a definite challenge to his words, Paul prodded, "Okay. Who's your favorite artist?"

Alex had never passed up a challenge in his life, but prudently kept his true opinion to himself in this matter. If he mentioned the name "Kandinsky," he'd spend the next hour babbling about one of his favorite subjects. To avoid a lengthy rant on technique and style, he gave an answer he hoped Paul would accept. "Oh, I don't know. Monet is okay."

Paul snorted. "Too easy. Everyone likes Monet."

He should have known the man was too smart to buy his feeble answer. Alex leaned back against the leather seat and considered how much to tell without appearing arrogant and bringing the conversation to a screeching halt. He recalled his first exposure to art, a cherished gift given to him by his mother. "Well, when I was a child I had a book illustrated by Maxfield Parrish. As I grew older, I developed a great appreciation for *Stars*."

Misunderstanding the reference, Paul replied with a puzzled expression, "A nude female?"

"It wasn't the 'nude' part." Alex contemplated the city passing outside the car window, the darkening evening the perfect shade of blue he remembered from the print, the lights reminiscent of the stars for which the artist named it. "I think it was more the woman's wistful expression as she gazed up at the night sky." Without knowing why, he voiced a sentiment he'd never before shared with anyone. "I believed I knew exactly how she felt. I've done the same thing, imagining myself anywhere but where I was."

"Was your childhood that bad?" Paul asked quietly.

Alex turned to face Paul, his gaze falling into a pair of sympathetic brown eyes. He hated whining about his "poor little rich kid" upbringing, but the truth was, he'd spent a lot of years envious of less financially blessed friends and their close-knit, loving families. "Imagine growing up where you could have anything you wanted for the asking."

"Many kids dream of that sort of thing."

"Yeah? What if you lived in a sterile world without loving arms or kind words? Your only contact a bunch of perfect, painted dolls, and the only conversation based on what you should and shouldn't do, and how to be a proper Anderson."

Paul winced. "Doesn't sound too thrilling when you put it that way."

The conversation stalled until Alex said, "Tchaikovsky."

"What?"

"You asked me who my favorite artist was. Art takes many forms, you know." The corners of Paul's mouth quirked up in a smile, and Alex knew he'd hit on yet another favorite topic.

"You like Tchaikovsky? Not Beethoven or Bach?"

Once again they'd found common ground on a topic. Few of Alex's friends shared his passions if, indeed, they possessed any besides partying, spending their family's money, and bragging over conquests. Paul, apparently, held many passions. Alex settled in for what he hoped might prove a lively debate. "Don't get me wrong, they're okay, just overexposed, and they never matched the fire of Russian composers, in my opinion. Who's your favorite?"

Their earlier conversation about books came to mind when Paul asked, "What genre?"

Alex should have known. The man probably once held the title of official high school geek. A sexy geek, but a geek nonetheless. That whole "President of the Chess Club" thing lurked in Alex's own past, however, so he wasn't in a position to point fingers. He'd still bet scholarly Paul beat him in the geek department. "Don't tell me you took Music Appreciation."

"Okay, I won't tell you," Paul replied with a grin.

Surprised? No. Impressed? Yes. "What do you play?

"Violin." Paul's eyes lit with passion as they always did when discussing a topic of personal interest. "I started playing when I was nine, right after my father died." His sudden frown and averted eyes gave warning enough of his revisiting a painful memory.

Before Alex could offer words of comfort, the vehicle pulled to a stop in an older, trendy section of town. Alex stepped from the car and reached back to help Paul, only to find the driver already there. He nearly growled at the proprietary hand Isaac placed on Paul's back, quickly schooling his frown into a more neutral expression—they were in public, after all. If nothing else, his pretentious grandparents had taught him how to keep up appearances.

He stood on the sidewalk waiting patiently for Paul, and together they passed under the twinkling lights and greenery-shrouded arbor leading into the stucco building housing the gallery.

Curious eyes observed their entrance, and they were immediately approached by a waiter who smiled and held out a tray filled with glasses of champagne, his wink and flirta-tious grin offering Alex more than a beverage. A few weeks ago, the offer would have been gladly accepted. Now, Alex had no such inclinations. A quick glance to his right showed Paul was oblivious to the exchange, busy speaking with an elderly matron, and for some unfathomable reason, Alex felt relieved.

He soon found himself caught up in the colorful displays carefully arranged around the studio. He hadn't been honest with Paul about his appreciation for the arts but didn't want to flaunt his wealth by disclosing the priceless classical pieces housed in Boston or the recently acquired collection of

Kandinsky woodcuts for his condo. Composers weren't the only things he admired hailing from Russia.

Alex hadn't known what to expect when asked to attend the opening, having never before heard of Edmond Strickland. Perusing a diverse collection of oils, watercolors, and sculptures, he respected the quality of the works on display and seriously considered adding a painting or two to his growing collection. One piece in particular caught his eye, and he wandered over for closer inspection: a beach at sunset, a storm gathering on the horizon. The somber grays, blues, and blacks of the oil-painted canvas created a striking contrast to the more vivid pinks and purples, and a single ray of golden sunlight penetrated a dark cloud, like hope shining through bleak circumstance.

Mesmerized, he imagined the roar of crashing waves battering the shoreline. In his mind's eye, brilliant flashes of lightning descended from a particularly sinister cloud, illuminating the tableau in whites, purples, and blues. A droning roll of thunder wouldn't have been out of place. The mastery enthralled him.

When his active imagination again conjured lightning from the violently roiling heavens, for one brief moment Alex spotted a solitary figure walking along the water's edge—a man with flame-red hair. Blinking hard to clear his eyes, he looked again, but saw only an extraordinary rendering of a stormy shoreline, nothing more.

"Yes, that's one of my favorites too," an intrusive voice said from his left. "I'm drawn to the whole somber ambiance."

Whole somber ambiance? What an overinflated prick! Alex glanced over his shoulder to find a rather smallish man with dark-blond hair, artfully arranged to stand at attention, each dagger-like spike tipped in navy blue. Unlike most of the well-attired guests, this man was dressed simply, in dark gray slacks and a lightweight sweater that blended well with the colors of the painting. The newcomer sipped champagne while studying the canvas, head cocked attentively to the side.

Agitation at being interrupted subsiding for the sake of good manners, Alex inquired with feigned interest, "What draws you to it?"

"Well," the stranger answered with a hesitant smile, "this piece brings back a special memory for me. I've always loved the beach, and one day a sick friend wanted to go, even though the forecast called for bad weather. So we—some other friends and I—bundled him up and drove down the coast, arriving about the same time the storm did. We found a little café and watched it roll in while we enjoyed coffee and bagels." He added wistfully, "That was the last outing I enjoyed with my friend." After a moment he recovered from his obviously unpleasant thoughts enough to ask, "What do you see?"

With nothing to be gained by answering truthfully, Alex gave an answer most of his acquaintances might expect—one involving monetary gain. "I see the product of an artist passionate about his work and a painting that'll make an excellent investment, particularly if the artist's passion continues with future paintings."

The do-it-yourself art critic frowned, clearly disappointed. "That's too bad."

"Too bad?" Alex asked, surprised at the genuine sadness in the man's voice.

"This piece is meant to be far more than paint, canvas, and a chance for financial gain."

Suddenly, a familiar voice interrupted their awkward conversation. "Oh, there you are." Both men turned to face the new arrival. "I was wondering where you were." Paul hurried over and kissed a stylishly stubbly cheek. "How are you, Eddie? It's been a while."

The man now revealed to be the reason for the gala smiled and said nothing, nodding his head toward the painting instead. Paul faced the wall and gasped. "Oh my God!" he exclaimed. "You captured the storm perfectly!"

With a smug grin, the artist responded, "I was inspired."

Tired of being ignored, Alex loudly cleared his throat.

Paul's eyes widened and he quickly stammered, "I... I'm sorry, Alex, forgive my manners. I'd like you to meet Edmond Strickland. Eddie, this is Alfred's nephew, Alexander Martin."

"Pleased to meet you," Edmond said, offering his hand and nothing more, eyes returning to Paul even while he addressed Alex. "Your uncle is a wonderful man, and a very dear friend."

"It's nice meeting you, as well," Alex lied, fighting a snarl. It seemed Isaac wasn't the only competition he'd have to face tonight. He pasted on a fake smile and attempted cordiality while scheming ways get Paul to leave earlier than planned— say, in five minutes or less. "Uncle Alfred sends his apologies and speaks highly of your work." He reminded himself that, regardless of a negative first impression, Edmond was his uncle's friend. That alone earned the man some measure of respect.

With a flash of blindingly white teeth, Edmond replied, "While I regret Alfred couldn't attend, I'm certainly glad Paul's here." To Alex's dismay, Paul blushed at the thinly veiled flattery.

Family friend or not, Alex took an immediate dislike to Edmond's easy familiarity and obvious flirting with the man who'd arrived with him. It might not have been an actual date, but Edmond didn't know that, and the blatant breach of etiquette grated on Alex's nerves. Ignoring the artist, he

THE WISH

directed his attention to his nondate. "I'm amazed by this painting," he said, seeing a chance to win approval since Paul obviously liked the haunting landscape too.

"It's beautiful," Paul agreed, eyes on the canvas and, thankfully, not on Edmond. "And has special meaning to the family." He peered up from under long dark lashes, brown eyes glowing with excitement. "Is this the one you'd like to get Uncle Alfred?" Turning to Edmond, he asked, "It's still available, isn't it?"

"Now, would I offer it to another without allowing you and dearest Alfred first dibs? But don't make a decision yet—I have another I'd like to show you."

The artist sauntered away, casting a coy glance over his shoulder to ensure Paul followed. Was it Alex's imagination, or was the man deliberately being provocative, and not to him, which he expected, but to Paul? Also, what did "special meaning to the family" entail?

Noticing he'd been deserted, Alex followed the two men. Paul stood stock-still, staring in rapture at another seascape— an almost perfect replica of the painting of Douglas, Jacob, and Byron that had recently hung in Alfred's office. The lighting, beach, and surroundings resembled the original, as did the bathing suits. The only differences were the children themselves. Instead of the Sinclair boys, the youngsters in the painting were unmistakably himself and Paul, or rather, how they'd looked at approximately ten and five years old, respectively.

The likeness of Paul held the bucket and shovel, much as his uncle Byron had in the original, while a young version of Alex admired the bright blue sails of a toy boat, an occupation previously held by Douglas. The smaller child, Jacob, who'd been building a sand castle in the background, was noticeably missing. A red "Sold" sticker dangled from the gilt frame.

"Edmond! Why?" Paul asked, his eyes glittering with unshed tears.

Before Alex could act, Edmond stepped in and wrapped his arms around Paul, clearly horrified at his reaction. "I cannot apologize enough. I had no idea the painting would affect you so," he murmured. "I suppose I should have warned you or arranged a private viewing." If his words hadn't rung true, Alex would have waded in and taught him a thing or two about causing pain to an unofficial Anderson, breeding and good manners be damned.

"Your uncle commissioned it months ago," Edmond explained. "Apparently he forgot to mention it."

Paul nestled into the hug, obviously comfortable with the close physical contact, causing a familiar stirring in Alex. Once again, his former rival inspired his jealousy, only this time Alex wasn't jealous *of* Paul, but *because* of Paul, nearly overcome with the urge to grab something heavy and bash the artist with it —repeatedly.

"Hey, handsome," he heard purred into his ear. Alex glanced to the right and came face to face with an attractive, decidedly drunken female. She staggered awkwardly on her stiletto heels and grabbed his shoulder to steady herself, giggling annoyingly. She epitomized what he called "Hollywood gorgeous": beautiful via money and cosmetic surgery, with lips too full and eyebrows fixed in permanent surprise from excessive facelifts. He'd also be willing to bet the breasts she'd been given by genetics weren't nearly as large and perky as the ones currently spilling over the plunging neckline of her dress.

"Excuse me, I'm with someone," he growled, peering over

her shoulder to discover he'd lied. Paul and the hedgehog, as Alex privately dubbed Edmond, were nowhere to be seen.

It took some time to convince her he wasn't interested, and he wondered, given her pouting reaction, if she'd ever been turned down before. Probably not, judging from her ample charms, but those didn't last forever, and someone younger and prettier always waited in the wings to take their place in the spotlight.

Arguing with the tipsy, surgically enhanced female, it occurred to him how much alike they were. Only his looks were natural and he was blessed with charm, unlike this silly creature. The results were the same, though. They could snare whoever they wanted and had never crossed paths with anyone worth keeping, apparently, if they were both still alone in their thirties. Well, that was about to change for him, if he had anything to do with it.

He finally escaped when the inebriated woman found another prospect, one more eager to chat her up. Attempting nonchalance he didn't truly feel, Alex hunted for Paul, unwilling to allow Edmond any more time with him than absolutely necessary.

Alex's first search of the gallery ended empty-handed. On his second round, he found Edmond merrily chatting with a group of tuxedo-clad gentlemen and leaning into the embrace of an older Hispanic man. Alex felt a little better seeing him occupied with another, but his anxiety peaked about the noticeably absent Paul.

From behind a partially opened door came a familiar voice, though he'd never heard the dejected tone before. "I'm sorry, Jordan, I need to be getting back."

Jordan? The guy who'd betrayed Paul?

Easing the door open, Alex stared into what appeared to be

a store room, judging from pedestals, racks, and packing crates haphazardly strewn about the cramped space. In a far corner, Paul stood with his back toward the door, body rigid and hands on his hips. About to intervene, Alex froze when another man stepped into view.

"Oh, babe, please stay," a masculine and surprisingly smooth voice pleaded. "I've missed you so badly."

The stranger turning entreating eyes on Paul was drop-dead gorgeous, with wheat-blond curls and dark, wide-set brown eyes. Dressed to perfection in an expensive tuxedo, he made an impressive sight. However, he couldn't hold a candle to Paul, in Alex's opinion.

"Don't call me that," Paul hissed from between clenched teeth, body trembling with barely controlled emotion. Alex hoped for righteous indignation.

"I made a mistake," the faithless man whined, and Alex couldn't agree more. "Please, Paul. Please give me another chance."

The room grew quiet, and Alex waited for the words that would make one of Paul's prospective suitors happy and leave the other disappointed. Tears dampening his cheeks, Paul turned and confronted his former lover, hands balled tightly into fists at his sides. "I told you before: I don't believe in reruns. No matter how many times you watch the show, the characters never change, and neither does the ending."

"Oh, I *have* changed, really, and if you give me a chance...." The handsome snake in the grass stepped forward, arms spread wide. Alex tensed, ready for battle. He retreated into the shadows when Paul sidestepped the embrace.

"No, Jordan. I'm sorry, I can't do this again." Paul lifted his pointed chin defiantly. "I notice you've waited until now to talk to me. My uncle's been dying for months. Did I even once receive a phone call asking about his health? No, you only tracked me down tonight because you think he left me money."

"It's not like that!" Jordan protested. Even from ten feet away Alex could tell the man lied.

"Please, just go," Paul hissed, body trembling like a tightly wound spring. Alex knew from experience how hot Paul's temper flared and hoped Jordan did too. Though he might despise Edmond personally, the man didn't deserve to have his party interrupted by a fistfight.

Shoulders slumped in defeat, Jordan slunk away. "Well, you have my number if you change your mind. I really do love you, Paul." Alex ducked behind a stack of canvases. Jordan cautiously opened the door and slipped through, bored expression and rolling eyes belying his words.

Creeping from the room moments later, Paul's tear-streaked face proved he'd indeed loved Jordan, and possibly held lingering feelings for the jerk. Didn't Alfred say the affair ended over a year ago? With the turmoil caused by Byron's illness and the subsequent upset of the Anderson household, quite possibly Paul hadn't the time or energy for closure, and a year wasn't actually a long time.

Easing back into the crowded gallery, Alex located Edmond and confirmed that, as a commissioned piece, the painting of the two boys had been sold to Byron Sinclair as a gift for his lover. Recalling his uncle's words, "You'll know it when you see it," he realized he'd been set up. The matter had already been taken care of, confirmed by Edmond's offhand remark, "… when I talked to your uncle last week to arrange delivery." Why, the sly rascal. It seemed his uncle provided an opportunity to make up with Paul. Well, there was certainly one thing Alex believed might help.

After much discussion about pigments and hues, Edmond

named a price, and Alex pulled out his checkbook. He paid for the storm scene, suspecting he'd been given a discount due to his uncle and because he asked the artist not to tell Paul, implying the painting would be a gift. Paul's obvious adoration of the work insured that Alex couldn't let the painting go to anyone else, "special meaning to the family" notwithstanding. If Paul liked the painting, he'd have it, even if Alex had to be sneaky in giving it to him. However, Alex swore to himself to pay Edmond back in full for naming such a low price, even if not monetarily. Connections within the artistic communities of Houston and Boston would make it well worth the artist's sacrifice.

After shaking hands and promising to attend the gallery's next event, Alex headed off in search of Paul, hoping to prevent another run-in with Jordan. Alex found him in front of the commissioned painting. "Can we go home now?" Paul asked without meeting Alex's eyes.

"If you'd like," Alex replied, though it was exactly what he'd wanted to ask.

Paul face appeared red and blotchy. "I'd like," he said, rushing past on his way to the door, calling over his shoulder, "Would you say goodbye to Edmond for me?"

Wanting nothing more than to simply leave and save Paul from unpleasant memories, Alex felt obliged to accomplish one final task. "Certainly. You go out to the car. I'll be out in a minute."

Having already said their goodbyes to Edmond, he used the excuse to seek out the sleaze from the storeroom, needing to prove the man a slut with no true feelings for Paul. Alex found Jordan, as artfully arranged and as much on display as any of Edmond's creations. He carefully pushed back his sleeve to reveal his Rolex, pasted on his most beguiling smile, and sauntered over, snagging a glass of champagne from a passing tray. "Mind if I ask you a question?" he began, presenting the glass to his quarry. His fingertips caressed Jordan's palm.

Assessing eyes raked over him, measuring his worth, widening appreciatively at the expensive watch. Alex must have passed inspection, for Jordan accepted the champagne with a playful grin. One long, elegant finger circled the rim of glass. "Thanks," he said with a seductive purr. "I'm Jordan." Stepping close enough to rub his body against Alex, Jordan leaned in and whispered, "What's your question?"

"You've already answered it." The blatant display and hand groping Alex's ass left little doubt about what Jordan assumed the question would be. "Now, if you'll excuse me," Alex said, forcibly removing the hand from his posterior, "I have someone waiting who'd never offer himself to the highest bidder." Ignoring Jordan's stuttering outrage, he spun on his heel and followed Paul out the door, winking at the sniggering waiter who'd borne witness to the exchange.

His smug triumph lasted until he climbed into the waiting car. Paul huddled sullenly in the far corner of the backseat, and Alex fought the urge to go back inside and give the fickle asshole a piece of his mind. Fortunately for Jordan, getting Paul home took priority.

His heart sank when Paul slid farther away, distancing himself. That wouldn't do. Paul needed comfort right now, not solitude. Unable to stand the man's obvious discomfort any longer, Alex wrapped an arm around Paul and pulled him close, ignoring the indignant "Hey!" and halfhearted resistance.

"Shh...," Alex murmured. "You need it, take it." Paul stopped protesting and snuggled into the embrace, relaxing against Alex with a heavy sigh. Buckling them both in, Alex met Isaac's eyes in the rearview mirror, commenting, "Traffic's a bit heavy tonight."

Understanding his meaning, Isaac nodded. "Yes, it is. Maybe I should try another route." He took a right at the next traffic light to take the long way home.

If holding Paul was all Alex could hope for, he'd make it last for as long as he could.

CHAPTER FIFTEEN

"He's sleeping pretty soundly," Paul observed, gazing down at Alfred's peacefully slumbering form. "I was hoping to say good night."

"We can't wake him," Alex replied, "he needs his rest." He and Paul stood shoulder to shoulder, watching the steady rise and fall of the blankets. His rational mind told him to say good night, but he hesitated. Paul still appeared unhinged by the encounter with Jordan. An idea sprang to life. Though he anticipated Paul shooting him down, he asked, "How about a cup of tea?"

Paul's eyes clouded with suspicion. Then his wary expression softened, and with a barely perceptible nod, he agreed.

Considering Alfred's office the best choice, being neutral territory, Alex led Paul there and settled him into one of the comfortably padded leather chairs. "I'll be back in a moment," he said, before hastily retreating to the kitchen. He returned moments later with a loaded tray, thankful Paul hadn't disappeared.

After pouring them both a cup of tea, Alex leaned against

the desk, waiting for Paul to speak. When minutes ticked by silently, he lost patience. "Want to talk about whatever's bothering you?"

"There's nothing to tell." Paul stared at his hands, picking imaginary lint from his jacket.

Paul lying? That's a first. He wished the man felt comfortable enough to confide in him, although he admitted he'd never done anything to earn the man's confidence.

Then Alex remembered a surefire way to get Paul talking: mention one of his many passions, like books, music... or art. Eyes straying to the blank wall, he effectively changed the subject. "The new painting is going to look good there." It struck him how both paintings, the new and the old, shared a similar style, not only in subject matter, simple enough to copy, but in technique. "Did Edmond paint the original?"

Paul peered over the top of his glasses, eyes red-rimmed. "Yes, back in college. He swore he'd flawed the piece somehow and sold it for a fraction of its worth. In return, Alfred gave him backing and connections. They've been friends ever since, which is why we were invited tonight."

Recalling Paul's earlier comments, Alex urged, "Tell me about the storm scene."

Paul sighed, running his fingers through his hair, resignation in his eyes. "You know about the Jeep, right?"

"Not the whole story." Alex dropped into the adjacent chair, careful not to crowd Paul. As far as he knew, the Jeep was the only gift of any financial value Paul had ever accepted, so there must be an interesting reason why he'd made an exception to his "no gifts" policy.

"It happened during a visit last September," Paul began with a sad, barely discernible smile. "Uncle Byron always loved the ocean, and, since he'd had a few pretty good days, he begged us to take him to the beach.

"Eddie arrived shortly before we left, and he and Uncle Byron talked privately for a while. Once they emerged from the study, the four of us took the Jeep down the coast." Paul appeared small and lost, and Alex regretted asking such a pain-inspiring question, but he needed to hear what he'd missed out on, knowing in his heart he should have been in the café Edmond described with the rest of his family, sharing the memory. Now he'd have to make do with the remembrances of others.

"When we got there, the weather turned bad and Alfred got worried, wanting to come home. Uncle Byron insisted, 'We came all this way and I'm not tucking tail and running from a few rain clouds.'" A bittersweet smile flitted across Paul's face. "Who were we to tell him no? In the end we watched the storm from the safety of a café. Edmond went out to the beach and took tons of pictures. The result now hangs in his gallery." Paul lowered his voice to a scant whisper, the tremulous smile fleeing. "That's the last time Uncle Byron left the house for anything other than doctor visits."

Alex desperately wanted to give Paul the painting but couldn't if the giving caused more grief. Still, how shameful for something with priceless emotional value to wind up with someone who wouldn't appreciate the sentiment that went into the creation. Though he'd wanted to surprise Paul, possibly on his next birthday, Alex now envisioned his plan backfiring. Settling for a direct approach, he threw caution to the wind. "Would it bother you if I bought that painting?"

Paul frowned, furrowing his brow. "Bother me? Why would it bother me?"

Alex shrugged. "It may bring back bad memories."

"It's a happy memory, Alex. We had a great time, and...." Paul looked young and vulnerable when he confessed, "I wanted the darned thing the moment I laid eyes on it, although I knew I couldn't afford the price. I was afraid it might wind up with someone who'd only consider it an investment, never understanding how precious it is. I'll never forget that day—ever."

Remorse slammed into Alex, reminded of his earlier words to Edmond, even though he'd lied. Of course then he hadn't known the painting's true value. He'd loved the work on its own merits; however, buying the painting for Paul far surpassed any pride of personal ownership. "Where do you think we should hang it?"

Paul stared at the wall, apparently lost in thought. After a moment he said, "The front hallway, where visitors will see it."

"Good idea. You still didn't explain about the Jeep. Not that you have to, mind you. That's between you and your uncle." Curiosity nibbled at Alex.

"No, that's all right. Uncle Byron left it to me knowing I'd argue, goading me with a reason he knew I'd agree to."

"What was that?" Apparently, it wasn't often Paul accepted gifts. Byron must have made an extremely clever argument.

"He mentioned the day at the beach when I'd driven the Jeep." Paul grinned sheepishly. "He also pointed out that my poor car isn't going to last much longer and how he'd rather see me in the Jeep than standing on the side of the road."

"Both extremely good points. But he always was an excellent attorney."

"I know." Paul's smile dimmed somewhat. "That's the first time I let him win, or the second time, rather."

Alex remained silent, knowing Paul would clarify only if he wanted to. This time, his patience paid off.

"Did you happen to notice an attractive man with curly blond hair at the opening tonight?" Paul asked.

Alex knew full well who Paul meant, but wasn't about to admit to eavesdropping, especially now, with Paul hovering on the edge of confiding. "I may have bumped into him," was all Alex cared to confess.

"That was Jordan, my ex. I didn't expect to see him tonight."

"Is he the reason you wanted to leave?" Although Alex knew the answer, he needed to hear the story from Paul's own lips.

"Yes."

Alex had listened to Alfred's side of the story. How much did Paul know of the whole truth? "You said 'ex'. What happened, if you don't mind my asking?"

Paul snorted. "You're probably the only one who doesn't know, so what's telling you gonna hurt?" He drained his teacup and placed it on the desk. "Through my college years I worked and saved, wanting to open my own business when I graduated. I thought I had life figured out. First came the store, next a house, the perfect man and the perfect life—even a kid or two." A self-deprecating laugh escaped. Paul took a picture from the desk, staring at the two men whose relationship they both envied, sorrow etched on his handsome features.

"All my life, I've watched my uncle and Alfred, wanting to be like them. I thought I found 'the one' one night at a party." He held the picture out to Alex, pursed lips and the slump of his shoulder radiating disappointment. "I couldn't understand why Jordan even paid attention to me. I was nobody, and it took me far too long to figure out his reasons.

"You see, he didn't believe I didn't have money, thinking me rich because of my uncle. For two years he and I were happy, or at least I thought so, though I never completely understood why he wouldn't come with me to Bishop. I loved him and convinced myself he loved me too.

"He begged me to buy a property here, where he could stay when I went back home. No matter what I said, he never believed I wasn't rolling in money. Tired of his constant demands, I showed him my bank statements and loan payments, proving I barely made ends meet."

Alex knew the rest of the story, but remained quiet, unwilling to implicate Alfred. As much as Paul loved Alfred, he also valued honesty. What would he do if he knew Jordan had been paid to break his heart? Alex should have realized Paul's shrewdness wouldn't leave the truth undiscovered.

"Jordan wanted more than I had to offer and began making demands," Paul said. "Nothing I did made him happy. He even had the nerve to suggest I sell the store!"

"Then what?"

"Two hundred thousand dollars, Alex!" Paul barked, jumping from his chair to pace frantically before the desk. "That's what I was worth to him! Two hundred fucking thousand lousy dollars!" Wounded eyes glittered with tears that soon overflowed onto his cheeks, sliding down his chin to fall to the floor.

"What did he do?" Alex asked, fighting the urge to find Jordan and give the man a few choice words—or his fist.

"Alfred gave him the money to go away," Paul admitted with a defeated sigh.

Paul knows? "You're not mad?"

Paul laughed, a sound totally devoid of humor. "Oh, I was for a while, until I discovered how Jordan amused himself while I was away. Something Alfred knew and hadn't told me, hoping I'd find out on my own while shielding me as much as possible. Jordan was in deep trouble, Alex. Seems he has a gambling problem and used his connections to me and our uncles to get credit."

"You knew?"

"No," Paul said, nibbling at his lower lip. "Not at first. I turned a blind eye to his faults because I loved him. When I found out, he said he was sorry for what he'd done. He even went to counseling and started working on honestly paying off his debts. I gave him another chance."

Oh, *hell* no! Alex didn't believe in second chances, conveniently forgetting a second chance was, in essence, what he himself wanted. "You mean you stayed with him after he used you?"

Regardless of Jordan's many transgressions, Paul jumped to his defense. "Jordan didn't have the advantages we did, like a family, a home. He had problems we can't even begin to imagine."

"That's no excuse in my book," Alex growled. He stood and joined Paul in his pacing. "Let me guess: he didn't stop gambling."

Paul puffed his cheeks, blowing out a huffed breath. "I think he did for a while, though not for long. He just learned to hide his weaknesses better. Anyway, it gets worse."

"How could it possibly get worse?" Alex felt strangely indignant, even though Paul had been slighted and not him.

"To put it mildly, he didn't get lonely whenever I went to Bishop."

Alex chose not to comment. Alfred had alluded to the man's infidelity, but apparently being a slut wasn't the full extent of Jordan's misdeeds.

"And he owed a bookie money," Paul continued, "a *lot* of money."

Alex easily imagined what happened next. "When Alfred offered to bail him out, he took the money and was gone the next time you came back, am I right?"

"Yes. I'm the biggest sucker on the planet, aren't I?" Paul hung his head. "Go ahead, tell me what a sap I am."

The arrogant bastard Alex once pretended to be would have agreed; however, that version of him hadn't survived long after arriving at his uncle's house. The new and improved Alex answered truthfully, "No, you're not a sap. Too forgiving, maybe; a sap, no."

Paul's next question took Alex by surprise. "How do you do it, Alex?"

"Do what?"

"Sleep with people you don't care about. How do you do that? Isn't it lonely? Don't you want to wake up with someone you love, who loves you?"

Though Alex had never thought of his independence in quite those terms before, Paul made an excellent point. "Like our uncles?"

"Yes," Paul replied, nodding, "like them. Don't you want something more than meaningless sex?"

Alex decided he had nothing to lose by telling the truth. "Of course I want something more." Bitterness crept into his voice. "I've never found anyone who saw past the money to who I really am."

"*What?*" Paul shouted, eyes widening. "All you've ever known were poor excuses for lovers like Jordan? Someone who'd walk away for the right price?"

Judging from his reaction, Paul definitely didn't travel in the same circles Alex did, where such behavior wasn't only accepted, but expected. Maybe Alex hung out with the wrong people. "Pretty much," he replied.

"How awful for you. Have you never had anyone to love you for you?"

The answer was a resounding "No" even if Alex chose not to voice it. The truth was, even in bed with another living, breathing human being or two—hell, even in the middle of a crowded club with his so-called friends—Alex felt alone. He didn't like solitude nearly as much as he pretended to.

Capturing Paul's angular face between his hands, he forced Paul's head up until their eyes met. "What do you see when you look at me?" Alex leaned in, lips inches away from Paul's. He wanted badly to close the distance. Hearing Alfred's words replaying themselves in his head stopped him. He'd sworn to take responsibility for his actions, and he'd made a promise he intended to keep.

Glistening eyes, grieving now for someone else's loneliness and not because of a manipulative ex-lover, studied him intently. Paul took a deep breath and then answered, "I see someone who was given everything he wanted and nothing he needed."

"What do you think I need, Paul?" Given the man's unique insight, Alex genuinely anticipated the answer.

It didn't disappoint; Paul kissed him. Though merely a brief meeting of lips, it meant more than Alex could ever explain.

"Do you still want me?" Paul murmured as he withdrew.

The question was even more unexpected than the kiss, and when Alex hesitated, Paul asked again, "You still want to sleep with me, right?"

Part of Alex yelled *"Yes!"* but no way would he accept the offer, not under the circumstances. Though it killed him to do so, he shook his head. "How's a pity fuck from you different from what I have now? I don't want you to sleep with me because you feel sorry for me, or so I can wipe away the memory of another man.

"You don't want me, Paul. I don't know what you want, but I'm certain it isn't me." How ironic that, after all his fantasies of having Paul in his bed again, now knowing he wasn't betraying his uncle, he couldn't accept the offer. "You know, if someone had told me earlier tonight that I'd be turning you down, I'd have said they were crazy. You may have uttered the words, but you don't mean them, and it's you, Byron, and Uncle Alfred who taught me not to settle. I'm a little late getting the message, but it's finally sunk in. Good night, Paul." With those words, Alex did the hardest thing he'd ever done— turned his back on what he wanted most in the world and went to bed alone.

CHAPTER SIXTEEN

LATER, lying in bed, Paul mulled over the unexpected turn of events. Would wonders never cease? Aside from the teasing, innuendo, and blatant offers, when it came down to the real deal, Alex had said no. Unfortunately, the offer was dead serious, even if, upon further reflection, Paul's timing left a lot to be desired.

Damn Jordan for showing up tonight! Paul had loved him fiercely once, or rather, loved Jordan's false advertising. Now it no longer mattered whether the man dealt with his issues. His gambling habit only tipped the iceberg when it came to their problems. He'd never be capable of a mature, loving commitment without being on the constant lookout for someone better, richer, or more powerful.

Players didn't change. At least, Jordan couldn't; could Alex? Had he truly repented of his philandering ways?

Paul's conscience pointed out that he'd been forgiving enough to stay with a man who'd used him, but judged Alex before meeting the guy. His libido added, *That was one hell of a night in his bed.* While not enough to base a relationship on, it beat anything from Paul's past.

Under Alex's superior façade hid a complex man who doted on Alfred and had truly cared about Byron. And when Paul hurt, seeking comfort in Alex's embrace seemed totally natural. He recalled consoling arms holding him in the car. No words were necessary; actions spoke louder. Plus, Alex had kept his promise, with the exception of one kiss in the garden, which, truthfully, Paul had quite enjoyed.

Tonight, when asked point-blank, Alex said no. Did integrity lurk beneath the conceited, unfeeling mask, causing him to refuse? Well, if Alex ran, Paul would give chase. Mind made up, he announced into the quiet of his bedroom, "Alex Martin, you will be mine."

Of course, it wasn't simply the room witnessing his confession. With his eyes closed, he didn't notice the gathering shadows crossing the floor and disappearing through the bedroom door.

WELL, well, how promising. Especially since Byron had expected Paul to be harder to convince, relying on Alex's famed skill as a seducer to win over his naïve nephew. How could he forget the boy's innate ability to find good in everyone?

He'd worried when the gigolo made an appearance, given Paul's onetime love for Jordan. In the end, the fiasco advanced Byron's plans, paving the way for a little soul baring. The following conversation saddened him, and he grieved the wrongs done to both young men that shattered their youthful dreams. If understanding grew from shared pain, however, the grief might prove worth the end result.

As shocked as Paul at Alex's refusal, after hearing his nephew's declaration, Byron hurried to find the other half of the equation and gauge Alex's reaction. Following a fruitless search of the blue room, Alfred's office, and the kitchen, Byron finally located Alex in the gym, beating the hell out of the heavy bag.

Oh, quite promising indeed. Apparently, Paul had gotten under Alex's skin. It wouldn't be long now.

Elated at the night's progress and proud of his lover for coercing their nephews into a date, Byron hurried to the bedroom he'd shared with Alfred for so many years, coming to an abrupt halt just inside the door. Triumph turned to terror. Alfred lay upon the bed, clutching his chest. His pain-clouded blue eyes met Byron's, opening wide.

"Byron!" Alfred croaked.

Byron froze. Alfred could see him—because Alfred was dying.

CHAPTER SEVENTEEN

A LOUD crash jolted Paul from his bed, and he skidded to a stop in Alfred's bedroom a moment later, dashing to the bedside and frantically tearing through the nightstand for a nitro bottle. He popped a pill under Alfred's tongue like he'd been instructed to do in case of an emergency.

Alarmed when no color returned to Alfred's pasty complexion, Paul reached for the phone and dialed 911. Next he called Isaac, telling him to open the gates for the paramedics.

"Hold on, please, hold on," Paul chanted, finally noticing the disaster that had woken him from a sound sleep. A bookcase lay on its side, dozens of heavy, leather-bound tomes littering the floor. He couldn't spare a thought for how it could have toppled, too busy hoping he'd arrived in time.

"What the hell is going on? I was going to the kitchen when I heard...."

Paul gazed up at Alex with fear in his eyes, clutching Alfred's hand.

"Oh, dear God!" Alex shouted, rushing to the bedside.

"Uncle, talk to me!" A faint rasp was Alfred's only response. "Paul, did you...?"

"Yes, I gave him nitro and called 911."

As if on cue, a clamor arose in the hall and William's seldom-heard voice urged, "This way, gentlemen, last door on the left."

A gurney and two paramedics rushed in and Alex stepped aside, gently pulling Paul away from the bed to allow the emergency workers room.

The blue-clad technicians took Alfred's vitals and asked a few questions. Then they hoisted him onto the gurney, strapped him securely in place, and hurried down the hall and out of the house. The entire process took only a few minutes and then they were gone, along with Alfred.

Alex manhandled Paul into the Jeep's passenger seat before climbing under the steering wheel to follow the bright strobes of the ambulance.

"Hey, lover, what are you doing here?" Alfred muttered. "You're not supposed to be here, are you? Didn't you go away somewhere? I'm supposed to meet you, aren't I?"

Byron beheld the man who'd stolen his heart only to cherish and protect it for so many years, torn between wanting his lover alive and happy and the overwhelming need to be reunited. "I never left," he answered.

"You've been here ever since...."

Seeing in his lover's gaze the moment he remembered the gulf separating them, Byron watched the lines around Alfred's eyes and mouth ease, streaks of gold creeping into his lovely silver hair. "Ever since you asked me to wait for you," Byron finished for him.

"You can do that? Stay, I mean?"

With a tender smile, Byron explained, "Everyone gets one final wish."

In a voice slowly returning to its once youthful vigor, Alfred asked, "Anything?"

"Well, not anything. It has to be truly important to you; important enough to fight for."

Alfred's pale cheeks slowly regained their color. *It won't be long now.* Although Byron eagerly anticipated being with his love again, he silently mourned for their nephews, who'd doubtlessly take Alfred's death, following closely on the heels of his own, hard. He prayed they'd turn to each other for comfort instead of letting despair rip them apart.

Apparently considering the possibilities, Alfred ventured, "What becomes of you if I want to stick around? I've been without you long enough."

"Don't worry about me, love, I asked to wait for you. If you're here, here I'll stay also."

"Well, you know what I truly want: to see the house filled with Alex and Paul's children."

Byron quietly listened to the voices that'd helpfully guided him thus far, smiling at their answer. "I do believe you've picked a winner, babe." By this time, the vestiges of silver had fled Alfred's hair, and thirty years disappeared from his features, though the vision sat superimposed over the image of an elderly man with gray skin, lungs struggling for breath in a death rattle. Byron's smile faded. Although it meant they'd be together again, watching the love of his life slipping away spiked a dagger to his ghostly heart. "Just a little while," he whispered, fading into the shadows to wait.

"BYRON? Byron!" Alfred screamed as his lover disappeared. A deafening alarm shrieked in the background.

"We're losing him!" came someone's frantic cry, the last thing Alfred Anderson heard with his mortal ears.

WITH a white-knuckled grip on the steering wheel, Alex tailed the ambulance. If he hadn't already accepted the truth, the litany of heartfelt, pleading prayers murmured from the passenger seat would have proved Paul's love for Alfred. Alex pushed his own fears aside to get them to the hospital safely, believing in his heart they'd never arrive in time. Alfred was a fighter; if he chose to, he'd beat his illness and live years longer, though anyone could see his heart wasn't in it. With Byron gone, he didn't want to continue, regardless of how much he loved his surviving kin. Some might call it selfish, but the man didn't have a selfish bone in his body. Alfred simply loved Byron that much.

Following the ambulance to the emergency room receiving doors, Alex instructed Paul to get out while he parked the Jeep. With a terrible sense of foreboding, he watched the paramedics pull the gurney from the vehicle, wheeling into the building and disappearing into an area marked "No Admittance."

The sliding glass doors slid open to the sound of Paul's indignant voice arguing with a uniform-clad nurse. Both appeared relieved by Alex's approach. Paul, clearly frustrated, exclaimed, "Alex, you have to fill out the papers! They won't let me admit Alfred because I'm not his family!"

"I'm sorry, sir; it's hospital policy," the nurse blurted.

Placing a supportive hand against Paul's back, Alex feigned calmness. "Don't worry; I'll take care of it." To the nurse he said, "I'm Alex Martin, Alfred Anderson's nephew. May I have the papers, please?"

She handed him a clipboard full of forms, pointedly ignoring Paul, and Alex leaned against the counter, scribbling the necessary information. Paul stood a few feet away, forlornly staring toward where the gurney had disappeared.

The doors opened and an orderly stepped out, eyes sweeping the waiting room and alighting on Alex. "Mr. Martin? I was told to come and get you."

"I have to finish up here," Alex replied, pointing to Paul with his pen. "Would you mind taking him back?" His raised eyebrow dared the orderly to even mention the word "family."

"Certainly," the young man replied without hesitation, turning to the quietly sniffling Paul. "If you'll come with me?"

"Alex?" Those soulful brown eyes appeared so lost, and the last brick in the wall around Alex's heart crumbled and fell. He'd have gladly given all his worldly possessions never to see such misery there again.

"It's okay," he murmured, fighting the urge to offer comfort while trying not let the sinking feeling in his gut show on his face. "You go on and I'll be there in a minute."

Rushing through the papers, he handed them over to the nurse. The orderly reappeared at his side. "If you could come with me, sir." No further words were necessary; Alex read the message loud and clear on the man's face. Alfred was dead.

The orderly pushed the button to activate the doors and they whooshed open. Alex found Paul slumped in a chair, face soaked with tears. A nurse stooped beside him, attempting to offer comfort. Alex dropped into a chair on Paul's other side, pulling him into a hug.

Paul buried his face in Alex's neck, sobbing. "Shh," Alex crooned. "It's okay, they're together now. They're happy."

"I don't want him to go!" Paul cried. "First Uncle Byron and now Alfred! What will I do without them? I don't want to be alone!"

"You aren't alone, you've got me." Though he said the words as comfort, he meant them with every ounce of his being. He loved Alfred, too, and would dearly miss his uncle. Right now, instead of sorrow, he chose to focus on the joy of having had such a wonderful person in his life, treasuring the time they'd spent together. The more he'd learned of his uncle, the more he understood that, as much as Alfred loved the living, his heart remained with Byron, and every day he awoke alone had been sheer agony.

Suddenly, it hit home for Alex that he was alone now, too, and though Paul might need him, he needed Paul more.

CHAPTER EIGHTEEN

"WHERE'RE you takin' me?" Paul slurred as Alex navigated him toward the staircase, carefully helping him up each step.

"We both need some sleep."

Having taken a doctor-prescribed sedative, a drug-induced fog clouded Paul's mind. He waved a sluggish hand toward the hall. "My room's down there," he stated, somewhat mystified that Alex didn't take him there.

"You don't want to be alone, remember? Besides, I think it's better if we avoid the east wing right now, don't you?"

"You're right." Paul nodded overenthusiastically, eyebrows furrowing when he tried to remember something important. Oh yeah. Books. "The bookcase! Someone gotta pick up books!"

Without his glasses, Paul glimpsed Alex through bleary eyes. Alex cocked a brow, and, being too tired to explain, Paul shook his head, mumbling, "Never mind," and he allowed Alex to lead him up the stairs and into the blue room.

Not much help in his befuddled state, Paul didn't fight when Alex pushed him back onto the bed and stripped him down to his boxers. Was Alex finally going to take what he'd been offered?

As if reading his mind, Alex said, "You're upset, you're exhausted, and you're drugged to the gills. I'm putting you to bed—alone—to sleep it off while I go make some phone calls."

Bolting upright, an ill-advised move that caused the room to spin, Paul pleaded, "No, don't leave me!"

A firm hand on his chest stopped him from scrambling off the bed. Peeling back the covers and tucking Paul beneath, Alex pulled them up to his chin. "Shh…. You get some sleep. I can make my calls from here if it doesn't keep you awake. Good night, Paul." Alex bestowed a chaste kiss on his forehead. "We'll talk tomorrow."

"Don't wanna talk," Paul whined sleepily, "wanna hold you." Wait a minute! Had he said that out loud? A dopey smile crept over his face. Yes, he had. "*In sedatio veritas…*," he mumbled absentmindedly to himself.

"Yes, under sedation the truth comes out," Alex replied. Before Paul could respond, he fell asleep.

Several times during the night, Paul swam to the surface of consciousness only to plunge back down into the welcoming embrace of oblivion. Once or twice he swore he heard softly spoken words, blaming the phantom conversation on the drugs when his sedated mind fabricated his beloved uncle's voice.

The night grew quiet and he woke surrounded by warmth. After a moment he registered Alex spooning against his back, one muscular arm thrown around his waist. Even in the early days with Jordan, he'd never felt so safe and secure. Snuggling into the reassuring embrace, he quickly fell back to sleep to the comforting sound of deep, even breathing.

Over a breakfast that turned to sand in his mouth, Paul listened carefully to Alex, who'd apparently been very busy the previous night.

"I know you may not want to talk about this, but we need to. Alfred made his own funeral arrangements. He's to be buried next to Byron in a simple graveside service with only family and close friends present."

Though Alex appeared to have no problem with those plans, Paul wasn't happy. "Several hundred people attended Uncle Byron's funeral and Alfred deserves the same!" Paul excelled at event planning and intended to make sure everyone understood how much Alfred Anderson meant to his nearest and dearest, and how much he'd be missed. First Paul needed to call the cathedral downtown....

Alex sighed, nipping ambitious plans in the bud. "He left a letter to be opened at his death, detailing what he wanted, saying, and I quote, 'Funerals are for the living.' Paul, Uncle Alfred held Byron's funeral the way he wanted. I know you'd go to any length for the man, as I would. He knew that, too, which is why he made his wishes known. Do you want to go against them?"

Defeated, Paul slumped back into his chair. "When's the service?" he muttered, agreeing under duress.

"Tomorrow, followed by the reading of the will. We have a lot of work to do in the meantime."

Once again, Alex cut off Paul's indignant protests. "Uncle Alfred left specific instructions. We both loved him dearly, but I never went against him in life, and I don't intend to now."

"Well, why listen to me?" Paul snapped. "It's not like I'm his family or anything!" As much as the truth hurt the night before, coming from an irritating nurse, he regretted them the second the words left his mouth. He took a deep breath, then, in a much calmer voice, said, "I'm sorry, Alex. I don't know what came over me."

Under-eye circles betrayed Alex's weariness, along with drooping shoulders. He leaned in to gain Paul's full attention. "Let's take things with a grain of salt, shall we? We're both on edge and bound to say things we don't mean. Make no mistake; you're Alfred's family, just like Martha, Bernard, and Isaac. You're part of the family he created for himself when his birth family turned their backs. Oh, they may not have disowned him outright; they chose instead to deny him their love and support. He replaced them with better people. You're one of those people."

Unexpectedly choked up by Alex's show of acceptance, Paul found himself at a loss for words. After a moment he quietly murmured, "Thanks."

The briefest hint of a smile flickered across Alex's face before quickly disappearing. "Don't mention it. Now, go take a shower. William's bringing some of your clothes to my room."

"You don't have to," Paul protested, "I can get them myself."

Alex once again provided the voice of reason. "Do you honestly want to be in that part of the house right now?"

He had a point. Paul didn't think he could bear to walk down the east hallway anytime soon, knowing what he'd find if he opened the door to the room across from his. Never again would he carry in a tea tray or a good book. Never again would he have a heart-to-heart chat with a dear father figure. Finally, he answered, "No, not really, and thanks."

Hurrying upstairs for a much-needed shower, he mulled over Alex's forcefulness and how he'd come to depend on the strength of another. Paul excelled at planning and organizing, but when the chips were down, the man he no longer considered his adversary had risen splendidly to the occasion. Together, they made one hell of a team.

After a brief shower, he toweled off and entered Alex's bedroom. Clothing from his closet hung inside the massive walk-in, and two open bureau drawers revealed his socks, boxers, and T-shirts.

Paul dressed casually, for comfort. The day, no doubt, would be grueling. He spared a moment to give quiet thanks he didn't have to go through the ordeal alone. His uncle had once told him, "Andersons make great guardian angels once you manage to get the pompous ass out of them." Paul agreed.

He glanced toward the warm cocoon he'd emerged from earlier. Long hours would pass before he could slip back between the cool, crisp sheets of the big bed. Since being invited, he intended to stay until asked to leave. If and when Alex evicted him, he'd have to convince the man otherwise. He mentally planted a flag and claimed the right side of the bed in the name of Paul Sinclair.

As STATED in Alfred's letter, funerals were for the living, and while Paul slept, Alex contacted everyone on his uncle's painstakingly prepared list. Alfred wanted his ending observed by only those closest to him and then for all involved to get back to the business of living, as he would have done, being a consummate businessman above everything else. Organizing such a hasty funeral, while a daunting task, didn't prove as impossible as Alex feared.

He spent the day with lawyers, accountants, a reporter, a security service, and numerous business associates of the deceased, while Paul met with haberdashers, morticians, florists, and family friends. As expected, the day taxed both their limits, and though he'd caught an occasional glimpse, Alex hadn't exchanged two words with Paul since breakfast. He'd barely managed to grunt out his thanks for the sandwich that arrived at lunchtime, eaten while tuning out the ravings of his great-aunt, Helena. For an entire hour, he listened to her whining and feeble excuses about why she couldn't fly out for the funeral, interspersed with personal opinions about everything from the casket to the venue, all arranged by Alfred months prior. That had been fourteen phone calls ago, and Alex feared the numbness in his ear might be permanent.

He'd been hopeful about the possibilities of a shared dinner, but Paul hadn't even brought the meal himself, something Alex trusted he'd have done if able to. Instead, William brought a plate loaded with a variety of fragrant dishes, explaining that Berkley's had sent a selection of their most popular menu items and a large bouquet of gladiolas. Though Alex hadn't particularly liked Thierry, he appreciated the gesture and made a note to send a thank-you before recalling that Paul usually took care of social niceties and more than likely had already sent a card.

With the day's tasks as finished as he'd had the energy to make them, Alex sat alone and contemplated the past twenty-four hours, allowing his personal grief to finally surface.

The invincible hero of his childhood was gone, pronounced dead on arrival at the emergency room, and Alex hadn't been holding Alfred's hand when his uncle died. However, when the doctors allowed him to see the body, his worries about a lonely death were put to rest. Lying still and quiet on the gurney, Alfred wore a brilliant smile. Deep in his heart Alex knew why. Byron had been waiting, just as Alfred had insisted mere days ago, and death no longer separated the two lovers.

Throughout the ordeal, Paul clung to him, refusing to let go. Alex didn't mind. Despite the circumstances, having a warm body pressed close provided comfort, and having a focus other than his own grief had given him purpose enough to survive the next few hours.

Wearily climbing the stairs to his bedroom, Alex recalled waking up to unruly hair and an armful of Paul. The words from their earlier conversation came back to him: *Don't you ever want to wake up next to someone who you love, who loves you?* For the first time in his life, not only was the answer "yes," but Alex also had a candidate in mind.

Entering his darkened bedroom, Alex breathed a sigh of relief to find his bed already occupied, as he'd privately hoped. By the moonlight shining in through the windows, wary eyes watched him undress as though expecting a reprimand for assuming the invitation to share the room was open-ended. That's exactly how Alex had intended the offer, though, and the big bed had never looked so inviting. Paul appeared incredibly young without his glasses, left sitting on the nightstand, and he lay among the satin sheets like he belonged there. Perhaps he did.

As Alex approached, mouth stretched wide in a yawn, Paul lifted the covers and he slid gratefully into the inviting warmth. When his guest would have retreated to the far side of the bed, Alex stopped him, murmuring, "Don't go." Questioning eyes locked with his instead of bashfully turning away as they normally did. Taking that as a "yes" to his unvoiced question, Alex swooped down, claiming Paul's mouth. Paul returned the kiss without hesitation.

Keeping his arms fully around his prize, a prize he had no intention of giving up anytime soon, Alex drew back enough to say, "I've decided to take your words to heart."

"Oh? What words?"

"I'm no longer going to sleep with people who don't care about me."

"Oh, that's good. Now get back over here." Paul pulled Alex closer with surprising strength.

The murmured demand was all the declaration Alex needed, and he rolled on top of Paul, bracing his weight on his elbows and grinding his stiffening erection against his lover's answering hardness.

Paul squeezed his hand between them to pull their cocks through the openings in their flimsy boxers, wrapping around both and sliding them provocatively together.

Alex hissed in pleasure, his mouth descending again in a demanding kiss, matching the rhythm of their bodies. Paul released their cocks and rocked their hips together. His image brought to mind a straight-laced librarian, but in bed he burned hotter than any club trick Alex had ever encountered, all the more enticing because he didn't do casual fucks. Having someone everyone else couldn't have was a heady rush, fueling Alex's libido and ego.

Fingers tangling in a rich mass of silky mahogany strands, he caressed Paul's tongue with his own, pulling it into his mouth and suckling, imitating a far more intimate act. He smiled at his partner's lusty groan. Slowly sliding down the tempting body beneath him, Alex moaned, his hard flesh finding friction against toned runner's thighs. If Paul could lay waste to his shirt, turnabout was fair play—he grabbed hold of Paul's cotton boxers and split the fabric apart with a satisfying rip, hoping they weren't the royal blue ones. Before Paul could protest, Alex took half of that amazingly full cock into his mouth, rolling his tongue around the head and working the underside with steady laps of his tongue.

Paul bucked and Alex grasped his hips, holding him in place and making him wait, to repay Paul's teasing during their last encounter. A frustrated whine was music to Alex's ears. Desire took precedence over finesse, and he worked Paul's cock like an eager novice, gaining as much pleasure from the giving as he would have from the receiving.

"I want you," Paul gasped. "Let me play too!"

Never breaking his rhythm, Alex shifted until his cock hovered inches above Paul's lips, slightly out of reach. Powerful arms wrapped around his hips, and with one swift lunge, his cock sank into Paul's mouth clear down to the root. Paul hummed with Alex buried deep in his throat.

If Alex hadn't known better, he might have thought Paul the slut he'd once accused the man of being. Now he understood that Paul's expertise wasn't the result of numerous partners. Any prowess stemmed from the fact that whatever Paul Sinclair did, he gave his all, wholehearted enthusiasm making up for any lack of skill.

The pent-up frustrations and sexual tensions of the past few weeks resolved with Alex and Paul thrashing upon the bed. Climax building, it took every ounce of willpower for Alex to pull away. "Not like this," he growled, crawling up the bed to gaze into lust-glazed eyes. "Can I fuck you?"

"No," Paul replied matter-of-factly.

What the hell? The man had teased him and brought him to the edge and.... Suddenly, the proverbial light came on, and Alex amended his question. "Can I make love to you?"

Instead of answering, Paul presented his exceptionally appealing backside, scrambling to the nightstand and then noisily rummaging inside. He handed Alex a square package and a familiar bottle. Worried about a coming accusation, Alex stammered, "I… I have absolutely no idea how those got in there."

Paul's teeth gleamed like pearls in the moonlight. "I do. It's where I put them."

The time for talking ended. Paul took control, tugging Alex's boxers off and then throwing them aside. He used his mouth to roll on the condom and then pushed Alex back on the bed before climbing on top. With a wicked grin, he lightly bit a pebbled nipple, a not-so-subtle reminder of who'd been the master before.

Alex's cock throbbed at the memory of that mastery, and he watched, puzzled when Paul's lithe body straightened, back arching, Paul hissing in pleasure/pain. *What's he doing?* The answer nearly stole Alex's control, mesmerizing him with the erotic image of Paul using fingers to prepare for something larger. Suddenly, tight heat gripped his shaft and Paul hissed, sliding down Alex's length, eyes closed tightly in concentration.

Wrapping his hands around slim hips, Alex fought the instinct to push up and bury himself in Paul's body, unwilling to take his own pleasure at the risk of causing pain.

Paul stopped midway down, panting, weight braced with his hands against Alex's chest. After a moment, he let gravity pull him down.

"I… don't… bottom… often…," Paul groaned through clenched teeth.

"Shh…," Alex crooned. "Take your time. We've got all night."

With another wicked grin, Paul assured him, "I intend to use every single minute."

Rising up until the head of Alex's cock barely remained inside him, Paul then reversed, sinking down completely, biting his bottom lip and rocking his hips in a grinding motion against Alex's groin.

"Oh, God!" Alex cried.

As Paul's body adjusted, so did his speed, and he rode Alex with enthusiasm, moaning with each upward stroke and hissing on the down, the sounds communicating less discomfort and more pleasure.

Alex wrapped his hand around Paul's bobbing cock, forcing a single drop of pearly fluid from the tip. Capturing the droplet on a fingertip, he brought the offering to Paul's parted lips. Paul greedily sucked Alex's finger into his mouth, tongue lapping the digit clean. Alex moaned and tightened his hold, stroking in earnest, matching the rhythm his energetic lover set.

Paul's tightening abs warned of impending climax, and Alex couldn't last much longer, either.

"Alex!" Paul gasped, doubling over, semen splattering Alex's chest and stomach. Rhythm faltering, he would have fallen had Alex not been holding onto his hips. Alex buried himself to the hilt, Paul's spasming inner muscles squeezing mercilessly. Abandoning the fight to prolong the pleasure, Alex let go, crying out and filling the latex sheath he wore.

Paul slumped into a boneless heap, and with his last reserve of strength, Alex rolled them to their sides, easing out of Paul's body with great reluctance. He grasped a scrap of torn cotton and cursorily wiped them both down. His lover scrutinized him with inquisitive eyes, and realization dawned that Paul probably assumed he'd now be dismissed from Alex's bed, as reputation dictated. Alex stripped off the condom and wrapped it in a tissue before dropping the evidence of their tryst in the trash can. It wouldn't do to flaunt such things around the servants, though they could think what they wanted about the torn boxers.

The old Alex would have been dressed and out of the door by now, or urging his partner to leave. The old Alex was a fool. Sated and weary, the long day catching up to him, he leaned in and kissed Paul soundly.

"Let's sleep in tomorrow," he mumbled through a sleepy haze.

CHAPTER NINETEEN

PAUL woke up alone and instantly feared the worst, until he found a note waiting by his glasses.

Paul,

I'd hoped to sleep a bit late and maybe have a little turnabout. I wasn't expecting my phone to start ringing before the sun came up. I didn't wake you because you were sleeping so soundly.

Alex

Paul hurried through a shower and spent the next few minutes trying to convince a persistent William he didn't need help dressing before finally relenting. The man merely wanted to do his job, a daunting task, considering whose shoes he attempted to fill. When no longer needed, the butler quietly left. Paul sighed. If William had been Bernard, Paul would now know the weather, the latest sports scores, the hottest Hollywood gossip, and the breakfast menu. William's "morning banter" amounted to: "Good morning, sir," and "Let me do that, sir." Paul did his best not to let his true feelings show, but he missed Bernard terribly.

Worry led him from the room, and he'd climbed halfway down the stairs before he heard Alex's irate bellow. "Out! I don't give a happy damn what you think is urgent! My uncle is being buried in a few hours, and I need to get dressed. My family's the only thing in my world important to me right now...."

Paul took the remaining stairs at a run, sliding into the office, hopefully in time to prevent murder. Having shared a house for weeks, he recognized the signs of Alex's patience reaching an end. Alex's short fuse burned hot, and when the dynamite exploded, there'd be no survivors. The four men crowded around the front of the desk had no idea of the danger they were in.

All eyes observed Paul's arrival, and he swore some of the men hissed like cats. Apparently, the vultures had landed, one of many reasons he'd shied away from wealth. Nothing drew the scavengers quite like a death when money was to be had.

With his usual diplomatic flair, Paul attempted to defuse the situation. "Gentlemen, I'm sure Mr. Martin's more than happy to meet with you at a future date. However, we're in mourning, and this isn't the time to discuss business. If you'd each leave your card with me, I'll set up appointments for you next week. In the meantime I'll ask you, out of respect for Alfred, to allow us some privacy."

Skirting the men, he carefully maneuvered his way to Alex, laying a restraining hand on an arm tensed to swing. He breathed a sigh of relief when Isaac appeared a moment later. They might be outnumbered, but not out-muscled.

The four scavengers cowered and stammered insincere

apologies, backing out of the room. The fact that Isaac stood every inch of six foot six, spent two hours in the gym every day, and had removed his suit jacket to reveal bulging muscles probably helped them decide on next week being soon enough. "I'll show them out, boss," Isaac said, literally herding the quartet into the hallway.

Chancing a glance up at Alex's face, still mottled red with anger, Paul tried to smooth ruffled feathers, keeping his tone conversational. "Something I should know about?"

Eyes trained on the departing vultures, Alex replied, "You have no idea, do you?"

"About what?" Anxiety set in.

Heavy hands found and kneaded his shoulders in a comforting gesture. "Our uncles were what some people call 'filthy rich'. You pointed out that they didn't live like kings. Now with them gone, every Tom, Dick, and Harry is coming out of the woodwork to try to get a piece of the pie. Tomorrow morning a new security system is being installed, and you're not to leave the house without me or Isaac. Do you understand?"

Paul's heart dropped to his stomach. Were they actually in danger? "No more morning runs?" *Damn, but I sound petty.*

"Until things calm down, I'd rather you use the treadmill." With another squeeze to Paul's shoulders, Alex added, "Don't worry; I'm sure everything will settle back down soon. Until then, we can't be too careful, you know? Especially not with scavengers prowling about."

Though a knot of uncertainty formed in his gut, Paul nodded. Dealing with scum definitely fell under the heading of "things Alex handles." He'd trust the man's judgment on this.

Once the front door slammed, shutting their unwelcome

guests out of their lives, the tension seemed to flow from Alex, the hardness in his eyes softening. "Now…." Throwing a quick glance toward the door, he captured Paul's lips in an unexpectedly thorough kiss. The reassuring contact ended too soon. "I wanted to wake up together this morning. Unfortunately, circumstances prevented it," Alex murmured, all traces of anger gone.

Unwilling to give up their moment easily, Paul pulled Alex back down. "Don't start something you don't intend to finish." Alex's lips relaxed into a smile when Paul resumed the kiss.

"Excuse me," had them shooting nervous glances toward the door. "Boss, I think you'd better get dressed, or we're gonna be late." Isaac leaned in the doorway, bulging arms folded across his chest.

Alex sighed and slowly stepped away. "He's right. I'll be back down in little while."

"Need some help?" Paul asked.

Alex grinned. "You think we're running late now?" He stepped into the hallway and out of sight.

Isaac sighed and Paul squinted at him sharply. Rather than the smirking glare he expected, Isaac wore a wistful expression. He noticed Paul watching him and remarked, "Don't worry; I know I can't have him."

"Oh, my God, Isaac! I'm sorry! You had feelings for Alex?" Paul had noticed him staring on occasion, sure, but Isaac had a reputation as a bit of a player. He stared at everyone.

"Nah," Isaac replied with a dismissive wave of his hand. "I always knew nothing serious would ever happen between us."

Inwardly relieved, Paul rolled his eyes and tried to make light of the situation. "You're not going to tell me it's because Martha would have your hide, are you?"

"No. Actually, flirting with Alex was a lot of fun over the years, in spite of her scolding. He's my boss now, and it has to stop. It's disrespectful, and that ain't Martha talking, that's my mama, God rest her soul. You've got nothing to worry about, anyway; he's not my type."

Throwing his arm around Paul's shoulders in a spirit of camaraderie, Isaac gazed down with laughter dancing in his dark-brown eyes. "Don't get me wrong, you're not bad, either. Still not my type, but not bad. I like a man with some meat on his bones."

They reached a silent agreement, and Paul knew he'd found an ally, or rather, inherited one. One of the few legacies from the uncles that didn't make him want to run and hide.

"C'mon, Mr. Sinclair," Isaac said, a sly grin betraying his playfulness. "It's gonna to be a long day. Let's go see what Theresa whipped up for breakfast." Muscular arm still around Paul's shoulders, nearly staggering him under the weight, Isaac led him down the hall and into the kitchen.

SECURITY was tight at the cemetery where Alfred would be laid to rest next to his partner. Unlike Byron's funeral, Alfred's was small and intimate. So small, in fact, that Alex recognized everyone in attendance. A dapper Bernard escorted a sniffling Martha, Isaac holding up her other side. Ushers directed them to the row of chairs reserved for the family of the deceased, set under a canopy at the gravesite.

Several couples attended, both gay and straight, whom Alex knew to be old friends of Alfred and Byron's. Former clients, many of whom graced the pages of the world's premier magazines, were also present to pay their last respects. Richard stood near the back of the group with the rest of Alfred's former law partners.

The funeral was by invitation only, and with the exceptions of Aunt Helena and an aging movie diva too ill to attend, every single invitation had been accounted for. Paparazzi armed with cameras and microphones fought to gain entrance into the walled sanctuary but were stopped by the finest security team Alex could hire on short notice.

He led Paul to the chairs and sat down next to him, purposefully placing a hand on one slender thigh, silently offering support while sending a clear message to any who might get ideas.

When Douglas Sinclair arrived, a member of the security detail led him to the family seating, per Alex's instruction. Paul gave him a soft smile and grateful eyes, greeting his uncle in hushed tones.

According to Alfred's hints concerning the contents of his will, within a few hours, Paul would be exceedingly wealthy, like it or not. Alex prayed his increased financial status wouldn't change so unpretentious a man, prepared to fight tooth and nail to prevent scavengers like Jordan from taking advantage.

The same minister who'd presided over Byron's funeral began the service with a prayer, and Alex listened, dry-eyed, to a touching eulogy. He figured others would think him unfeeling, but Andersons didn't mourn in public, and he privately felt he had no need to mourn. Alfred had lived a full measure of years with the love of his life and had now reunited with Byron. Any grief would be a private thing, leaving no photographic evidence to profit a snooping reporter.

After the last "Amen," Alex guided Paul to the waiting limousine with the rest of their acquired family, where he stood and chatted with his remaining uncle while Alex politely mingled and accepted condolences.

Social duties done, he crawled in beside Paul, who huddled into his side. Everyone who mattered either knew or suspected about them, and, gratified when Paul didn't seem to mind a little public affection, Alex held him all the way home.

"As with many of my better ideas, I borrowed this one from Byron," Alfred began, addressing his nearest and dearest through the power of technology and a video disk. "I've recorded private messages for each of you, to be shared as you see fit. Richard has the particulars and will ensure my wishes are carried out."

Richard distributed the videos, and everyone shuffled from the room except for Paul and Alex.

"Richard, would you give us a moment?" Alex asked.

The attorney left the office quietly, closing the door behind him.

"This is going to change everything, isn't it?" Paul asked, staring at the floor.

Alex cupped Paul's chin in his hand, raising it until misery-filled brown eyes met his. "Only if you let things change," Alex murmured quietly. "You yourself pointed out that our uncles didn't live like millionaires. If you suddenly find yourself rich, you can follow their example. You don't have to be something you're not."

"What about us?" Paul whispered. "What will this do to us?"

"Only what we let it." Alex wrapped his lover in a crushing embrace and kissed Paul thoroughly, daring fate to take away what it had recently given him.

Tears shimmered in Paul's eyes when Alex reluctantly released him. "I guess we better do what Alfred wanted," he said, holding up his video.

"Yeah, I guess we'd better."

With a final, fleeting kiss, Paul left the office, and Alex listened until his footsteps faded.

He poured a martini and then turned on the video before sinking into the desk chair. His uncle appeared gaunt, and judging from appearances, the recording had been made mere days ago. "Alex," Alfred began, "I don't have much time, and deny if you will, but deep down we all know the truth. My days are numbered. I thank you for your firm belief that I'd—how did you put it—'outlive us all'? Sadly, reality is a cruel, cruel thing.

"I think you know my final wishes for you. Instead of wasting our time on legalities, I'd much rather take this opportunity for one more little heart-to-heart with you. Everything associated with the Anderson family is yours, as is your due. Any joint property owned by Byron and myself will be divided evenly between you and Paul, with the exception of the stipends set aside for the household staff. All real estate but the house Byron gave you outright is jointly owned by the two of you.

"I gave the Bishop house to Byron the year after we met, and one day I hope you'll learn why he left it to you. Of everything you've inherited, I also hope you realize the most important things aren't material." Blue eyes focused and intent, Alfred implored him, "I want you to take care of Martha, Bernard, Isaac, and especially Paul."

Given the conversations they'd had about that particular subject, Alex knew the high esteem in which Alfred held his lover's nephew. Now, sharing his uncle's love inspired no jealousy. Alex finally understood that the old man loved them equally, as sons.

A wryly smiling Alfred confessed, "Byron asked me on his deathbed to do everything in my power to get you two together. He firmly believed you're kindred spirits. I agreed to his wishes because I love him, even though I know I can't make love bloom where it won't. What I ask is for you open your heart, if not to Paul, then to someone else. Don't wind up a lonely, bitter old man, Alex. Victoria wouldn't be happy with me if I didn't look out for your happiness."

Everything clicked for Alex. From the first night, when Paul prepared one of his favorite meals at Alfred's suggestion, to the arranged dates at Berkley's and the gallery opening… it was all part of one great master plan. Even the faux power failure that forced the candlelight dinner showed his uncle's hand at work, fulfilling a promise to a dying lover. It humbled Alex, the lengths Alfred had gone through to make others happy, especially when his own health issues should have been his primary focus.

He wished he could talk to Alfred once more, for so much remained unsaid. Now, all he could do was listen.

"You may not realize it, Alex, but you've been groomed for years to take my place. I never dreamed passing the torch would happen so soon. Richard has the necessary papers ready for you to sign, plus one I've never mentioned before. It's completely optional, of course, although it's something I'd like you to seriously consider. There are documents drawn up to legally change your name to Anderson, or rather, drop the Martin, naming you Alexander Anderson."

As many times as Helena had suggested a name change, this was the only time his uncle had ever broached the subject. Sheer spite had kept him from changing his name when his grandparents tried to force the issue. If he'd only known that was what Alfred wanted, Alex would have gladly ditched any reminders of his father long ago.

Then came the words he'd often heard throughout his life, words he himself had rarely said, though he meant them. "I love you, Alex, and consider you to be my son. Take care of yourself and those you love. Always remember this one bit of advice." Expression stern, his aging uncle imparted his one last bit of wisdom, the Anderson family creed: "Never give the bastards the upper hand."

Alfred concluded with a simple, "I love you, son." The video faded to black.

Alex's heart sank. How many times had Alfred said those words over the years? The only time he'd ever returned them since reaching adulthood had been a few short nights ago, when he'd felt isolated from the others in his uncle's life.

Did the man even know how much Alex loved him? Only a few small words—why had he withheld them? Dear, sweet Byron never once heard them from Alex's lips, though he'd been as free with his declarations as he'd been with his kindness and hugs.

How about Paul? Would Alex lose whatever chance he had with the man if he didn't learn to open up and express how he felt?

This time, no shadow slipped into the room to offer comfort as his heart broke. Alone in the office, sitting in the same chair Alfred had sat in to impart a few final words, Alex truly grasped the error of his ways.

PAUL ventured down the hallway to his old room for the first time since Alfred's passing, and the place didn't seem nearly as inviting as it used to. Unable to help himself, he eased open the door to his uncle and Alfred's shared room, memories playing through his mind of running in and bouncing on the massive bed in days gone by, waking them up early on a Saturday morning. Even before realizing he was gay, it seemed perfectly natural to find the two men sleeping spooned together.

He entered the deserted room with quiet reverence, half expecting to hear the booming voice of his uncle or the more cultured tones of Alfred bidding him welcome. Only then did he recall being awakened the night of Alfred's heart attack, and his eyes darted toward the towering bookcases on the far wall. Alfred's massive book collection sat stacked neatly on the shelves, and he bet not a single volume was out of place. Bernard would have attended to it himself, despite William's, or anyone else's, protests.

His gaze fell on the pictures huddled together on a dresser, and he couldn't help smiling in spite of his grief. The images were carefully arranged in chronological procession, a lasting monument of a happy life.

The first picture showed two men, one young, one fast approaching middle years, dining together at a seaside cantina. Paul knew the photo well. A waiter snapped the shot during Alfred and his Uncle Byron's first vacation together in Cancun. No matter how many times his uncle told the story, Paul never grew tired of hearing it. He considered the trip to be the couple's honeymoon.

Though they were also the stars of another favorite photo,

the two parka-clad figures could have been anyone. The familiar men were completely hidden from view beneath layers of warm clothing. His uncle mentioned in passing how he'd always wanted to visit Alaska, and it didn't matter that it was early January, Alfred had insisted, "There's no time like the present," taking him north.

Beside the numerous framed images, Paul found a stack of photo albums. He reached out and petted one massive tome, labeled "Alex," exactly as his uncle left it, no doubt, waiting for its owner's return.

On impulse he opened the cover, finding more snapshots carefully arranged on the first page. A smiling blond baby stared out from the first—an infant Alex. The lovely but ill-fated Victoria held him in her arms. There were many more photos of the two, page after page, each showing Alex a little older. In every one, the boy's face glowed with good humor. Paul turned the next leaf and found a stark contrast to the smiling faces of the previous pages.

In this picture, Alex neither smiled nor appeared happy. Dressed in a navy suit, he seemed sad and lost, bearing little resemblance to joyful youngster of the earlier images. The years continued to pass with the turning of the book's pages. Occasionally, Alex appeared smiling, but the dim expression paled in comparison to the earlier pictures.

Finally, Paul reached a recent picture of a brooding Alex, taken no more than a few years ago, and suddenly understood why the man behaved as he did… or the way he used to. For a brief time before Alfred's death, Alex began to resemble more and more the cheerful child he used to be, the one Byron once described as carefree and mischievous. Paul only hoped the loss of his uncle wouldn't cause a setback. He quite liked the man Alex was becoming.

Knowing he couldn't put off the inevitable any longer, Paul finally closed the album and left the room, making his way across the hall to view the disk that would forever change his life.

He placed the video in the player and sat back on his bed, watching Alfred appear exactly how he existed in Paul's memory—behind his desk in the office down the hall. Dressed simply in a blue lightweight sweater, to those unfamiliar with the circumstances he probably seemed in perfect health for a man of his years. Paul knew better. The hollows in his cheeks were more a product of grieving and fading health than the result of high cheekbones, and his sky-blue eyes, from which his burning intelligence still shone, were somewhat distant and faded.

Paul had kept himself deep in denial for far too long. Watching the video instead of being face to face with Alfred forced him to acknowledge what had been before his eyes the whole time. Alfred Anderson had been dying, and no amount of love or well-wishing could have saved him. Torn between despair at Alfred's passing and relief that he hadn't suffered long, Paul settled back more comfortably to have one last conversation, albeit a one-sided one, with the man who'd played an all-important role in his life.

"If you're watching this, it means I'm gone," Alfred began, and Paul noticed his forceful, commanding voice had begun to waver. It still carried the same air of authority, but now it cracked when he talked, his tone husky. Alfred winked at the camera. "I'll give your love to your uncle."

Paul's eyes filled with tears as he recalled Alex's words, how the lovers were now together again, dismayed that his first thought upon hearing of Alfred's death had been for his own loneliness, while Alex, uncharacteristically, had focused on others.

Even in death Alfred proved how well he'd known Paul, saying, "You're probably thinking your heart's going to break about now. I'm sorry you had to go through this, but I'm not sorry you were in our lives. Byron and I both love you very much, Paul. You and Alex are our pride and joy, though we may not have told you often enough."

Paul disagreed. Never in his life had Alfred and his Uncle Byron failed to show their pride, and he again felt the stirrings of guilt at how he'd rebuffed their every gift.

"Paul," Alfred continued, "I know how you feel about the money, you've made it perfectly clear. Now listen to me; we want you to have it. Byron and I worked hard all our lives, made sound investments, and lived a good life. It's time to pass the torch.

"I don't know if you fully understood the working dynamic the two of us shared. The business deals were my domain, while charities and running the household were Byron's. Without your realizing, all these years when he took you to gallery openings and charity events were grooming for the role we hoped you'd one day fill. Alex, like yourself, was also being discreetly taught his place.

"You see, we wanted you to be a team and eventually take over from us. In our arrogance, we thought we had years before we'd need you to fill those roles. How horribly wrong we were." Though Paul believed it a trick of the lighting and camera angle, Alfred's penetrating blue eyes seemed to stare straight through him. "I hope you'll forgive our presumptions, but we want the two of you to continue the work we started.

"It's my hope you'll live in the house we built, even if it

means frequent trips to Bishop to check on your own business. We could never ask you to give up something you've worked hard for. As you might have guessed, money won't be a problem for you, and out of love for me and your uncle, it's my wish that you'll accept your inheritance graciously. You don't have to change your life or even your spending habits. A great deal of good can be done with lots of money in the right hands."

Alfred shook his head, heaving out a heavy sigh. "Already the vultures are probably circling, talons out to swipe whatever they can. Would you rather those greedy bastards have what Byron and I worked our whole lives for?" Alfred answered his own question. "Of course not."

He paused to drain his teacup, and then a hand, possibly Bernard's, reached out from off-camera and took the delicate china from him. After a moment, Alfred continued. "Now that we're alone, I can tell you this. The full extent of what we've given you is on file with Richard. There's one stipulation. Martha, Bernard, and Isaac are to be cared for. They each were given enough to live reasonably on, though you know as well as I do that's not what I meant. I probably don't need to say this because I know what kind of person you are—make sure those three people aren't alone."

As if Paul needed to be told to look after his family.

"Which brings me to my next topic," Alfred said. "Alex. I know the two of you got off to a rocky start, and I admire the way you've managed to put your differences behind you. Please watch out for him for me, Paul. He's walled himself off from emotional attachments. Although he may seem cold and aloof, that's a façade. Deep down, he's a good man and worth the effort of getting to know. He can also protect you, for he knows how to deal with the scavengers.

"Paul, don't close your heart because one heartless soul

hurt you. If someone special comes along, give him a chance. That's all I ask of you. Take care of yourself, and if it's possible, Byron and I will be watching over you. I love you, Paul, and I'm proud of you and your strong personal convictions. You're a son of my heart, if not my body."

Tears fell in steady streams now, from Paul's eyes and from Alfred's. With a long last look into the camera Alfred said, "I love you, son." The image disappeared, leaving Paul alone in his darkened room with his misery.

A soft tapping on his door sounded a few moments later. Furiously wiping tears from his cheeks, he called, "Yes?"

The door slowly opened, and a tall figure stood silhouetted in the doorway. "Can I come in?"

In answer, Paul patted the bed next to him. Alex closed the door, crossed the distance in long strides, and climbed on the bed. Paul pulled him into a fierce embrace, and their choking sobs rocked both them and the bed as they shared their misery. When they calmed, Paul rubbed Alex's trembling back and murmured soothing nonsense. Eventually Alex fell into a restless sleep, and Paul held him while he napped, studying Alex's tear-streaked face. Surprise, surprise. It seemed Alex Martin did know how to love after all. That was good, because Paul decided he wanted Alex's love for himself. If the man even dared trying to rebuild the "arrogant bastard" walls between them, well, Sinclairs were nothing if not persistent—what the uninitiated might call stubborn.

Another knock sounded later and Theresa announced dinner. Paul started to wake Alex, then noticed blue eyes, unnervingly reminiscent of Alfred's, were open and watching him. "Let's go eat," Paul said.

Alex scrutinized him for another long moment before easing off the bed and holding out his hand. Paul reached out and Alex pulled him to his feet, enfolding him in a nearly painfully tight embrace. "Thanks," Alex whispered. Just as softly, his mouth descended, delivering the most emotionally charged kiss of Paul's life. Paul hoped there were plenty more where that came from. He could get used to them.

CHAPTER TWENTY

"You found the perfect place for the painting." Paul and the newly named Alexander Anderson lay curled together in the big bed in the room now known as "their room." Light jazz provided a tranquil backdrop to their recovery from another memorable round of getting acquainted. Across from them, the painting *Stormy Horizon* hung, having found a place, not in the front hall as originally planned, but in their bedroom, the former blue room, for the private enjoyment of the new masters of the house. By mutual agreement, they'd closed off the master bedroom for now, leaving their uncles' sanctuary exactly as it had been when the two men shared it.

"I couldn't agree more." Alex sipped a martini and admired the painting; still occasionally plagued by illusions of lightning when he stared too long. Then, in the scant millisecond of imaginary brilliance, he saw them—two men walking hand and hand down the windswept beach. Though logically he blamed his overactive imagination, he wondered if Paul somehow witnessed the phantom images too. "I know our uncles are together now, I can almost see them walking down the shore, hand in hand."

Paul smiled. "You know, I was thinking the same thing."

Well, at least he hadn't accused Alex of insanity. "Paul?" A curious gaze met Alex's, and he tried to think of the right words to say, never having been in this position before. "You know everything's going to be different now, right?"

"Different how?" Paul expressive features shaded with concern. "You're not talking about the money, are you? Because I'd like to forget about that for now."

Alex sighed. He needed to let Paul know how he felt; however, as badly as he wanted to, he couldn't seem to come out and say the words. He tried another approach. "Actually, I meant us."

Paul cocked an eyebrow. "There's still going to be an 'us' when this is over? I'm not simply a calm port until the storm passes?"

Alex thought long and hard about the question. Given his past history, he understood why Paul might be skeptical. "I'd like there to be," he admitted.

Paul smiled, one simple gesture telling Alex all he needed to know; that, and a mind-blowing kiss.

Snuggling contentedly into Alex's chest, Paul fell asleep within minutes, leaving Alex to his musings. He had absolutely no experience with relationships, never having let anyone get close to him before. Terrified he'd lose what he'd been waiting a lifetime for, he swore to make their relationship work, for although the words hadn't been said, he was pretty sure he wasn't alone in how he felt.

Oh, he'd wait until they'd had time to grieve for the two great men who'd been like fathers to them both, and then he'd do things properly. There'd be wine, dinners, and the occasional weekend in Bishop, presumably the reason Byron gave him a house there. There'd be art galleries, books read by the fire, and long walks on the beach. When he finally managed to convince Paul of the depths of his commitment, they'd talk to Lee and maybe finally fill the house with the happy, childish giggles Alfred intended.

He hoped the poor tykes didn't inherit their mother's temper. An image appeared in his mind of a little boy with dark hair. Wouldn't it be nice if the boy had Paul's smile or eyes?

Alex lay entwined with the man he was coming to love more with each passing day, thoroughly convinced he wanted to see those laughing amber eyes and goofy grin every morning when he woke up. He decided then and there he'd learn to say how he felt even if it killed him, because if he didn't, losing Paul surely would.

If things worked out maybe he did stand a chance of having a relationship like his uncle's, as he'd always wanted. And many years from now, when the end finally came? His eyes strayed once more to the painting. He contemplated the two ghostly lovers he'd seen, who resembled Alfred and Byron. Was there ever truly an end, if you didn't want there to be?

The music still played when Alex fell into a contented sleep, one arm thrown possessively over his lover. If he'd been awake he might have noticed two shadows in a darkened corner of the bedroom, twined together, dancing.

ABOUT EDEN WINTERS

You will know Eden Winters by her distinctive white plumage and exuberant cry of "Hey, y'all!" in a Southern US drawl so thick it renders even the simplest of words unrecognizable. Watch out, she hugs!

Driven by insatiable curiosity, she possibly holds the world's record for curriculum changes to the point that she's never quite earned a degree but is a force to be reckoned with at Trivial Pursuit.

She's trudged down hallways with police detectives, learned to disarm knife-wielding bad guys, and witnessed the correct way to blow doors off buildings. Her e-mail contains various snippets of forensic wisdom, such as "What would a dead body left in a Mexican drug tunnel look like after six months?"

In the process of her adventures she has written fourteen m/m romance novels, has won several Rainbow Awards, was a Lambda Awards Finalist, and lives in terror of authorities showing up at her door to question her Internet searches. When not putting characters in dangerous situations she's a mild-mannered business executive, mother, grandmother, vegetarian, and PFLAG activist.

Her natural habitats are airports, coffee shops, and on the backs of motorcycles.

Keep up with Eden and Rocky Ridge Books by joining the newsletter.

edenwinters.com
Edenwinters@gmail.com

Small-town mechanic Joey Nichols gets dumped hard, but novelist Troy Steele can help him find his way to revenge, and past it to love in this Lambda Award Finalist/Rainbow Award Finalist story.

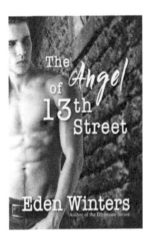

Noah Everett devotes himself to getting rent boys out of the life, but doesn't count on Jeremy Kincaid finding his home in Noah's heart in this Rainbow Award Finalist novel.

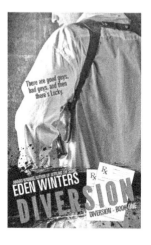

Diversion (Book 1)

Lucky Luckylighter, an unlikely drug enforcement agent, and his partner Bo Schollenberger get together while solving their first case in Diversion, Book 1 of this Rainbow Award-winning series.

More in the series:

Collusion

Corruption

Manipulation

Redemption

Reunion

Tradition

Relation

Suspicion

Decision

Made in the USA
Las Vegas, NV
11 October 2022